# PIGEONS OF DEATH

## LUKE RYDER
BOOK 4 .

## JOHN G. BLUCK

ROUGH
EDGES
PRESS

Rough Edges Press
An Imprint of Wolfpack Publishing
701 S. Howard Ave. 106-324 Tampa, FL 33609

roughedgespress.com

Paperback ISBN 978-1-68549-736-1
eBook ISBN 978-1-68549-735-4
LCCN 2024937306

# PIGEONS OF DEATH

# ONE

*TODAY MARK WILL DIE*. Sweat ran down the small of the assassin's back, but he ignored it. His eyes focused on the grand old Spicer mansion, gleaming in the sunshine, surrounded by a lush, expansive lawn. A well-dressed crowd of partygoers loitered on the thick grass eating, drinking, and gossiping. They were accustomed to the hot, humid air as was the killer. Today it was eighty-four sticky degrees.

White tents shaded folding tables laden with the finest foods money could buy. The party on the Kentucky horse farm was the perfect cover for murder. The bigger the crowd, the easier to blend into it and escape.

Like a cobra, the killer slithered into the throng and began to stalk his prey, waiting for the ideal moment to strike.

\* \* \*

FROM THE WIDE steps of his English country-style mansion, Mark Spicer, aged forty-two, peered down at the sizable crowd on his horse-training farm's lawn. This outdoor party would be the finest he'd staged.

In the distance, beyond thousands of feet of brown wooden fences, dozens of beautiful, athletic horses grazed. Curious, the closest animals watched the well-attired guests who stood on the soft turf.

Holding his heavy, glass beer stein, Mark felt its sweaty coolness as he went down his front steps to greet his visitors. Loud chatter told him people were having a fine time as they filled their plates.

A well-known Kentucky thoroughbred trainer, Mark loved large gatherings. He enjoyed socializing and relished people-watching. Sundry body types, fine clothes, and gestures attracted him.

Mark noticed a person who seemed to study him. Uneasy, Mark shifted his gaze a dozen feet to the right and saw his young wife, Carmen. Her cover-girl figure reminded him how lucky he was.

Standing near a handsome young man, Carmen smiled, laughed, and tossed her lengthy, dark hair behind one shoulder. Leaning close to him, she whispered in his ear. His face turned red.

Jealousy again struck Mark like a slap in the face as it always did whenever she flirted with other men.

Mark's eyes drifted to other young women—their body shapes, faces, and movements. He felt the pull of desire, and he smiled.

Someone tapped Mark's shoulder. Mark turned and saw the wealthy horse enthusiast, Rex Hightower, and his wife, Estrella.

Rex scanned the crowd. "Nice get-together."

"Thanks." Mark trained his eyes on Estrella, where they lingered. She wore a low-cut dress suitable for hot weather.

Rex grinned, put a protective arm around his wife's waist, and caught Mark's attention. "When are you going to give me a chance to buy one of those top-notch thoroughbreds of yours?"

Mark shrugged. "Whenever you outbid everyone else."

Rex cocked his head. "You mean I need to outbid that Mexican sugarcane farmer, Mateo Guerra, who's bought your finest horseflesh for the last three years?"

"Yep." Mark fixed his eyes on two young colts grazing in the distance. "I'm training new horses. Call me later, and you can watch them run."

"Thanks, Mark. It would be better if they stay stateside instead of going to Mexico or Saudi Arabia."

Mark shrugged. He glanced at Estrella and winked. "Bring Estrella with you when you visit."

She smiled. Rex snatched her hand. "See you soon." He'd spoken over his shoulder as he led her into the crowd of guests.

* * *

MEANWHILE, miles from Mark's lavish party, a tall, middle-aged man with black hair balanced on the edge of an examination table. Almost naked in a patient's gown, Deputy Sheriff Luke Ryder waited in a Lexington medical office. The disagreeable odors of medical alcohol and floor wax invaded his nose. He wondered, *Am I gonna be allowed to resume normal duty?*

A tap echoed from the door. Dr. Ralph Sanders entered. His yellowed teeth and foul-smelling breath caught Luke's attention. Luke held his breath.

Turning to a computer screen, the orthopedic surgeon pointed to an x-ray of Luke's lower left leg. "Your tibia is healing well."

Luke saw two screws in the bone x-ray but could see no fracture.

The doctor bent down and examined Luke's left leg. "How's it feel?"

"Okay, 'cept on rainy days it pains me."

The specialist grinned, exposing his amber-colored teeth. "Your surgeon in San Diego did a great job putting your tibia back together."

Luke recalled his recent Alaskan vacation cruise. Pirates

had hijacked the ship. During a fight, one of them had smashed Luke's leg with a heavy glass ashtray, cracking his shinbone. Later, during a final struggle with the buccaneers, Luke's injured tibia had snapped in half.

Luke pushed away from his reverie. Dr. Sanders was saying "...often takes up to six months to fully heal this sort of injury."

"Am I cleared to return to full duty?"

The physician paused. "Yes. But if your leg starts to hurt a lot, call me."

"Thanks, Doc." Luke hustled to put on his clothes. He had to return to his office to finish police paperwork—not his favorite activity. Later that night, though, he anticipated having dinner with his girlfriend, Layla, and Sheriff Jim Pike at the Holler Bar.

Luke couldn't wait to relax with Layla, eat a hamburger, and talk with his best buddy, Jim.

\* \* \*

MARK SPICER SMELLED THE SWEET, cut grass, which had been mowed that morning. Sunshine warmed his face. As he observed scattered groups of guests near his classic, well-kept mansion, barns, and training corral, he felt he was the master of his destiny.

Behind him Mark heard flapping wings. He turned to see two pigeons fly across the sky and over the party guests, toward his huge barn.

*Those birds better not shit on the crowd.*

Instead, the pigeons fluttered through the open hay door in the barn, in which Mateo's racing pigeons lived—and where the Mexican also boarded his horses.

Mark saw David Braga's stocky, bull-like form approaching. Mateo had insisted his Mexican colleague, David, become Spicer Farm's barn manager to keep close tabs on Mateo's expensive thoroughbreds. David also ensured Mateo's pigeons were well cared for.

*His birds are as important to him as his horses.*

David stopped near Mark. The Mexican's gleaming-white, strong teeth contrasted with his swarthy, tanned skin and his short, black hair. "Great party, Mark."

\* \* \*

CALM, holding a paper plate of hors d'oeuvres, the assassin wove his way toward Mark and David. The men were engrossed in conversation, not paying attention to anything else. Mark set his beer mug behind him on a banquet table.

The killer focused on six nearby people who were filling their plates with food.

*Go away, damn it.*

As if answering the assassin's wish, the six began to walk toward another group of partygoers.

*Ahh. Thank you.* Like a lethal cobra, the killer glared at Mark. *Now I'll get you.* He slipped a packet from his pocket and inched toward Mark's beer mug. He held the mini envelope under a paper plate.

Engaged in conversation, neither Mark nor David paid attention to the man standing behind them.

With stealth, the executioner poured a tasteless, odorless white powder into Mark's drink.

*Ha, ha.* The killer tried to suppress his smile, but the corners of his lips turned up a trifle as he stepped backward. At the same time, he dropped a plastic bag on the grass. It held four fentanyl-laced oxycodone pills.

*Adios.* The assassin melted into the throng of guests. *Mission accomplished.*

\* \* \*

DAVID WITHDREW a photo of a young woman from his wallet and handed the snapshot to Mark. "This is my daughter, Juanita."

Mark recalled David was a widower. While examining the picture, Mark nodded. "She's lovely." Mark found it hard to believe a rugged father could've sired such a delicate young woman.

David's eyes were bright, and Mark felt their intensity. David grinned. "I wish to invite you and your wife to Juanita's wedding next month in Tijuana."

Mark wondered, *What's it like in Tijuana? Would it be similar to scenes in old-time Wild West movies?* He'd never been to Mexico or the West Coast of the United States. Mark figured he'd also get to see Mateo again if he attended Juanita's wedding.

Mark beamed and handed the snapshot back to David. "I would be honored to attend, but I should ask my wife first."

David laughed. "I understand."

Mark picked up his cold mug and swigged his beer. He enjoyed its coolness as it flowed down his throat. "I believe she'll want to go."

David nodded. "Tijuana's beautiful in September. You'll find plenty to do."

Mark started to feel groggy. "It'll be nice to see Mexico." He noticed his words were slurring. His eyelids seemed heavy, and for a moment he could only focus on David's white teeth.

David grinned. "I'll show you around the city. You'll love it."

All of a sudden, extreme weariness hit Mark. He blinked to keep his eyelids from closing.

*Has the heavy, humid air made it hard to breathe?* Mark gazed in David's direction. "The heat's hit me." He noticed two garden chairs. "Let's sit."

David nodded. The men sat.

Mark lifted his mug to his lips, tilted back, and drank. He shook his head to rid his brain of cobwebs.

"You okay?"

"Beer makes me drowsy." Mark found it hard to pronounce words. He fought harder to keep his eyes open.

\* \* \*

THE KILLER SLIPPED OUT of the crowd and headed toward a group of buildings. *I'll wrap this up.* After going into a large horse barn, he found its bathroom, dropped the opened packet into a toilet, and pushed its lever. The flushing sound seemed to cleanse him, wash away his sin. He watched as the envelope spiraled down into the drain. *Easy, wasn't it?*

Feeling invisible, he took his time to walk back into the large, happy gathering.

\* \* \*

DAVID FELT a twinge of fear and leaned forward. "Mark?"

In a trancelike state, Mark peered into the crowd on the lawn and slumped in his chair.

David shook Mark's shoulders.

Mark's mug slipped from his fingers and fell onto the lawn. Beer poured into the lush, green grass and soaked into the soil. David smelled the spilled beer as it began to evaporate. He noticed the pupils in Mark's eyes were mere pinpoints. Then his eyes closed.

Mark's breathing slowed. He snored but also struggled to breathe. David knelt next to him and touched his pale skin. It was cold and clammy—not right on a hot, muggy day.

David grabbed Mark's shoulders, and Mark fell sideways, limp. David raised his voice, "Mark." His heart racing, David eased Mark down onto the soft grass. Mark's lips and fingernails had turned blue. David had seen the same thing happen to a friend in Mexico who'd died after taking drugs. David yanked his cell phone from his hip pocket and dialed 911.

"What's your emergency?"

"The owner of Spicer Farm collapsed." As David spoke faster, his Mexican accent became more pronounced. "I think it's a drug overdose."

"An ambulance and police are on the way. Do you have Narcan?"

"Yes. I'll get it." David stood straight, still grasping his phone. He began to sprint toward the horse barn where he kept Narcan in a cabinet. As he gained speed, he yelled, "Help Mark. An ambulance is coming."

The party guests quieted. Loud conversation morphed into concerned whispers. A growing crowd moved toward Mark, who was lying on the grass. Like curious cattle, they herded around him.

David strained and ran yet faster, pushing his body to its limit. His breathing was ragged. Lightheaded, he gasped for air. Sweat streamed down his forehead, burning his eyes. He smashed against the side door of the barn and bounded inside. Rushing into his office, he yanked open a gray metal cabinet, banging its door into the wall. Items tumbled aside as he clutched a box of two Narcan doses. Turning around, he ran back toward Mark. Gasping for breath, he pushed himself to run faster. As he slid to a stop on the grass near the crowd, close to Mark's limp body, he sucked air into his lungs. "Let me through." His face felt flushed.

His fingers slippery with sweat, David ripped the top off the Narcan cardboard box and took out a nasal drug dispenser. He sprayed a dose into Mark's nose.

The distant wail of sirens became louder and louder. David's heartbeat increased. He waited two minutes and squirted a second dose of Narcan into Mark's nostrils. David touched the man's throat. No pulse.

*"Jesus Cristo,"* David heard himself say. "Live by drugs, die by drugs."

\* \* \*

JACK HARTFORD, an emergency medical technician, guided his ambulance across the beautiful, green lawn near the Spicer mansion toward a crowd. He slowed. Two men pointed the way to Mark's body, circled by onlookers. Jack stopped his vehicle and snatched an oxygen tank and a defibrillator.

Meanwhile, Jack's EMT partner, Ginger Falcon, grabbed a box of Narcan and followed him.

As Jack approached the people near Mark, he saw a man giving him mouth-to-mouth resuscitation, while another thrust his palm downward on Mark's chest.

With Ginger behind him, Jack shoved his way through the muttering crowd to Mark's body.

Jack saw two spent Narcan dispensers on the grass. Glancing up at the crowd, he yelled, "What'd he take?"

David stepped forward. "Could be oxycodone or fentanyl."

After putting an oxygen mask over Mark's mouth and nose, Jack turned on the gas. He checked Mark for a pulse. There was none. Jack ripped off the oxygen mask, and Ginger cut away Mark's shirt. As fast as he could, Jack placed sticky defibrillator pads on each side of Mark's chest. He pressed the shock button to try to restart Mark's heart. The man's body jumped.

After twice trying to shock Mark back to life, Jack gave him an injection of adrenaline. He shocked Mark again, but Mark remained lifeless. Jack cast his eyes downward.

Crying, Carmen neared Jack. "How is he?" Her mascara smeared as she wiped her eyes. Her body shook.

Jack stood. "Sorry, ma'am. He's dead."

Carmen fainted, collapsing onto the soft Kentucky bluegrass next to her husband.

Jack began to walk toward his ambulance to get smelling salts. In the distance, he saw the sheriff's squad car turn onto the long, gravel driveway.

# TWO

GRAVEL CRUNCHED under Sheriff Jim Pike's police vehicle as he drove it along Spicer Farm's long driveway. Flashing ambulance emergency lights guided him to the scene. Well-dressed people lingered on the lawn near the farm's mansion and huge main barn.

Taking care to leave a clear exit path for the ambulance, Jim parked his SUV. He scanned the crowd of partygoers. Members of Lexington's elite and owners of neighboring horse farms milled about. When Jim opened his car door, sticky afternoon heat assaulted his body.

Jim nodded at the EMT. "What happened, Jack?"

Jack neared Jim and turned toward Mark. "This man's dead." He spoke in a low voice. "Appears he OD'd. I found this on the grass." Jack thrust a plastic sandwich bag toward Jim.

Jim frowned. *How many times have I told EMTs not to disturb the scene?*

"Don't you want it, Sheriff?"

"Set it on the grass."

Jim turned to a newly arrived deputy near him. "Randy, set up inner and outer perimeters. I've got extra crime scene tape and tent stakes in my SUV if you don't have enough."

"Yes, sir."

Jim turned to another deputy. "Sarge, get a clipboard and start taking names of everyone. Get witness statements if they saw anything."

\* \* \*

FROM FIFTY FEET AWAY, Steve, owner of the neighboring Kobold Farm, watched Carmen, who slumped on the grass, weeping. Even in painful distress and sorrow, she was a striking, beautiful woman. Thin, with prominent cheekbones, an upturned nose, and dark eyes, she was a rare, nearly perfect woman on the outside. Yet, inside she was flawed—rumored to sleep with any man handsome or wealthy enough.

Memories of touching Carmen's soft, nude body made Steve yearn for her once again. Their lustful, drunken love-making had occurred just one time when Mark was out of town. *Was our coupling merely another of her short-lived affairs?*

\* \* \*

JIM SAW a familiar van driving up the long gravel driveway. A cloud of dust trailed the truck. It had "County Coroner" painted on its white sides in gold letters. Jim watched as the coroner's vehicle stopped near the ambulance.

Dr. Mitch Corker wrestled his lanky, ancient body out of the meat wagon.

Jim walked toward Mitch, and he noticed the timeworn man needed a haircut. His scraggly mustache could use a trim, too, though his blue eyes appeared young. They were full of life, even though his face was creased and leathery.

Mitch scanned the area. "Where's Luke Ryder?" Mitch squinted. "I'd think your hotshot deputy would be on the scene."

Jim sighed. "He's at UK Hospital getting his leg checked."

"How's he doing?"

Jim shifted his stance. "He hopes the doc will clear him for full duty."

Mitch nodded and craned his neck toward the body in the grass within the core crime scene surrounded by yellow barrier tape. "What's the situation?"

"The EMT thinks it's a fentanyl overdose."

Mitch slouched. "Of late people been fallin' like flies sprayed by bug killer."

The two men walked to Mark's body after donning shoe covers. One of Mitch's knees crackled when he knelt near the body.

# THREE

DAVID HELD his secure satellite phone. His hand shook. *I must control my emotions.* He touched Mateo's name on the screen of the device.

Repeated buzzes indicated Mateo's phone was ringing in Tijuana.

"*Hola*, David."

"Boss, I have depressing news. Mark's dead."

"How did it happen?" Mateo's voice sounded higher than normal.

"He died of an overdose. Pills, I think." David's stomach was nauseous. *How will I take care of business with Mark gone?*

Mateo's voice cut into David's thoughts. "I didn't think Mark was a user."

David exhaled. "Carmen could've let him try her pills. She's a boozer and an addict." *Didn't I tell Mateo years ago the woman had problems?*

"Mark must've changed a lot since the last time I saw him." Mateo sighed.

"Boss, on a brighter note, I've lined up a sale to Ali of another of Mark's horses."

Much of David's job was to find customers for Mark's thoroughbreds. After a deal was struck, Mateo would first buy the horse from Mark for cash with drug money. The customer would then wire clean money to Mateo's shell company to purchase the thoroughbred. Customers had no idea drug money was being laundered because the company was called Spicer Horse Payments Corporation.

Mateo coughed. "Good work, David. I'll send Rafael to Kentucky with the cash for the new Ali deal next week." Mateo liked Ali's foreign funds because they were harder for authorities to track. "Ali's always quick to wire his payment."

David's brow furrowed. "Since Mark's dead, how do we proceed?"

"You handle the books. Make it appear our purchase happened before Mark died. Or you can make the books show the farm sold the horse to us."

David blinked. "Okay."

"You've been a master helping Mark and me clean cash, putting it into a lot of small accounts, paying vendors and the farm employees with folding money, etc., etc." Mateo paused for at least two seconds. "Mark never informed Carmen about our cash-for-horses deals, correct?"

David tried to remember if Mark had ever given him a hint about whether or not he'd told his wife anything about the illegal part of the farm's business. "As far as I know, she doesn't know a damned thing."

"Superb. Continue handling the books, paying bills, receiving payments, and cleaning the cash for the farm. If she asks, say you'll be happy to continue doing the farm's paperwork because it will make her life easier."

David gulped. "What do I do with your payment for Mark's horse when the courier arrives?"

Mateo huffed. "Put the cash in Mark's safe."

"I don't know the combination. He always handed me cash when I asked for it."

"Buy a modern safe. We'll worry about the rest of Mark's

cash in his old safe later on." Mateo paused. "I liked Mark. But we must adjust to new times." Mateo hung up.

David decompressed. He recalled it was rare for Mateo to show emotion when someone died. He seemed to care more for horses and his racing pigeons than he did for human beings. Because so many pigeons were roosting in the barn, David had had to hire two Mexican friends to take care of them. He stood and gazed at the floor.

David remembered how years ago Mateo had started a pigeon racing club, *Club de Las Aves*. Pacing back and forth, he pulled other memories from his brain. They played back to him like ancient newsreels. When Mateo had first met Mark, Mateo had grinned like the Cheshire cat in *Alice's Adventures in Wonderland*. He had told Mark he owned a successful sugarcane farm, which was a lie. Then Mateo had asked Mark to hire David to be the Spicer Farm barn manager.

Close-up images of Mateo's and Mark's lips appeared in David's vivid recollection. Mark had said, "Sure."

Mateo had also asked, "Would you permit David's pigeons to roost in your barn?" David remembered his surprise when Mateo had uttered those words.

Mark had shrugged. "I don't see why not."

Mateo had joked, "Racing pigeons is like horse racing, but the stakes are far lower."

As he again played back this sentence from his memory, David sat at his desk. He knew the birds often carried messages and light parcels. Small backpacks the color of the birds' feathers could contain drugs. Each pigeon was capable of flying illegal, addictive pills worth thousands of dollars on the street.

# FOUR

## 8:00 P.M., SATURDAY, AUGUST 3—HOLLER BAR

A HALF HOUR LATE, Luke approached the Holler Bar, his feet disturbing the gravel in the parking lot. The cinder block tavern was a community gathering spot in the holler, a small wooded Kentucky valley. The neon sign in the watering hole's dirty front window was on, glowing deep red though the sun wouldn't set for three-quarters of an hour.

*The place must be near full*, he thought.

Luke could smell stale beer as he grabbed the front door's handle. A recovering alcoholic, he fought to forget alcohol. It always tempted him. The bartender and waitresses knew what he wanted when he entered—a tall glass of ginger ale.

Luke pulled the door outward. Twangy country music vibrated the air inside the establishment. The bar was jam-packed with weekend revelers.

The odor of alcoholic drinks mixed with the smell of hamburgers and a potpourri of hot foods. His stomach rumbled as his eyes adjusted to the dim light. He saw his African American girlfriend, Layla Taylor, sitting with Jim, and Mitch, the coroner.

Layla waved. She held a half-eaten club sandwich in her left hand. A tall, dark beer was on the table near her.

Luke grinned and waved back. Though he'd missed on-the-scene police work while his leg was healing, he'd had extra time with Layla and her daughter, Angela. The six-year-old had started to call him Daddy. Luke doubted he'd make a decent father, although he did like playing with the little girl.

Luke walked to Layla, Jim, and Mitch's table. Before sitting, he waved to Lucy, the waitress. She flashed an okay sign. Then she strolled to Joe, the bartender, to fetch a tumbler of ginger ale.

Luke pulled a chair across the rough wooden floor and sat. "I have news. The doctor cleared me to return to regular duty."

"Good. I need your help on a high-profile case."

"Which one?"

Jim glanced at Layla and then back at Luke. "Mark Spicer, the horse trainer, died this afternoon of an overdose during a party he was holding at his farm."

Luke eased back in his chair. "Ain't he the top thoroughbred trainer in the country?"

"Yep." Jim paused as Lucy, the waitress, set a glass of ginger ale near Luke.

Jim glimpsed at Layla. "Can you keep what I say quiet?"

"Of course."

Jim winked at her and then turned to Luke. "It was murder," Jim said in a low voice. "Mitch, tell Luke what you found."

Mitch turned to Luke. "Twenty times more fentanyl was in Mark's system than was needed to kill him. I've never found such a concentrated, lethal dose in a corpse before." Mitch glanced behind him to make sure no one could hear him. "Mark dropped his beer on the lawn as he fell. It soaked into the soil, but an ounce of beer remained in his mug. An enormously high amount of fentanyl was in the beer, according to Alice Strom, your CSI."

Luke examined Mitch's timeworn face and then spoke. "How'd you get results so fast?"

Mitch smiled. "There's a new-fangled quick test strip. It also indicates fentanyl concentration on a sliding scale."

Luke nodded. "Sure beats waiting for an outside lab to do more complicated analysis."

Mitch shrugged. "Yeah, but because this is a homicide, we still need to send samples to an outside lab to get a confirmation my analysis is on target."

Jim got Mitch's attention. "When are you going to release the body to Mrs. Spicer?"

"I'll do an autopsy next week. We'll release the body when the autopsy is done. We'll retain some organs, tissue, and fluids."

Luke cleared his throat. "Could it be suicide?"

Mitch shook his head, gesturing no. "I saw him a lot this year. He was happy."

Luke took a breath. "But you never know what people hide."

"True, but Jack, the EMT, found a plastic bag of oxycodone pills near the body. Alice tested them and found fentanyl's in them, but nothing like the extreme concentration she found in Mark's beer."

Luke nodded. "Someone wanted it to seem like an accidental OD?"

Mitch squinted. "Yes."

Jim leaned forward. "Alice checked the bag for fingerprints. She found none, not even Mark's." Jim took a sip of ale. "It's lucky that Jack wore medical gloves. He picked up the bag. I can't count the number of times I told him not to disturb the scene."

Luke studied Jim's eyes. "What do you want me to do?"

"Lead the investigation."

"Thanks. It'll be a challenge."

Jim moved closer to Luke and lowered his voice. "You need to be creative, cuz we don't want the killer to know we realize it was murder."

Luke nodded. "We gotta investigate, but how should we

proceed?" He trained his eyes on the bar at the far side of the room. "I'll mull it over while I order a burger. Lucy's too busy to take my order. She's scurrying around like a squirrel hiding acorns."

Jim laughed. "You have a way with words, brother."

His stomach aching for food, Luke neared Joe, the bartender. Luke nodded in Lucy's direction. Lucy was carrying an overloaded tray to a crowded table. "Lucy's busy. I'd like a triple-layer burger with everything on it. I'll wait."

"This is on the house for being considerate." Joe plopped a glass of ginger ale on the bar.

"Thanks, Joe." Luke sat on a barstool. He decided he'd give Joe a tip to hand to Lucy.

Luke heard loud voices to his left and smelled body odor. Two scruffy men were chatting. Both wore blue jeans, hadn't shaved for days, and had deep tans. The first one said, "Carmen sure as hell did in Mark."

The second man eyeballed his pal. "You positive?"

"Carmen screws all the nice lookin' men she meets."

"If she kilt him, no way the cops can prove it. OD deaths happen every day."

"I'm not gonna stick around to find out. I got me a better job next door on Kobold Farm—two bucks extra an hour."

"I'll join you."

"You should, buddy."

The two men got up and carried their drinks to a table in the bar's far corner. Luke figured he should thoroughly investigate Carmen, but what was the best way to approach her?

* * *

LUKE CARRIED his tray of food to the table where Jim, Mitch, and Layla sat. Luke glanced at Jim. "I overheard two Spicer Farm guys sitting at the bar. One thinks Carmen killed Mark." Luke reckoned everyone at the farm had to be investigated. Someone had to go undercover.

Jim riveted his eyes on the dartboard on the far wall and then turned to Luke. "I bet you think the same thing I do. We need to check out the farm from the inside."

"Yep." Luke gestured at the two men in the corner of the barroom. "A Spicer worker said he's quitting."

Jim slid his chair closer to Luke. "This week's issue of *The Holler* had a want ad for a stable hand at the Spicer Farm." Jim scratched his scalp. "One of our people should apply for the job."

Luke nodded. "Who?"

Jim pursed his lips. "You worked undercover twice before."

"Somebody could recognize me from my picture in the Jenkins murder article."

"People forget what was in the newspaper three days ago. The Jenkins article's a year old." Jim scratched his nose. "Shave off your mustache, but let your beard grow. Wear ratty clothes and skip a bath before you apply."

Luke sighed.

"You're the perfect person for the job."

"What about ID?"

"We'll fix you up with a brand-new driver's license. We could call you Lucas Blanco."

"Okay," Luke heard himself say. He was often mistaken for a Latino because his mother had been from Italy. He'd inherited her dark hair. His beard was black, and his skin was swarthy. Because of his appearance, he could easily pass himself off as a rugged farm worker.

Jim squinted. "I'll call the driver's licensing office first thing Monday."

Luke saw Layla frown. He thought, *She's tryin' to hide her displeasure*. She hadn't liked it when he'd gone undercover at NASA earlier that year. He knew stable hands lived on the larger horse farms. Even if he were allowed to commute to the Spicer Farm, he'd have to spend countless hours there, day and night. How long would this undercover stint last? Weeks? A month?

Luke noticed Jim had been silent for a while, thinking.

"I'll tell everybody you're taking an FBI training course in Arizona for two weeks."

"How should I contact you?"

"Call, text, or email me on my personal cell phone."

Luke nodded.

Layla cleared her throat in an exaggerated way. "Gentlemen, if you're done talking shop, I have an idea. Let's play pool. I won't see Luke often in the next week."

Jim patted Layla's shoulder. "Don't worry. He's on a simple fact-gathering mission." Jim stood. "You're my partner, Layla."

She smiled at Mitch. "Be advised. I'm the champion pool player in this bar." She put her hands on her hips and laughed.

Luke wolfed down the rest of his burger and pointed at Mitch, the coroner. "Let's prove her wrong."

As he stood, Luke wondered how he could allay Layla's fears and make her feel less lonesome. Could he stay at home with her one or two nights a week?

# FIVE

LEXINGTON DRUG DEALER Ethan Wood sat on a rusted kitchen chair in his dilapidated house. The high humidity made him feel hot and sticky. *I'm goddamned tired*, he thought. Depressed, he glanced at his drinking buddy, Malcolm, who sat on the other side of the kitchen table. Malcolm picked up a cool can of beer.

Ethan planted his elbow on the worn table and leaned on his fist. His filthy clapboard house hadn't been painted for years, and he didn't have a decent fan. Even with the kitchen and attic windows opened, the inside of the house was stuffy and humid. It smelled of mold. The kitchen temperature was much hotter than the eighty degrees his outdoor thermometer read.

Ethan frowned and studied Malcolm. The man's remaining teeth were a yellowish brown, stained by cigarettes and coffee. With his scarred face and the gap between his upper left canine tooth and the rest of his front teeth, he could've passed for a retired boxer.

Malcolm blew smoke from the side of his mouth and set his burning cigarette in the ashtray on the table. "Yur in big trouble."

Ethan bit his lip and then took a breath. "I've been selling drugs to Carmen for years. When the cops find out, they'll charge me for Mark's death. If I leave town, they'll be suspicious. But I'm gonna go."

"Lay low, brother. Wait. It'll be unlikely the cops will learn you sold drugs to her."

"I doubt it." Ethan grabbed a beer can from his noisy fridge and twisted the container to free it from the six-pack's plastic rings. He popped the can's tab, gulped the brew, and licked his lips. "Even if it's an OD, the cops will be after me."

"They're always after you."

"Yeah, but because of Dalton's Law, I'd get years added to my sentence if they convict me."

"What's Dalton's Law?"

Ethan took a short breath. "It's a Kentucky law. It's been on the books for eight years. If they convict me for sellin' pills with fentanyl in 'em, I'll have to serve at least eighty-five percent of my sentence."

"They's been puttin' fentanyl in lots of drugs these days." Malcolm grunted. "It ain't yur fault them Mexicans add it to their pills."

"My supplier, David, told me they've been workin' hard to improve the pills. They bought new, modern equipment to make the chemical levels more accurate."

"What difference would it make? They're gonna put fentanyl in drugs anyway."

Ethan took a sip of beer. "They figure too many customers are dying. Fewer users, less money." He paused. Ethan's inner voice told him, *The DEA won't stop going after us even if the pills are better*.

Malcolm shifted in his chair. He snatched his cigarette and sucked smoke into his lungs. He coughed and set the butt in his ashtray. "I heard a rumor Carmen killed Mark by puttin' pills in his beer." Smoke leaked from his mouth as he spoke.

Ethan glared at Malcolm. "I've known Carmen for years. She has no idea David is smuggling cartel drugs, and Mark was laundering money. She believes David and I race homing pigeons. You'd think she woulda figured out the pigeons carry drugs." Ethan paused and glanced at Malcolm. "I screwed her once. She's as loose as a bitch in heat, but she's not evil."

Malcolm shrugged. "Now she's free to find a younger man. And she could've kilt Mark for his money."

"My gut tells me no." Ethan paused. She's naive."

"Naive?"

"She's not wise to the ways of the world."

Malcolm crushed his empty beer can on the floor with his heel. "Would the *Nuestro Club* cartel kill Mark?"

"No. He was useful cuz he laundered money. I bet he tried drugs and overdosed." Ethan hunched his shoulders. "I wonder if Carmen will trust David to run the farm for her. The Mexicans will want to keep using the Spicer Farm to smuggle drugs and launder money."

Malcolm peered through the dirty, half-opened kitchen window at the sky. "A half-dozen of them birds of yours are flyin' this way." He pointed out the window. The sounds of flapping wings were louder.

Ethan stood. "I gotta go upstairs and get the packets off the birds before they finish eatin'. Wanna see how I do it?"

Malcolm shrugged. "Okay."

The two men climbed the creaking steps to the attic. The birds pecked at birdseed in troughs. Ethan shut the window and counted the pigeons. "They're all accounted for."

Malcolm squatted near the feeding birds. "How'd you train 'em to go back and forth between the farm and your attic?"

Ethan captured a bird and began to remove its packet of pills. "They sleep in the Spicer barn and return to eat at my place. The birds go back and forth two times a day. David's men reload the pouches."

"They fly to other places?"

"Different groups of birds supply Louisville, too. A separate bunch of pigeons fly pills from Mexico in stages. It's kinda like the Pony Express. David says Mateo came up with the idea of smuggling drugs across the border cuz he'd found out pigeons carried cell phone parts into Brazilian prisons back in 2015."

Malcolm scratched his greasy scalp. "But a bird can't carry a whole hell of a lot."

"Birds can carry up to two and a half ounces." Ethan tossed the pigeon's pack of pills into a plastic bag. "They average sixty miles an hour."

"Wow." Malcolm batted a mosquito away from his face. "For a pigeon to fly from Kentucky to the Mexican border, they gotta travel close to 2,000 miles."

"David says the best birds can fly 1,100 miles when they race. The Mexicans set up a pigeon racing club as a cover."

"Are they smugglin' all their drugs using birds?"

"I don't know." Ethan let go of a pigeon and tossed another drug packet into the plastic bag. "The Mexicans got lots of birds. See all the pigeon shit in this attic?"

Malcolm grinned. "You gotta give David and his pals credit. They outsmarted the DEA, the border guards, and the cops."

Ethan put a tie wrap on the bag. "I hope I can dodge the local fuzz. But I gotta feelin' I'm up shit creek."

# SIX

LAYLA FIXED BREAKFAST—SCRAMBLED eggs, bacon, buttermilk biscuits, grits, fried potatoes, and coffee. *It's a true country breakfast*, Luke thought.

When Luke went into the kitchen, Layla wrinkled her nose. "You smell like you slept with the animals."

"I gotta stink like a stableman when I apply for the job at the Spicer Farm."

Layla hugged him, but she turned her head away from his scratchy beard. "You need to shave." She smiled, took a half step backward, and turned. Then she grabbed the frying pan from the stove and slid eggs onto three plates.

Angela, Layla's six-year-old daughter, sat down on a chair at the kitchen table. "Good morning, Daddy."

Luke patted Angela's head. "You, too, honey."

Layla turned to face Luke. "You're her dad, now."

Luke blushed through his tanned skin. "I'm doin' what's natural."

Layla focused on Luke's eyes. "What's today's plan?"

"I'll drive to Frankfort to get my new driver's license. Then I'll head for the Spicer Farm."

"Why not shower?"

"You got to live the part like actors do." He peered across the room. "In case I didn't tell you—stable hands live at the big farms five days a week."

Layla blinked and, for a moment, fixed her eyes on the linoleum floor. "How many days will you be working at the Spicer place?" She cocked her head at Angela.

Luke asked himself, *Will Angela repeat what she hears?* He took his time to figure out how to answer. "Let's see if I learn how to take care of horses in four or five days."

After eating most of her breakfast, Angela broke into the conversation. "Excuse me, Maw, I'm done."

"You're excused."

After Angela left, Luke whispered, "I wish I could be with you every night, but I gotta go undercover."

"Why you? You still complain about leg pain."

"Nobody in the Sheriff's department but me has experience with horses and has been undercover."

Layla leaned toward Luke and kissed his lips. "Angela will miss you reading to her at bedtime."

Luke peered toward the bathroom where Angela was brushing her teeth. "I'll miss readin' to her, too."

"You doze off before she does when you read." Layla laughed and studied Luke. "In five minutes, I need to drive Angela to her enrichment classes."

Luke nodded. He often wasn't home when Layla drove Angela to summer school. He was running late, and he began to shovel food into his mouth. He glanced at Layla. "I gotta get going."

Luke's mind wandered. *What weapons should I take with me, if any?*

# SEVEN

LAYLA STOPPED her rusted sedan and helped Angela out of her car seat. The little girl hugged Layla goodbye and ran to the front door of Renee's Daycare School, where Angela was taking summer enrichment classes.

Layla smiled as she watched her child enter the building. Luke's sister, Renee, had founded the school, and Layla worked there during the regular school year, but not in the summer.

After Layla got back in her car and started it, she asked herself yet again, *Why'd I forget to take the pill?* She'd missed taking a birth control pill in week three of her current cycle. Her period was now three days late. She sighed. *I better stop at the drugstore to pick up a pregnancy test.*

Yesterday, she'd wondered whether missing one pill during the month could result in pregnancy. A medical foundation's website taught Layla the pill is ninety-nine percent effective, unless a woman neglects to take a pill during certain times of her cycle. Forgetting a pill when Layla had meant her chances of conception had increased by six percent. Taking a morning-after pill would've been wise, but she hadn't done it, and it was too late now.

*How am I going to tell Luke if I'm pregnant?* She knew she

wanted his baby. *Will he marry me?* He loved her. She knew it, but he'd been married before. *Would memories of his contentious divorce convince him not to remarry?*

Luke had told Layla about Emma, his ex-wife. Emma couldn't become pregnant because she had a hormone imbalance. He hadn't said whether or not he wanted to have children. But he did tell Layla the sad story of how Emma got hooked on pills. She'd been in a car accident and had broken her leg. Her doctor had prescribed oxycodone pills for her pain. Soon she had become addicted to them. Luke said Emma had been depressed before the car wreck, probably due to her inability to have children.

Emma later started taking meth. Luke had tried to convince her to go to rehab, but she wouldn't do it. They had argued, and later they divorced. Luke had said he was sorry for Emma, but he admitted he was relieved his marriage to her was over.

Layla wondered, *Did Luke start overusing alcohol because Emma's addiction stressed him? Did his marital troubles sour him on fatherhood?*

* * *

FIVE MINUTES after Layla left to drive Angela to school, Luke's mobile phone rang.

He touched the "answer" icon. "Hi, Jim."

"You can leave for the driver's licensing office, Luke. It's all set."

"Okay. I'll go directly to the Spicer Farm after I get my license."

"Keep me posted." Jim hung up.

Luke attached his holster with his SCCY miniature handgun to the right side of his belt. He was happy to do real police work again.

After donning a pair of worn blue jeans, he scanned his closet. He snatched a black, long-sleeved work shirt with a hole in one elbow. *Perfect.* He slipped the shirt on but didn't tuck it in. It hid his mini, ten-shot plus one-in-the-chamber, 9mm weapon.

He wondered, *Does the SCCY have enough firepower?*

He picked up his Smith & Wesson pistol and a second magazine loaded with a dozen cartridges. He inspected the weapon.

*I could lock it in a toolbox.*

After searching his workbench drawer in the garage, he found a padlock and keys. He glanced around the garage and saw a toolbox the size of a shoebox. He unlatched it. The Smith & Wesson and its magazine fit in it with little room to spare.

He padlocked the gun in the box and then spotted a sturdy, oversized paper shopping bag. He balled up a newspaper, shoved it into the bag, and set the metal box on top of the crumpled paper. After he put the bag on his pickup's passenger-side floor, he tossed a layer of trash over the bag, including an unwashed milkshake container, hamburger wrappings, two soda cans, and an oily rag. He smiled. *Should do the trick.*

He grabbed a moth-eaten woolen Army blanket; his new, state-of-the-art crossbow; and his quiver with eight arrow-like bolts in it. If he ended his day before darkness came, he'd find a place to target practice with the bow to prepare for deer hunting season. He wanted to learn to load his bow faster.

Most people could reload a crossbow in sixty seconds, but Luke knew that practiced hunters could do it in fifteen or twenty seconds. On the slim chance he'd get a second shot at a deer, he'd have a better chance to kill it if he could reload quicker.

After carrying his crossbow, quiver, and blanket to his clunky truck, Luke set the items on its hood. A metal-on-metal groan sounded when he yanked the passenger door open.

The passenger seat in the cab was worn through. Padding stuck out of it. Luke put the bow and the quiver on the seat and tossed the Army blanket over them.

Luke sat in the driver's seat and turned the ignition key. The battered truck started, coughed, dieseled, and quit. The smell of gasoline and exhaust smoke blew through the driver's side window. After turning the key again, Luke heard the ancient truck rumble to life, and he headed to the driver's licensing office.

# EIGHT

## 10:00 A.M., MONDAY, AUGUST 5

ETHAN, the drug dealer, had a pounding headache. He rolled over on his unmade bed and buried his face in a pillow, hoping the soft pressure on his forehead would kill his pain. He was also nauseous. *Too much beer*, he thought. He'd spent hours the previous night drinking with Malcolm.

Ethan's cell phone rang with a painful, shrill sound. He glared at the phone.

*It's Carmen.* The thought of speaking with her made his nausea grow. *God damn it.*

As the phone kept ringing, he wondered if he should ignore Carmen's call.

*No, I gotta answer. I need all the news I can get about what the cops know about Mark's death.*

"Hi, Carmen." Ethan knew he should tell her not to blab to the police about how she got her drugs. He'd beg her to keep her mouth shut, if necessary.

"I'm running low."

Ethan felt bile rise in his throat. "This is the final time I'll sell to you. A guy in Louisville can take over from me."

"What's going on?"

"I could be convicted for Mark's death and get twenty to

life. They'll figure Mark used your drugs, which I sold to you. I'm leaving town."

"I didn't give my drugs to Mark. He wasn't an addict."

"I believe you." Ethan paused. "But do you realize Mark also could've gotten drugs from David? He's been laundering cartel drug money for years using your farm. Mark was in on it."

"What?" Carmen huffed. "David's a barn manager, not a crook."

"He has another job besides barn manager. David brings in drugs from Mexico, and I'm his Lexington pusher. Mark sold horses for cash to a Mexican from Tijuana by the name of Mateo to launder drug money."

Carmen sounded like she was hyperventilating. "Did David kill Mark?" Her voice trembled.

"I doubt it. Calm down and sit, if you're standing." Ethan pictured Carmen's curvaceous body and beautiful face.

*It's a shame she's out of touch with what's happening. How's this naive babe gonna deal with a Mexican cartel?*

"Okay, Carmen. I'll sell you a super-big bag of pills. You should have enough 'til you can get in touch with the guy in Louisville. They could even last a year."

"Okay."

Ethan imagined Carmen being attacked by David. But David was always kind to women. Then again, what if Mateo ordered David to kill Carmen to make it easy to buy the farm and continue to launder cash?

"I shouldn't have told you about the Mexicans. But if I were you, I'd take all the cash you can find, put it in an overseas account, and plan to disappear."

"Where would I go?"

"Maybe Canada?" Jumbled thoughts zipped through Ethan's brain. "You could also tell David you know about the drugs and money laundering, and you want to cooperate with him and Mateo…"

"I'm not a criminal."

"Ask David for pills. Say you want to cut out the middleman."

"I'll consider it." She sighed. "But it scares me." Carmen's voice was shaky. "What would you charge for a bag of pills that'll last a year?"

"Five grand."

"It's a lot."

"Check Mark's safe. He was rolling in cash."

Carmen exhaled. "Let's meet at the usual place tomorrow morning at nine-thirty."

"See you then."

Ethan reckoned he'd get rid of the pills he had on hand. "We'll talk tomorrow about what else you could do." He paused. "Have you heard anything from the cops?"

"Not a thing."

"Be smart. Don't mention your drug use. Don't tell the cops anything."

"Okay. Bye."

\* \* \*

CARMEN DISCONNECTED from her call with Ethan. *I need cash fast.* She didn't have the combination for Mark's safe. *Maybe there's cash in Mark's safe deposit box?*

She left Mark's office in the Spicer mansion and walked to her sports utility vehicle to drive to the First Federal Bank. She had Mark's safe deposit box key, her credit card, and her checkbook.

*I better not write a check for five thousand dollars. Could be cash in the box.* She switched on her electric vehicle and drove toward Lexington.

# NINE

GRASPING HIS VIBRATING STEERING WHEEL, Luke hummed a country tune as his pickup traveled along meandering country lanes. He felt refreshed and enjoyed the bright sun and the blue, cloudless sky.

As his truck passed enormous horse farms, he saw miles of lush, green grass and grazing thoroughbreds on each side of the narrow country road.

The grassy-smelling air rushed past his face and whipped his black hair. When he guided his pickup around yet another bend, the well-kept Spicer Farm came into view on the right side of the lane.

He took his foot off the gas pedal. Dark chocolate-colored wooden fences stood behind a roadside rock barrier and surrounded the huge farm.

Luke's decrepit pickup truck coughed and chugged as he turned onto the farm's gravel driveway. The feeble vehicle passed under a hand carved sign. It included outlines of horses and "Spicer Farm" in sculpted, eight-inch letters.

Because he'd slowed, he could smell gasoline mixed with a slight odor of hay as his vehicle approached a sandy horse-training corral. It was in the middle of an expanse of thick turf.

He was used to Kentucky's sticky summer weather, but

this morning he felt hot under his heavy work shirt. Sweat rolled down his back beneath the worn garment. It hid his pistol belt on the right side of his belly.

Buildings surrounded the central corral and lawn in a horseshoe-shaped layout. As his truck crunched the driveway's gravel, Luke slowed down to better examine the farm buildings.

The two main structures were a combined barn and stable and an imposing, graceful mansion. It had to be at least a century old.

The country house was three stories tall with six gables sticking out from a gray slate roof. At the highest point of the stately home, a black, wrought iron weathervane shaped like a racehorse pointed westward.

A wide set of steps led up to the mansion's extra-wide, wooden front door. Luke guessed it was ten feet tall.

*The mansion must have at least a dozen bedrooms,* he thought. He noticed a large, man-made pond seventy feet from the magnificent home and wondered if it was stocked with fish.

Airborne dust billowed behind Luke's truck as it chugged forward like a slow-moving tractor. He guided his vehicle along the horseshoe-shaped driveway past the mansion. At the far end of the looped drive, he stopped by the enormous barn.

From his driver's seat, Luke studied this structure. It had an A-frame roof at least 150 yards in length with a coffee-colored vinyl covering. The roof was three stories in height. As he peered upward at the structure, he saw an open hay door in the gable. He could see a pulley system meant to hoist bales of hay and straw to the loft above the barn's floor.

Yellowish straw bales sat near the building waiting to be stowed in the barn. As he wondered if he'd soon be moving bales into the loft, he heard flapping wings. Five gray pigeons reduced their speed and fluttered through the hay door opening.

A sign posted alongside the front door near the hay bales read, "Office at the rear." A horse whinnied inside the stable.

*I gotta remember I'm Lucas Blanco,* Luke thought as he got out of his vehicle and slammed its door. He patted the cheap wallet in his rear pocket. The billfold held his new Kentucky driver's license, including his picture. In it, he appeared rough. His mussed-up hair and unshaven face fit the image he wanted to portray, somebody not apt to be a lawman.

The door near the bales opened, and a stocky man with a body like that of an NFL football player emerged. He scowled at Luke and sized up Luke's beat-up truck. "Don't park your fuckin' junk heap there. Makes the farm seem cheap."

Luke plastered a smile on his face. "Where can I park?"

"Behind the shed." The man pointed, and then spit onto the dusty gravel.

Luke tried to appear humble. "Where do I apply for the stable hand job?"

The man frowned. "Inside in the office. See David. This morning he hired a stable hand, but a mucker quit this morning."

"Thanks."

The gruff man turned and walked away.

The mucker job would be dirty and low-level enough he'd get it, Luke reckoned, as he returned to his truck. He moved it out of sight behind the tool shed the blunt man had pointed out.

*Dressin' and smellin' like a bum could pay off.* Luke pushed his hair out of his eyes and approached the barn's entry.

# TEN

TWO HUNDRED-FIFTY-POUND, six-foot-tall Terry Trigo sat in the second-story loft of the Spicer Farm's main barn. A dozen carrier pigeons fluttered into the loft through the hay door as the muscular Latino watched.

Attached to its leg, one bird had a special, sealed tube with a black ring painted on it.

*I gotta catch the black-banded bird first,* Terry thought.

The capsule contained a coded message. The other eleven birds carried gray, feather-colored backpacks filled with counterfeit oxycodone pills.

Terry recalled that David had told him that as early as the 1930s, smugglers had trained pigeons to fly drugs into the United States. Back then, the birds flew too high to be shot down.

Terry removed the capsule and eleven backpacks from the pigeons. After slipping the capsule with the dispatch into his hip pocket, he poured the addictive pills from the backpacks into a plastic bag. The drugs had arrived after having been carried in stages from Mexico.

Each bird's pack contained 150 to 180 pills, depending on the bird's size and how far it had to fly. The street value of the drugs a single pigeon carried was at least $5,000. Depending on demand, one or two teams of birds made two round trips per day, transporting their illicit cargo on the last leg of the Kentucky-Mexico route.

Terry decided to hide the drugs first, and then deliver the capsule with the coded note to David.

After climbing down the stairs and exiting a side door of the barn, Terry made his way to a termite-eaten post at the corner of the corral.

Surveying the area, he saw no one around and slipped the bag of illegal drugs into the hollow post.

When one of David's pushers requested pills, Terry or another pigeon handler would go to the post to fulfill the order. Pills would be loaded into pigeon backpacks for distribution to pushers. Teams of birds flew specific circuits to a half-dozen drug dealers in Lexington, Louisville, and the surrounding region.

Once Terry had safely stored the pills in the post, he plodded to the barn to deliver the message tube to David. *What did the coded letter say? Had it come from Mexico?*

\* \* \*

DAVID SAT in his office at his gray steel desk. He knew that Gabriel was going to drive to Nashville that night. Gabriel, the night shift pigeon man, was often David's choice to transport a cage of carrier pigeons 215 miles to the Nashville safe house.

Once in Tennessee, the homing pigeons would be ready to fly narcotics and messages back to the Spicer Farm after new product arrived from Mexico. Because of their instinct to return to their homes (in this case the Spicer Farm), and the birds' ability to find their way, their kind has been used for thousands of years to carry messages and lightweight items.

David smiled. *Mateo's a smart one.*

Mateo had started his pigeon racing club, *Club de Las Aves*, to learn how to send messages via pigeons, and also as a way to cover up his illegal smuggling.

Mateo feared the Pigeon Racing Cooperative would

cancel his membership, and his *Club de Las Aves* would be disqualified from competition, if the co-op found out he had a criminal record. He'd therefore dreamed up his alias, Mateo Guerra.

*It's strange Mateo has come to love pigeon racing when his real business is smuggling,* David mused.

Mateo raced birds in courses from 100 miles to 600 miles long. His average race was 300 miles in length.

A knock at David's office door cut his thoughts short. "Come in."

Terry entered and handed David a small sealed tube.

"Thank you." David glanced at it. A bird on the final leg of the pigeon circuit had arrived from Mexico.

After Terry left, David unscrewed the cylinder's top, removed a thin roll of lightweight tissue, and smoothed it flat on his desk. He grabbed a Spanish *Bible* from his bookshelf. Mateo had the same edition at his headquarters in Mexico.

David studied the cipher written on the lightweight paper. Each chapter, verse, line number, and word number led him to a specific word in his *Bible*.

He wrote decoded words on a separate piece of the special featherweight paper. In Spanish, the note read, "Since M is gone, build lab. Will send pure F. Store until lab ready to make product at your locale."

David set the two flimsy papers on a cheap dinner plate. He lit a match and touched the papers. A flash, similar to the output of a powerful camera strobe, resulted. Both papers had disappeared, leaving no ash.

David had once asked Mateo how he'd thought of such a safe way to send messages and dispose of them. Mateo had said he'd seen a traveling magician's show in Tijuana. The itinerant entertainer had snapped his fingers, and a sheet of paper disappeared in a bright flash.

After the show, Mateo had given the entertainer a generous tip and asked him about his magic paper. The man explained the paper was called magician's paper, and he'd bought it on the Internet.

Mateo searched the web and discovered the paper was easy to buy. After doing detailed keyword research, he learned flash paper is treated with nitric acid. When the acid-soaked tissue burns, it doesn't produce smoke or ash.

Curious, Mateo had combed the Internet for the history of flash paper. One Internet source said the Soviet Union's KGB had used it to transport secret messages like the one David had just received.

David rubbed his head. Mateo had given him his marching orders.

*I must hire men who can keep their mouths shut and build a drug lab.*

Then David remembered he needed a new man to muck the stalls. He could explain hiring a mucker to Carmen, but how could he justify employing a construction team?

# ELEVEN

LUKE OPENED the back door of the Spicer Farm's horse barn. Stalls lined both sides of a wide passageway the length of the skinny redwood building. The top Dutch doors of all the stalls were unlocked, and a half-dozen inquisitive horses, their heads sticking out into the aisle, noticed Luke. The equines were beautiful. Even to the untrained eye, they appeared to be the finest of thoroughbreds.

A hundred yards away, daylight streamed through a doorway wide enough to lead a horse outside.

Luke's eyes focused on the closest animal to him, a white horse on his left. Its curious, liquid eyes probed him like an x-ray, while its soft, brown ears aimed in his direction. Luke's gut told him this animal was friendly and craved companionship.

Near each of the stalls, Luke noticed tack hanging on hooks—harnesses, bits, reins, halters, and bridles.

While he surveyed the tack, a brilliant light flashed through the crack under a closed door. *Did someone take a picture?* A sign above the door read, "Barn Manager, David Braga."

Luke stepped to the door and tapped on it.

"Come in." The man's voice had a slight Spanish accent.

Luke opened the door. He noticed a middle-aged, stocky

man with shiny, olive-colored skin and black, close-cropped hair. He held a cigar and motioned Luke into his office. As the man drew smoke into his mouth, he appeared to savor it.

Luke leveled his eyes at the Latino. "I saw yur stable hand want ad."

"I already hired a man for the job." The barn manager grinned. His bright-white teeth seized Luke's attention. "But you are lucky. A stall mucker quit this morning."

Luke smiled.

The swarthy man stood, crushed the butt of his cigar in his ashtray, reached across his desk, and offered his hand.

Luke shook it. The Latino's grip was firm.

"I'm David Braga."

"I'm Lucas Blanco."

David pointed to a spindly wooden chair next to his desk. "Please sit." He slid his Spanish *Bible* to the far side of his desktop. "Tell me about yourself." David sat.

"I grew up on a farm. I know all about animals, includin' horses."

"Why do you want a job at Spicer Farm?"

"I'm tired of workin' fast food jobs. I figgered I'd do what I know about."

"You a drug user?"

"No." Luke hoped he hadn't sprinkled in too much poor grammar to fit his fake identity. But in any case, his day-to-day grammar wasn't perfect anyway.

"Are you Latino?"

"Half. Paw was from the holler, and Maw was Mexican." Luke figured what he said was sort of true. His mother had been from Naples, Italy. In the fifteenth century, it had been under Spanish rule. Back then, the citizens of *Napoli* spoke Spanish. He was certain he could pass for a first-generation American of Mexican heritage.

David squinted. "You can start today. It pays $10.25 an hour in cash-money."

"Thanks, Mr. Braga."

"Call me David." David pointed out of his window at a clapboard, one-story building. "Hands get three free meals a day in the bunkhouse. We require you to stay rent free on this farm five nights a week."

"I gotta git my clothes from my rental room."

"Go after work tonight." David took a breath. "After you fill out the paperwork, report to Bruno Chavez. He'll explain your duties. He's the guy who has the body of a *toro*."

"I bet he's the one who told me how to find yur office."

"It was him. He left a minute before you arrived." Studying Luke, David grinned, flashing his white teeth. "Welcome, Lucas."

The men shook hands again.

David took documents and a pen from a desk drawer. "Fill these out." He set the papers and pen on his desk near Luke. "Can you write?"

"Yeah."

David nodded at a card table. "You can sit and complete the paperwork. I need your driver's license to copy it for our records."

Luke took out his worn billfold and handed the license to David.

David started toward his office door. "Be back soon."

Luke snatched the forms and a pen and dragged the wooden chair to the folding card table.

After removing an evidence bag from his pocket, he held his hand over David's crushed cigar butt. It felt cool. *It seems safe enough to grab*. He used the bag to snatch what was left of the cigar and bagged it.

*Better not start burning in my pocket*. He reckoned he'd feel heat before the butt burst into flames if a spark was still inside the stogie.

As Luke began to fill out the boxes on the documents, he wondered how he'd deal with Bruno. The man could be a problem. He had an attitude and would be hard to work for. Then Layla's image popped into Luke's mind. *How am I gonna tell Layla I have to stay overnight in the Spicer Farm bunkhouse most of the week?*

\* \* \*

AFTER LUKE FINISHED the Spicer Farm employment papers, David came back to his office and returned Luke's driver's license.

"Thanks." Luke passed a fistful of paperwork to David.

David scanned the documents. "I saw Bruno at the far end of the stable, by the wide doorway. He's waiting for you."

"Yes, sir." Luke nodded and exited the office.

As Luke began to walk past the expensive horses toward the entrance of the barn, the white horse on his left whinnied. Luke had learned years earlier each horse has a distinct whinny, and equines can identify each other from their unique sounds.

Luke knew that horses neigh when they ask for friendship. Often a whinnying horse is lonesome, trying to find a welcoming herd. He wondered, *Does the white one want to be my buddy?* Would the steed come to regard him as a pal and no longer neigh when Luke walked by?

Luke saw Bruno's silhouette, his massive body backlit by sunshine beaming through the wide entryway in the distance.

As he neared Bruno, Luke heard a light brown horse nicker. The sound was like a weak, purring whinny. The animal took a good look at him. From the animal's nicker, Luke realized the horse was hungry. All the animals were checking Luke out as he walked by them.

When Luke was a dozen feet from Bruno, a superb, ebony stallion snorted with his head held tall—a sign of alarm. The animal glared at Bruno. Was the tall horse afraid of the bull-like man? Had he mistreated the beast?

Bruno sneered. "David hired you. Lucas Blanco, correct?"

"Yep. Yur Bruno?"

"Uh-huh. I got plenty for you to do."

"Okay."

"Muck the dirty stalls. Ernie Duke will show you how." The massive man paused. "Wash the horses when I or Ernie says. Feed them when we tell you and give 'em the feed mix listed on the clipboard at each stall."

Luke nodded. *Bruno's a control freak.*

Bruno fiddled with his mobile phone. "Ernie will be back in five minutes. I gotta go." The sturdy man turned to leave, but stopped and again faced Luke. "Oh yeah, new hires gotta meet the owner, Mrs. Carmen Spicer."

"Yes, sir."

"She knows yur coming. I called her." Bruno flushed through his tough, tanned skin. "After lunch hour, knock on the servant door at the back of the mansion. The maid will let you in."

Luke puzzled over why Carmen wanted to see all employees, even those with the lowliest jobs. He was happy he'd have a chance to size her up and get a first impression of the sort of woman she was. Was she the kind of person who would murder her husband or hire a hitman? Luke glanced at his watch. "I'll be on time."

"Take a shower in the bunkhouse. You smell like a stray dog." Bruno showed his disgust.

"I ain't got my bath stuff from home yet."

"Soap and towels are near the shower." Bruno exhaled. "Take off your boots before you go in the house." He turned on his heel, farted, and left the barn.

Luke wondered if Carmen had seen his newspaper picture from a year ago. If so, would she recognize him? He wished his beard would grow faster.

He leaned against the wide doorway and waited for Ernie.

# TWELVE

CARMEN ENTERED the First Federal Bank in Lexington with Mark's safe deposit box key in her purse. Her pulse started to pound.

A pudgy manager stood up from his desk and approached Carmen. "Mrs. Spicer, I'm sorry to hear of your loss."

"Thank you." Carmen felt herself shake a trifle. She'd not gone to the bank often and then only when Mark was with her.

Carmen figured the manager was assessing her. His eyes locked with hers. "How may I be of assistance?"

"Did Mark have any accounts besides our checking account?"

"No, but I can set up a savings account for you if you'd like."

"Maybe later. Right now I'd like to open Mark's safe deposit box."

"Of course. Follow me, please."

After filling out a form the manager had given her, Carmen went with him into the vault. They both inserted their keys in the bank box's locks. The manager pulled the drawer-like, heavy container outward. "Ring the bell when you're done." He left.

*I hope cash is in the box.* Her heart pounding, she made a quick survey of the contents of the heavy-duty metal container.

She noticed a purple satin bag. Fingers shaking, she peeked in the pouch. A dozen precious stones—a diamond, emeralds, and an assortment of gems she could not identify —were inside.

*I could go to a jeweler and sell them. But it'll take time.*

Reaching in the bank box, she found an envelope with a rubber band wound around it. She opened it and found a bundle of greenbacks. In less than a minute, she thumbed through the bills. She counted $1,200 in cash.

*I could write a check for cash for thirty-eight hundred.* She paused. *But what if Mark had been murdered? What if the cops see I've written a check for cash and find out I've used the money to buy drugs?*

She wondered if she was paranoid.

*Mark would never take illegal drugs, and the cops know it. He rarely even had a beer.*

She spotted a sturdy cardboard envelope secured with a string. She unwound the twine and found a yellow card labeled "safe combo" in the envelope. A set of numbers was on the card.

*Ethan said money had to be in the safe.* She stuffed the cash in her purse and put the combination card in her wallet.

After the manager locked the box, she thanked him and drove home.

She asked herself, *How much money's in Mark's ancient safe?*

# THIRTEEN

SOMEONE WAS WHISTLING a classic oldies tune outside the stable doorway, out of sight. Luke pushed himself away from the door frame and peered around the entrance's right side toward the excellent whistler.

A tall, thin man walked toward Luke. The bony man's shoulder length, red hair straggled behind him and blew in the gentle but humid breeze. He saw Luke and stopped warbling. "You Lucas Blanco?"

Luke had a positive feeling about the rail-thin man. "Yep. Are you Ernie?"

"Yes."

Ernie extended his hand.

Luke squeezed the man's calloused hand, but not too hard because he could feel Ernie's thin bones and sinews. Ernie appeared to be in his fifties. "I'm pleased to make yur acquaintance."

"Me, too." Ernie slid a can of chewing tobacco from his jeans pocket. "I thought you'd have a Mexican accent."

Once again, Luke had to lie. It was part of being under-cover. "My maw was from Mexico, but my paw was from the holler."

"I heard if you speak a second language, you'll have less

chance of having a stroke." Ernie leaned against the door-frame. "Could you teach me Spanish words?"

Luke was glad he'd figured out what to say next because he didn't speak a word of Spanish. "My maw wouldn't talk in Spanish around me cuz she wanted me to become a true American."

"I'm outta luck. Bruno refuses to teach me any Mexican lingo." Ernie studied Luke's eyes. "I bet you figured out Bruno's an asshole."

Luke shrugged. *Bruno's gonna be a problem.*

Ernie squinted. "He's always an angry bastard. He spends the majority of his time tending pigeons instead of worrying about the horses."

Luke was quiet. *No way I'm gonna judge people too fast on this farm.* He figured he'd stay clearheaded and keep his eyes and ears open. His goal was to uncover facts about Mark's murder and learn how people on the farm interacted.

Ernie stood straight and fingered his tobacco tin. "We should talk about your job. Ever work on a farm?"

Luke nodded. "Yep. I tended all sorts of animals includin' horses, but I ain't never dealt with racehorses."

"You'll learn. Kentucky farm boys have common sense." Ernie winked. "You'll start with basics, like mucking stalls. I'll add chores later." He tapped a clipboard and handed it to Luke.

A schedule attached to the board listed stall numbers, horse names, and a timetable. Luke smiled. "It's a lot of horseshit to deal with."

"You got a sense of humor." Ernie laughed. "See the column with groom names?"

"Uh-huh."

"Tonight, I'll add your name. Usually, we have five grooms. Two quit. We three—me, you, and Terry—will have to work harder 'til David hires two people to help us."

"Okay."

"Start by mucking the white horse's stall. I'll take him out for exercise." Ernie fished in his tobacco tin with his index finger and his thumb to snatch a clump of chewing tobacco.

He stuck the lump in his mouth between his cheek and lower jaw. "Let's go."

As Luke and Ernie neared the stall, Ernie spit tobacco juice on the floor and pointed to an alcove. "We keep the muckin' tools yonder."

Luke grabbed a pitchfork, a broad shovel, a stable broom, and a bottle of odor-control solution. He laid them in a wheelbarrow. After slipping on rubber-soled galoshes, he picked up a pair of heavy-duty gloves. He glanced at Ernie. "When I walked by the white horse, he was calm."

"Whitey's the most peaceful thoroughbred I come across in years." Ernie laughed. "I wish folks at this farm were as good-natured as Whitey."

"What do you mean?"

Ernie spit tobacco juice. "Bruno's an SOB. And Terry—the other groom—is gruff. David's okay. But after the owner, Mark, died of a drug overdose Saturday, Carmen, Mark's wife, put David in charge of training the horses. He's stressed."

Luke's brain went on alert. "Mark Spicer OD'd?"

"Yep. It was on the TV and even in the Lexington and Louisville papers."

"I don't pay no attention to the news."

Ernie took a step toward Luke, who'd grasped the wheelbarrow's handles. "Mark wasn't a drug user. I never even saw him smoke a cigarette. Once in a while, he'd have a beer, though."

Luke leaned toward Ernie. "You sayin' he all of a sudden decided to start takin' drugs?"

"Hell no. People think Carmen slipped pills into his beer during his annual party."

Luke started to roll the wheelbarrow. "I gotta meet with her after lunch. She's a killer?"

Ernie shrugged. "You never know about people, but she does make passes at the decent-looking men she comes across. A number of folks call her a nympho." He paused. "I heard she slept with David."

"Wow." Luke picked up speed as he pushed the wheelbarrow toward Whitey's stall.

Ernie chuckled with a quiet voice. "It's like a soap opera set on this farm."

Luke reckoned he'd do a thorough investigation of Carmen, but how? He was lucky she would meet with him after lunch. He'd have to shower, comb his hair, and put on deodorant, if he could find any. He hadn't counted on meeting Carmen so soon.

How much time would she spend speaking with him? He was a mere stable hand, trusted to clean stalls but not anything else. Luke's train of thought changed, and he began to think about the many duties he'd have on the farm. In the next five days, would David and Ernie let him feed and water the expensive horses, bed them down, and tack them up—put on their bridles and saddles, and exercise them?

Ernie smiled. "Deep in thought, Lucas?"

"I'm wonderin' if y'all will let me ride one of them expensive beasts."

"Could be. Let's see how you do." Ernie patted Whitey and then turned to Luke. "Don't forget to get lunch at noon in the bunkhouse."

"Okay." Luke felt exhilarated. Riding a racehorse would be a first for him. He beamed as he came close to Whitey and gazed into the animal's vivid eyes. *I hope I'll git to ride you.*

While Ernie was leading Whitey away, Luke was in the stall scraping up horse shit with the shovel. He judged it wasn't as smelly as dog feces.

He tossed the horse waste in the wheelbarrow. He guessed he'd need fifteen minutes to muck the stall. Then he'd clean up, eat lunch, and meet Carmen.

*Is she like a black widow spider? Did she do in her mate?*

\* \* \*

LUKE PUT AWAY the mucking tools and the wheelbarrow and then started for the bunkhouse to shower and eat lunch. He smelled of horse shit, urine, dirty straw, and his own body odor.

He pulled on the bunkhouse outside door and came face-to-face with a burly Latino man who stood six feet tall and had to weigh in excess of 200 pounds.

The massive man's brown eyes sized up Luke. "You smell like garbage that's been sittin' in the sun too long." The Latino spoke in a strong Mexican accent. He sneered and took a step closer to Luke. "Move aside, scumbag."

Luke stepped into the elongated room. "Where's the shower?"

"Far end of the building." The man paused. "You the new guy—Lucas?"

"Yep. What's yur name?"

"Terencio Trigo. Call me Terry." He cocked his head. "Talk to me in Spanish."

"I don't know many Spanish words cuz my maw didn't want us to learn it."

"She wasn't proud of Mexico?"

"I don't know. She's dead."

"She's lucky she can't see you today." Terry stepped toward the door and bumped Luke's shoulder and side as he went by.

Luke wondered if the big man had felt Luke's SCCY pistol under his shirt when they'd collided. Luke kept silent.

Footsteps on the rough, wooden floor told him someone was nearing him from the rear. He turned and saw Ernie, his dangling, red hair framing his grinning face. "I saw you meet Terry. I told you he's gruff."

Luke shrugged. "At least he gave me directions to the shower."

"After you clean up, let's have lunch together. I'll fill you in about different folks."

"Thanks. I'll be out in five minutes."

\* \* \*

LUKE STOPPED at the lunch table where Ernie sat. The redheaded man turned and saw Luke. "You smell like a cleaned-up whore drenched in perfume."

Luke shrugged. "I come across a cologne bottle near the bars of soap." He glanced at a banquet table stocked with apples and bananas as well as a platter of scrambled eggs. Coffee, juice, and water decanters stood near the fruit. An industrial-sized refrigerator was shoved against the counter.

Ernie gestured toward the fridge. "Sandwiches are in the fridge."

Luke wiped his wet hair away from his forehead. "It's a money saver to get food for free."

"Pay's low, but the benefits are okay."

After selecting fruit, coffee, and a roast beef sandwich, Luke plopped his tray onto the table across from Ernie. "I'm as hungry as a bear after hibernation."

"Appears to be true." Ernie focused on Luke's soiled shirt and blue jeans. "Carmen won't like your clothes."

"Nothin' I can do about it."

"Check the closet near the shower room. You'll find clothes left by ex-employees."

"I'll take a gander at them." Luke bit into his sandwich.

Ernie took a sip of black coffee and swallowed. "Try to impress Carmen. Get on her good side, and you'll keep your job."

"Any more tips?"

Ernie scratched his scalp, and dandruff flaked down onto his shirt shoulders. "She gets hurt feelings if you don't pay attention to her."

Luke wondered, *What's Ernie trying to say?* Was he hinting she needed men to dote on her? "What kinda attention does she want?"

Ernie sighed. "She likes men, and she wants us males to like her. Frankly, I think she's a nympho."

Luke took a bite from a banana and set the half-eaten fruit on his tray. "Wasn't it you who said she sleeps around?"

"It was me." Ernie used a fork to push scrambled eggs

around on his plate. "She chases guys cuz she's eighteen years younger than Mark. Even though he's dead, I doubt she'll settle on one man."

*Was Ernie mistaken about Carmen? Had she picked a replacement husband and poisoned Mark, or would she prefer to remain unmarried?* The farm and horses were worth millions. Mark must've put money in the stock market. "You said according to rumors, Carmen slept with David. You think they'll marry?"

"Nope. She dumped David." Ernie set his fork on his plate. "David's too old for her and is a widower with a grown daughter. Even if they married, she'd be screwing other men, and the marriage would end in divorce."

Luke rubbed his fast-growing stubble. "So David slept with the wife of the owner of this farm?" Luke raised his eyebrows.

Ernie sighed. "It's hard for a red-blooded man to resist Carmen. If I were you, I'd please her, but stop short of hoppin' in her bed."

"I already got a girlfriend."

Ernie gulped coffee from his paper cup. "Carmen's got a condition, and everybody on this farm knows it."

Luke stroked his chin with his left hand. Was Carmen as loose a woman as Ernie claimed? Did she feel alone? Had Mark neglected his young wife? Luke turned to Ernie. "What kinda condition you think she has?"

"Besides being a nympho, she'd depressed. She tried suicide two months after marrying Mark." Ernie shook his head. "I'd think she'd still be mourning his death. But I bet she's already checking around to find another man to play with."

Luke wondered why a woman who'd married a millionaire horse trainer would want to kill herself. "You think she takes pills for depression?"

"No, but I heard she dabbles in hillbilly heroin."

Luke cocked his head. "Oxycodone?"

"Mostly, but the pills got fentanyl in them, too."

As Luke finished eating, he asked himself if Carmen

would've shared her pills with Mark. Luke frowned. "You think Mark figured since Carmen was takin' pills, he ought to try 'em?"

"No. But odds are she poisoned him with them." He got up. "I need to get back to work."

Luke stood. "I should get moving, too. I don't want to be late to my meetin' with Carmen."

"You've got this." Ernie walked away and left his empty paper cup on the table.

Luke surveyed the area. No one was around, and Ernie was already outside. Luke pulled an evidence bag from his pocket. Using a clean paper napkin, he bagged Ernie's cup.

\* \* \*

## 1:10 P.M., MONDAY, AUGUST 5

Luke rapped on the servant door on the backside of the Spicer mansion. He heard footsteps on the wooden floor inside the rear entryway. The shiny brass doorknob twisted, and the door swung inward. A Hispanic maid in a starched uniform took a moment to size him up. "Yes?"

Luke smiled. He figured he seemed threatening because his black stubble was growing into a short beard. "I'm supposed to meet Mrs. Spicer. I'm the new stable hand, Lucas Blanco."

The maid opened the door all the way. "Come in. Carmen is expecting you." She eyed his footwear. "Your boots are clean enough. Come with me."

"Yes, ma'am."

As Luke followed the maid down a carpeted corridor, he glanced aside into impressive rooms paneled with expensive hardwood. The oaken floors shone like a buffed luxury automobile.

Luke's eyes took in sights of ornate, antique solid walnut tables, chairs, and bookshelves. He also saw handcrafted teak pieces decorated with carved flowers and vines. A mahogany curio cabinet had leaded glass doors. Its wooden panels included detailed horse farm scenes crafted from different kinds and colors of inlaid, exotic woods.

*This place stinks of old money*, Luke thought.

The young maid stopped near a wide doorway framed in oak. Its door was ajar. "Carmen, Lucas Blanco is waiting to see you." The maid left.

Carmen sat behind a massive, ancient wooden desk. Her eyes were puffy and red.

*She's grieving the loss of Mark. Or is she a killer who regrets her actions?*

In a split second, she seemed to assess him, and then forced a smile.

She stood. Dressed in short shorts and a sleeveless, striped black and white blouse, her modern appearance was in stark contrast to the classic contents of the mansion.

"I'm pleased to meet you, Lucas. Come in and sit." She pointed to an expensive wooden chair next to her desk. She wiped one of her eyes as if to prevent a tear from dribbling down her cheek.

"Nice to meet you, ma'am." Luke stepped forward. He imagined she was trying to resume her normal activities to overcome her sorrow.

Carmen offered her hand, and Luke shook it. He felt her softness and weak grip. Her skin was creamy, not tanned, and she wore light pink lipstick and little makeup. Her eyes were dark brown, and their pupils were smaller than they should have been inside the dim office. Luke speculated whether or not she'd taken oxycodone or other opioid drugs.

They both sat.

"Lucas, you can call me Carmen. We're on a first-name basis on this farm." Luke thought she was not concentrating because she paused often as she spoke. "Welcome to Spicer Horse Farm. David spoke to me about you. Are you from the area?"

"I'm from the holler. My paw was from Kentucky, but my maw was Mexican." A twinge of regret for having told a lie traveled through Luke's body, though his undercover job required him to lie when needed.

"David said you grew up on a farm and are experienced with animals, including horses?" Carmen slurred her words.

Luke sat up straight. "I tended many an animal."

Carmen peered deep into Luke's eyes, and the corners of her mouth curled up.

"Maw and Paw passed away. I'm divorced."

"Then you don't mind getting free room and board in our bunkhouse? Our policy is for hands to live on the farm at least five days a week."

Luke pasted a smile on his face. "It's a good deal." He asked himself, *How can I ask a grieving woman about herself, her dead husband, and how he died?* Luke figured he'd be fortunate to learn anything unusual from her at this early stage of the investigation.

Carmen leaned closer to him. She had a long, classical face, dark eyebrows, and hip-length, brunette hair. "David, Bruno, and Ernie will instruct you on your everyday duties."

Luke speculated about her. Was she a trophy wife? She must've married Mark for his money. If he couldn't satisfy her sexually, she may have slept around. Yet, she cared for Mark enough to be sorrowful, though not overly so. Or was she a skilled actress, able to cry on command?

He heard himself ask, "Anything else, Carmen?"

"Yes, I'm going to need your help. Let me explain why." She glanced at a heavy oak curio cabinet. It contained fine china and antique knick-knacks. She focused again on Luke. "But before I do, I don't know whether or not you heard my husband, Mark, died."

Luke forced himself to blink. "Yes, I've heard. I'm sorry for your loss."

"Thank you. His death was a shock." She blinked, and a tear streamed down her cheek. "I'm dealing with a lot. Mark wished to be cremated, but that can't happen until the coroner releases his body."

"It's a stressful time."

Carmen wiped her tear away. "Mark wanted a celebration of life service rather than a funeral. I'm going to ask a friend to help me plan it, since neither Mark nor I have close living relatives who can lend a helping hand. I think it might be best to hold it in a month. By then I'll have had time to come to grips with my new situation."

"I understand."

She sighed and glanced across her office. "Sorry I went off on a tangent. So why do I need your help? You may have noticed the dreary furniture in the house."

Luke nodded.

"This dark art nouveau stuff makes me feel sadder, more depressed. It's lucky—or maybe unlucky—that I ordered modern furniture a couple of weeks ago to put in my office."

Luke wondered what she was getting at and why she'd taken so long to get to the point.

"The new office furniture will arrive tomorrow. So I need a man to clear out this office. I'd like you to help." Her pale cheeks colored pink. "Maybe this project will help keep my mind off Mark's death and worrying about planning his service."

Luke couldn't believe his luck. "I'm glad to help." He could spend time with Carmen and perhaps learn background information relevant to Mark's murder. But he'd need to figure out how to encourage her to share information with him.

She stood. "I'll call David and let him know you'll be assisting me."

"When should I come back?"

"I'll have someone find you when the new furniture comes." She paused and spoke into an antique intercom. "Lilia, please come to my office to escort Lucas out."

Luke stood. Lilia arrived within twenty seconds.

"Nice meeting you, Carmen," Luke said as he left. "See you tomorrow."

# FOURTEEN

DRESSED IN A NAVY-BLUE HOODED SWEATSHIRT, a stranger walked along a cracked, weedy Lexington sidewalk. It ran next to a tall, bushy hedge. After glancing around and seeing no one, the man pushed aside branches and stepped through a narrow gap in the towering bushes. He could see his intended destination, an ill-kept, two-story shack of a house. Peering through the windows, he saw no lights were on. This was the home of Ethan, the drug dealer.

The prowler had learned Ethan kept his battered motorcycle parked under the eaves of his rundown house when he was at home. The dense, overgrown bushes hid the bike and the intruder from the public sidewalk. This suited the criminal. He halted next to Ethan's motorcycle, which stood on a narrow walkway between the hedge and the west side of the house. Curious, the intruder peered upward at its weathered gray clapboard wood. Paint had peeled and flaked off it over the years.

*I better get on with business.* He reached into his jeans pocket and took out an electronic GPS tracker. He'd bought the inexpensive device online with an untraceable gift card.

The directions for the tracker said the user could attach it under the bike's seat.

After releasing a latch to lift the seat, the intruder stuck the gadget, encased in a magnetic box, under the "saddle." He then snapped the seat back into place.

*Now I can watch his comings and goings. I'll act at the optimum time and place.*

The wretch felt a pleasing sensation and relief because placing the tracker had been so easy.

*Soon the deed will be done.*

# FIFTEEN

## DINNER TIME, MONDAY, AUGUST 5—LUKE'S RENTED FARM IN THE HOLLER

LUKE'S GASOLINE-POWERED pickup crunched gravel and sputtered to a stop in the driveway of the farm he rented. He pulled his cell phone from his hip pocket and touched Jim's name on the mobile's contact list.

"Anything to report, Luke?"

"I just arrived home from the Spicer Farm. I got hired."

"Things are going our way." Jim's voice sounded happy.

"The barn manager, David, said folks think Carmen Spicer poisoned Mark. It's said she takes oxy pills. I met with her."

Luke heard Jim shift his phone in his grasp. "Learn anything from her?"

"Nope. But I gotta help her move furniture outta her office tomorrow. I'll see what I can wangle out of her then."

"Anything else?"

"David's friendly, but I met two impolite Mexicans. I got a bad feelin' about them."

"What did they say?"

"Nothing helpful. My gut tells me they have records."

"What are their full names?"

"Terencio Trigo. He goes by Terry." Luke heard Jim shuffle paper. "He's gruff."

"What's the name again?"

Luke spelled it, and then he spelled Bruno Chavez's name as well. He scratched his beard. "I met a redheaded man, too. He seems okay. He's a groom—Ernie Duke, regular spelling."

"Anything else?"

"I picked up David's cigar butt and put it in an evidence bag. Also, I snagged a paper cup Ernie was drinking out of."

"Excellent. Get all the DNA you can."

"Will do. I'll call you tomorrow if I find out anything important." Luke was silent and then spoke. "Oh, yeah. I'm staying at least five nights a week in Spicer's bunkhouse."

"Excellent. You'll have plenty of time to nose around."

"Yeah, but I gotta tell Layla. She won't like it."

"Hang in there, brother."

\* \* \*

## EARLY EVENING, MONDAY, AUGUST 5

Luke had called Layla and given her his ETA. She'd set the table, and a chuck roast was in the oven ready to serve. Its aroma was perfect and inviting.

The screen door creaked open and slammed shut.

"I'm home." Luke entered the kitchen.

Layla turned to face him. She felt her lips form a smile. He appeared less scruffy, though he hadn't shaved in two days. He also smelled like he wore cologne.

She felt his strong muscles when they hugged. "You smell good. Did you take a bath before you left this morning?"

"No. They have a shower in the Spicer bunkhouse."

"You got the job?"

"Yep. That's the good news."

"What's the bad news?"

"They want me to stay overnight in the bunkhouse five days a week."

"Why?"

"Stable hands need to get up before dawn to tend the horses. If an animal needs help at night, somebody's gotta be available."

Layla felt her pulse speed up. *A fine time for him to be away just after I find out I'm pregnant.* She tried to stop herself from huffing, and then inhaled, and forced herself to smile. "I guess it won't be too inconvenient." She shrugged. "After all, you said you wouldn't be undercover too many days—maybe a week?"

"Something like that." He pulled a chair away from the kitchen table and sat at his place. "I gotta git up way earlier than normal to arrive at the Spicer place by dawn. I need to find my lightweight back brace in the garage, too."

"What for?"

"Carmen wants me to move heavy furniture."

Layla recalled a picture of Carmen she'd seen on the front page of the paper. Layla guessed the woman was a gold digger, young, beautiful, and already on the prowl for a youthful husband. "She's the widow of Mark Spicer?"

"Yep. Folks think she did in her mister."

*She better stay away from my man.* Layla aimed her eyes at Luke. "I have news, too. Let's talk after Angela goes to bed." Layla's guts rumbled.

"Okay."

Layla thought Luke appeared worried.

He shifted in his chair. "What is it?"

Layla grinned. "Don't worry. It's a nice surprise." She turned her gaze toward the living room. Angela was watching cartoons. "Angela, time to eat."

* * *

LUKE SAT on his living room couch waiting for Layla. She was tucking Angela into bed. He often read to the little girl at bedtime, but tonight Layla had insisted on doing it. *Why?*

*What's she gonna tell me? Is she going to move back to Louisville?*

A few minutes later, Luke heard a spoon clink from the kitchen as if Layla were stirring coffee in a cup. Fifteen seconds later she walked to him carrying two cups of steaming cocoa on a tray. She set it on the coffee table near the couch. The smell of hot chocolate was strong and sweet.

"Thanks, Layla."

Layla sat next to Luke. She picked up a cup of cocoa. "I have happy news." She took a sip. "How should I start?" Layla focused on him. "Taking birth control pills has been wonderful. Because of them, we've been uninhibited."

His words came to him out of nowhere. "Your free spirit's part of what I like about you."

He felt like she was peering deeper into his eyes. "The pill works great. It's ninety-nine percent effective. But one percent of the time, a woman can get pregnant."

Luke leaned forward and snatched his cocoa. He sipped the hot drink and pulled it away from his lips. "Are you sayin'…"

"If she forgets to take a pill at the wrong time in her cycle, birth control's less reliable—ninety-three percent effective." She glanced at her laptop computer. "I've been researching on the Internet."

"You're…"

"I forgot a pill. My period's three days late." She touched her belly. "This afternoon I drove to the drugstore and bought a pregnancy test. I'm going to have a baby."

Luke gulped. He felt his face flush and his heart beat faster.

"I want to keep the child." She studied his face.

He set his cup on the tray, kissed her, and grasped her hand. He laughed. "Me, a dad." His inner voice cautioned, *But can you be a dependable father? You're still a recovering alcoholic.* He glanced at his boots.

Layla squeezed his hand. "Raising a child is loads of responsibility, a lot even for two people to take on."

Luke nodded. "I hope I'll be a good father."

"You're fantastic with Angela. She calls you 'Dad' for a reason."

Luke's thoughts galloped ahead like an out-of-control horse. Being a father came with obligations. "Our lives will change." He wondered if he should ask Layla to marry him.

Did she want to be his wife? Would she say yes? Would she say no? Did he want a second marriage? His first one had been hell. Up to this point, he and Layla had enjoyed a fine relationship. He fixed his gaze on her face. With her liquid brown eyes, she seemed to be studying him, too. Was she trying to probe his brain to decode his silent thoughts?

Layla blinked. "You okay, Luke?"

"Yep. This is momentous." He paused. "We're a team, and we gotta stick together, soon all four of us."

Layla embraced him again. "Three of us are hugging."

He liked the soft, warm feel of her body. He felt at home. "I love you, Layla."

She held him and sealed herself against him. "I've loved you from the start, Luke." She kissed his lips. "Let's make love."

Luke felt his body warm up like a stoked steam locomotive. "I want you."

As they made love, he realized how fine she was. He felt proud. *I'm gonna be a father.*

He'd set his alarm for four a.m. He didn't care if he'd be sleepy when he got up. He had a lot to think about.

# SIXTEEN

## 5:00 A.M., TUESDAY, AUGUST 6

LUKE ARRIVED at the Spicer Farm an hour and forty-five minutes before sunrise. He parked his pickup in the lot behind the giant barn. A cup of coffee remained in his thermos. He unbuckled his seatbelt and began to sip the brew while resting in the blackness of his truck's cab.

Last night he'd made love with Layla. Afterward, he'd been awake for more than an hour. His mind had been busy with thoughts about his future.

*Will I make a respectable father?* He tried to analyze himself. Did he sell himself short? He'd had doubts about his ability to do his deputy sheriff job when Jim had hired him less than a year ago. Yet he'd done an okay job, even though he still lacked confidence.

Then he recalled the sorry excuse for a vacation when pirates took over his Alaska-bound cruise ship, the *Sea Trek*. He'd struggled to save his and Layla's lives while the buccaneers held the ship.

*Not just once, but several times, a fraction of a second had been the difference between life and death. How long's my lucky streak gonna last?*

*I gotta watch my ass. I'm gonna be a father.*

The warm, humid night air flowing through his truck's open window enveloped him like the breath of a beast. The day would be sticky. After rolling up the driver's side window, the truck door creaked with a metal-on-metal sound as Luke pushed it open. *I gotta oil it.* He eased the door shut and heard the constant hum of insects, crying out for mates.

A former Kentucky game warden, Luke knew cicadas buzzed during the day, but katydids—large, green bugs—called out at night. Crickets liked to start chirping when it was the hottest, late in the afternoon.

When Luke began to walk toward the bunkhouse, its door swung outward. Light from inside the building backlit a heavyset man's silhouette as he stepped outside. "About time you arrived, Lucas."

After Luke's eyes readjusted to the gloom, he recognized Terry, the stable hand. "You missed breakfast. Get your ass in gear. Stalls are waiting to be mucked."

Luke kept his mouth shut, but he nodded. *I don't want to rile this guy even if he deserves an ass-kickin'. I got an investigation to do.*

As Luke moved toward the bunkhouse door, Terry raised his voice. "Get workin'. I don't intend to do your chores."

Without meaning to, Luke spoke. "Last time I heard, you ain't the boss."

"What if I beat the shit out of you? Then you'll know who's yur boss." Terry stomped toward the horse barn.

Luke immediately regretted what he'd blurted out and said to himself, *Just what I don't need. Gettin' fired for fighting.*

# SEVENTEEN

CARMEN STOPPED her luxury sports utility vehicle in the parking lot by Fish Creek State Park. The sound of water flowing over the rocks in a woodland stream near the lot greeted her when she opened her vehicle's door.

Reaching into her biggest purse, she felt the fat bundle of greenbacks in a brown-paper sandwich bag she'd stowed there. The money made her feel relieved because with it she could buy enough drugs to satisfy her habit for the immediate future.

She recalled how she'd found Mark's safe combination in his oversized safe deposit box. Then she'd returned home from the bank and unlocked Mark's ancient, heavy-duty safe. It was jam-packed with greenbacks.

*Why'd he keep a safe full of cash? It would've been wiser to deposit it in the bank.* But then again, she could use cash to buy pills whenever she ran low, so she decided to leave it in the safe.

As Carmen stepped down and out of her sizable SUV, she snapped out of her reverie. She grasped her heavy purse with a firm grip. The air was humid, and today was going to be hotter by the time the afternoon sun beat down on

Eastern Kentucky. She'd dressed in a low-cut halter top and shorts to try to stay cool. That was an excuse. She knew her real goal was to dress to attract and impress men.

She squinted and surveyed the blacktop pathway running into the woods. No one was in sight. It was too early for most people to visit the park, except for joggers. Most people were at work or waiting to picnic at lunchtime.

The blacktop path led Carmen to a dense growth of trees, where the noise of the creek's running water increased. After fifty feet, the trail turned into a dirt path. A brown wooden sign read, "Deer Path Trail, one mile hike."

Rocks poked up from the dirt. She could stub a toe with her sandaled feet if she weren't careful. She felt guilty as she neared her rendezvous location, where she hoped Ethan waited.

*I'm an addict, sneaking around to get drugs.* Shame soaked her whole being. *What would Ma think of me if she weren't in heaven?* Repetitive, unwanted thinking began to plague her. *Should I end it all?*

She came around a bend in the path. Ethan rested on the park bench where he always waited when they met to exchange her money for his illicit, addictive pills. "Hi, Ethan." She smoothed her hip-length, dark hair. It was a pity Ethan was a drug addict and a pusher. He was handsome. She laughed in silence to herself. *But I'm an addict, too.*

Ethan stood. "Got the money?"

"Yes."

Ethan unzipped his cheap backpack.

Inside, Carmen saw a clear plastic bag containing oxycodone pills. Her heart began to pound. "I haven't seen so many oxy pills at once before."

"You're getting a bargain. I gotta leave town."

Carmen pitied Ethan. He was like her, a lost soul. It was depressing. She reached into her purse and pulled out her paper sack of cash. "All five grand's in the bag." She handed him the sack. "Count it if you like."

"I trust you." He swung the backpack toward her by its

strap. "Keep the pack. Narcan's in it, too. Keep the drugs out of sight. You didn't get them from me, if a cop asks."

"Okay. If you come back, call me, okay?"

"Sure. But it may be a while before it's safe and the cops aren't on my tail." He showed her a weak smile and walked into the woods.

*Where's he going to go?*

* * *

UNNOTICED BY CARMEN AND ETHAN, a man peered at them through binoculars from a spot concealed by thick, verdant bushes.

*I must deal with the pusher,* the man thought.

* * *

## 10:00 A.M., TUESDAY, AUGUST 6

Carmen stowed the bag of drugs under a blanket in the rear cargo area of her electric SUV. After climbing into the vehicle's driver's seat, she grabbed her cell phone and touched "David" on the device's contact list.

"Hello, Carmen. What can I do for you?"

"I have a shipment of office furniture arriving this afternoon."

Carmen could hear David sigh. "Okay." She knew he wasn't used to having a female boss. In Latino cultures, men are often in charge, she surmised.

"I need the recent hire, Lucas, to take the antique furniture out of my office and move the new items into it. I'll be back in a half hour to tell him what I need done."

"How about I send Ernie, instead? Lucas needs to learn his job."

"Ernie's skinny. Lucas is strong. The furniture is heavy." She figured David was thinking about how they'd had sex one day when Mark wasn't in town. She was surprised he didn't volunteer to move the furniture himself. Carmen reckoned he wanted her.

David's words broke into her memories of the lust they'd shared. "Yes, ma'am. Lucas will be waiting for you in your office."

"Great. Thank you." She imagined how handsome Lucas would be with a haircut and a shave. At once she felt guilt. She needed one real man, not a bunch of them. She understood she was justifying her liaisons with men as a way to find "Mr. Right." *I'm fooling myself.*

# EIGHTEEN

LUKE FOUND LILIA, the maid, in the kitchen. She smiled. "Need something?"

"A furniture dolly."

"One's in the storeroom down the hall." She displayed a puzzled expression. "What are you up to?"

"Gotta move furniture for Carmen."

Minutes later Luke stood next to a pile of furniture pads and a dolly designed to move bulky appliances. It had a sturdy steel plate to slip under heavy items and a hydraulic pump to lift them. *With the proper equipment, jobs are easier,* Luke told himself. He moved the dolly and pads into Carmen's office. He noticed his left shin, which had been broken three months ago, hurt a trifle.

Footsteps outside Carmen's office doorway caught his attention. He turned as Carmen entered the room. Her halter top showed cleavage and exposed her back. She wore short, low-cut socks, but no shoes. Pink lipstick accented her white teeth. She carried a lumpy backpack.

Her eyes were no longer puffy from crying, and she noticed the dolly. "You found the monster furniture mover." She slurred her speech. "It's a back saver."

"Yes, ma'am." Luke wondered if she'd been drinking. He knew how to spot alcohol and drug abusers. A recovering alcoholic, he attended LifeRing sessions at the Alcohol Treatment Center in Lexington. He'd often observed and talked with addicts.

She smoothed her dark hair, which fell below her belt. Her fingers vibrated as she stroked her hair. "Remember, call me Carmen."

"Sorry, Carmen. I forgot." Luke took a moment to examine her as she walked to her desk. She tossed the backpack on the floor next to her swivel chair and sat. He guessed she was an inch or two taller than an average woman.

She surveyed him, her eyes darting downward from his head to his waist.

Luke rubbed his chin. *It's a shame she's hooked on drugs or alcohol—or both.*

"You're in outstanding shape, Lucas. You need to be because these solid wood pieces are heavy enough to sink a ship." She trained her eyes on his.

Luke noticed the pupils in her eyes were once again constricted, smaller than they should be in the dim office light. He wondered if she'd taken an opioid drug. Next, he surveyed the old-fashioned office furniture. "Where should I start?"

Carmen stood and was unsteady on her feet. She scanned her desk, a table, and her bookcase. "Goddamn it, Lilia put my diagram someplace in the office, but where?" She grabbed a wine bottle from a shelf behind the desk, popped the loose cork from its neck, and poured rich red wine into a water glass. "Want a drink? It's cab."

"No, thanks." He told himself, *She's a different person when she drinks.*

She was moody. Was her mental state not only due to her drinking, but also a result of the toll Mark's death had taken on her? Was she a drug *and* alcohol addict? Had he prejudged her? She'd been under extreme stress. Her husband had died without warning, and his death had forced her to take charge of the farm with no training. Did she suspect her husband had been murdered? Had she killed him?

Carmen's voice took Luke away from his thoughts. "Suit yourself, Lucas, but please excuse me." Her eyelids drooped. "It's been a rough time for me."

"Losing yur husband must've been tough."

Carmen drank her wine like a jogger quenching her thirst in the blazing sun. She closed her eyes for a slow moment. She reopened them and seemed surprised to see Luke.

"Mark died of an overdose." She peered at the paneled wall. "He wasn't an addict. Someone at the party must've offered him pills." Teardrops flowed down her cheeks.

"Sorry for your loss."

"I've been trying to keep busy to cheer up."

"Who would'a slipped your husband drugs?"

She shrugged. "I don't know." Carmen dried a tear from her face with a tissue and finished her wine.

"Could be someone gave Mark extra-strong pills like oxy with Apache mixed in."

"Apache?"

"It's a street name for fentanyl. Apache's a hundred times stronger than morphine."

Carmen cocked her head and squinted. "You know about drugs?"

"Truth be told, I go to LifeRing meetings every two weeks cuz I used to have a drinkin' problem."

"It's like AA?"

"Yep. People with drug addictions attend, too." Luke peered into Carmen's dark brown eyes. Would she go to a meeting some day? "If someone has a drinkin' or a drug problem, I'd give high marks to LifeRing or AA. They do wonders."

Carmen's pale skin reddened. "Valuable information." She paused and took a deep breath. "You think somebody could've murdered Mark?" She spoke like her tongue was half-asleep.

Luke blinked. "I don't know."

She sighed. "I've asked my friends who could've given drugs to Mark. Nobody knows anything." She poured a second glass of cabernet sauvignon wine from her one-and-a-half liter bottle. It was close to empty.

Luke figured if Carmen wasn't lying about asking her friends if Mark had been given drugs, she wasn't his killer. Luke didn't want to push her too fast. "I'm ready to start movin' furniture outta here if you're ready."

She sipped her wine instead of gulping it. But she was buzzed and would be drunker if she finished her second water glass of wine. Had she taken drugs, too? Could she OD like her husband had? Luke touched his cell phone in his pocket. He'd have to dial 911 if needed.

Unsteady, Carmen sat on her swivel office chair. "Start with the oak cabinet. Move everything into the conference room across the hall."

Luke shoved the dolly's wide metal toe plate under the oak cabinet and placed a pad between it and the dolly's frame.

"I like watching you work." Luke noticed her words sounded less clear.

Luke rolled the heavy oak cabinet through the office doorway, across the hall, and into the conference room. Though his back was turned to her, he felt like Carmen was staring at him. After tilting the cabinet and slipping the metal toe plate from underneath it, he peered back through the conference room doorway and across the hall into Carmen's office. She was on her feet, pouring the bottle's remaining wine into her water glass.

Luke pulled the dolly behind him and stopped near her. "What's next?"

"Come closer." She showed a naughty smile. Her eyes drooped. "I see a bulge on one side of your stomach." Her hand darted out and pulled up his loose-fitting shirt. "Why are you carrying a gun?"

*What'll I say?* "I'm a gun guy." He blinked fast and then wondered if she'd made a pass at him. She was rumored to be man-crazy. He'd have to avoid her advances, yet not offend her. Otherwise she could stop speaking with him.

She wrinkled her brow. "What do you mean, you're a gun guy?"

"It's my hobby. I like to target practice."

Carmen studied him and appeared to gauge him. "I need a man to help me," she mumbled. Was she on the verge of passing out?

"I can help move furniture anytime you want."

"Yeah, but I need help with something else." She sipped her wine again and staggered. "I need a bodyguard."

Luke turned his head sideways and made a quick judgment. *She's either paranoid, or she's in real danger—or both.* He observed her with care. "I ain't never been a bodyguard, but if you'd like one, I could help you. Just the same, I can't watch over you twenty-four seven."

"You won't have to muck dirty stalls." She glanced at the ancient six-foot-tall safe along the wall. "I'll double your pay."

Luke figured this was a fortunate turn of events. He could get close to her, evaluate her mental state, and learn if she were her husband's killer, or had hired a hit man. Was the person who iced Mark threatening her? Was she bipolar? Could drugs and alcohol make her paranoid?

He figured he could consult with his ex-girlfriend, Carol Cuddy, a high school psychologist. Because she was exceptional at her job, she'd retired to start a private practice as a psychologist.

*She'll give me free advice.*

With an unsteady hand, Carmen set her empty glass on her desktop. "You're taking considerable time to decide." She swayed and sat on her swivel chair. "I'll sweeten the pot. You can stay rent free in the mansion. You can use a vacant bedroom next to mine. You'll eat better meals with me instead of eating bunkhouse food."

"I'll take the job." Luke felt elated. This was a break. But what would he say to Layla? He shouldn't say a lot, or he'd be in trouble.

Carmen extended her hand. "Shake on it."

Luke grasped her hand. It felt soft and feminine. "What about David?"

"I'll call him."

Luke touched the mini holster on the left side of his belt. Should he carry the pocket-sized pistol, or pack his hefty Smith & Wesson? *I should carry the smaller firearm. It'll attract less attention.*

After Carmen had hired him as her bodyguard, how would David react? If Mark's killer worked on the farm, what would the perp think?

Carmen's voice broke into Luke's thought pattern. "It's time for lunch. I'll have Lilia bring sandwiches and drinks."

Luke assumed food would absorb alcohol in Carmen's system if she didn't get sick first. Then he wondered if the furniture delivery had been delayed. "When will you git the new furniture?"

"After lunch. You can unpack it and place it then."

Luke decided to go back home to tell Layla his undercover work had changed. "I have to get clothes from my rented room."

"Take off after we're done with the furniture." Carmen spoke in a garbled but coquettish voice.

Luke nodded. *I gotta be careful how I deal with Carmen.*

# NINETEEN

LUKE SPENT the afternoon moving furniture out of Carmen's office and arranging her ultramodern pieces. *This is harder than I thought it'd be.*

Though Carmen had sobered up by late afternoon, he'd had a hard time getting her to reveal further details about what may have led to Mark's death.

By five p.m. the new furniture was in place. She stood up from her modern desk chair and walked to Luke. "I'll show you your bedroom." She led him down the hallway, stopped near a door, and unlocked it.

Luke took a step into the room and saw a double bed, a bureau, and an easy chair. He glanced at Carmen. "This is nicer than a fancy hotel."

"You deserve it." She stepped up to him. "Nice work today, Lucas." She squeezed his shoulder. "Are you going to leave to get clothes from your rented room, or stay for supper?"

*She's gettin' too friendly.* Luke took a half step back. "I better go cuz I gotta store the rest of my property in a friend's barn."

"When will you be back?" Carmen peered out of the window as if she thought someone was staring at her, but no one was in sight.

"Tomorrow morning."

"I wish you could stay tonight. Like you suggested, somebody could've killed Mark."

Luke nodded. *Carmen's paranoid, but someone did murder Mark*. It was fortunate she was cautious. "Lock your door tonight. Don't let anyone in. I'll be back before dawn. After breakfast, we'll make a plan."

"Okay."

Minutes later, Luke was in his pickup, driving toward his rented farm in the holler. He turned onto a gravel road, stopped on a turnout, and switched off the engine. It sputtered and then quit. The ugly smell of exhaust lingered in the humid air.

He accessed his phone's contact list and touched "Carol Cuddy."

*I gotta catch her before she leaves her office.*

"Luke. What's up?"

"Could I ask you psych questions about a suspect?"

"I should charge you a fee, but I won't." Carol had been Luke's girlfriend before he'd met Layla. After divorcing Emma, he'd slept with Carol on and off for years. But their friendship had become platonic.

"Thanks, Carol. Have time to talk?"

"Of course."

Luke pictured her pleasing face and wavy, red hair. Though in her midthirties, she appeared to be in her late twenties. *I'm glad Carol doesn't know Layla's pregnant. Is Carol ever gonna help me again after she finds out?* He cleared a frog from his throat. "Can you keep a secret?"

"Sure, if it's about a crime."

Luke scratched his itchy, fast-growing beard. "Have you heard how the horse trainer, Mark Spicer, died?"

"The paper said it was a drug overdose."

"It was murder." Luke paused. "His wife, Carmen, is a person of interest."

"You want me to analyze her?"

"Yes. I'll describe her." Luke thought a moment about

how to outline her character. He guessed she had emotional and mental problems.

Carol broke his train of thought. "Go ahead, Luke."

"She's an attractive young lady, twenty-four years old, eighteen years younger than Mark. It's said she sleeps around. Today, I moved furniture for her. She drank a lot of wine, and the pupils in her eyes were constricted."

"She's a drug and alcohol abuser?"

"Yep. Take it from a drunk like me." He paused. "She's also paranoid."

"Keep in mind what I'm about to tell you is a quick, off-the-top-of-my-head impression of Carmen based on scanty information. My initial opinion may be way off the mark. With that said, it's significant she's an addict. She could be a nymphomaniac. They often are hooked on alcohol and drugs. Nymphomania is an emotional condition. If she suffers from it, she feels guilty about her shortcomings and could be self-medicating."

"What about her fears?"

Carol breathed loud enough for Luke to hear her exhale. "Carmen could be paranoid if she believes someone wants to kill her. I think she needs treatment. Even if you don't consider her drinking and drug use, she's suffered a major loss. Plus she may also be bipolar, if she's a nymphomaniac."

"What else can you tell me about women like her?"

"They're obsessive, feel shame for their faults. They often try suicide."

Luke waved a mosquito away from his face. "She hired me as her bodyguard."

"So, she *is* fearful." Carol paused. Luke pictured Carol pursing her lips before continuing. "I'd be glad to try to persuade her to seek treatment."

"Thanks, Carol. That might have to wait until the investigation winds down." Luke took a moment to plan his next sentence. "I think she's gonna make a pass at me. She's got me stayin' in the bedroom next to hers in the Spicer mansion."

Luke heard Carol fumble her phone. "What's Layla going

to think when she hears you're sleeping in a bedroom near Carmen?"

Luke felt like his brain was running at top speed. He had yet to figure out how to speak with Layla about Carmen. "I don't know what to say, if anything."

Carol heaved a sigh. "It's fortunate you're not my beau anymore." After a moment she continued to speak. "As your friend, let me give you advice. Leave out the details when you talk to Layla about Carmen."

Luke thought, *Layla's pregnant. She's gonna be emotional.*

# TWENTY

OZZIE THE SNITCH phoned Jim at the sheriff's station with a tip. "I know who sold the drugs connected to Mark Spicer's death. If you can come to my place, I'll give you the details."

Jim felt a jolt of optimism because Ozzie's information could be critical to solving the Spicer murder. "I can be at your house in a half hour if traffic's not bad."

"Good. Could you give me a bit more than normal for this info?"

"Sure, Ozzie. See you soon." Jim hung up.

About to go home, Jim had already dressed in civilian clothes, slacks, and a sports shirt. They'd help him remain inconspicuous in Ozzie's Lexington neighborhood, Winburn.

South of Interstate 64, Winburn included low-cost homes, one-story apartment buildings, and wide streets. The area didn't appear blighted to the untrained eye, but crime was high in the neighborhood compared to the rest of the city.

A half hour later, Jim parked his personal sedan a block from the half duplex house Ozzie rented.

As Jim started to stroll along the sidewalk toward Ozzie's place, he noticed residential garbage and recycle bins stood at the curb. A toppled trash container blocked his path, and refuse lay scattered across the grass in the parkway and on the pavement.

The odor of ripe waste invaded Jim's nose, and flies buzzed nearby as he opted to walk on the street to go around the mess. He noticed weeds growing in the cracks in the street's blacktop. Most yards were neat, but not all of them had been mowed—a sign of a neighborhood in decline. An abandoned car with one flat tire stood a half block from Ozzie's place.

Ozzie had asked Jim to knock on the back door of his unit. Jim's feet felt the thick sod. But his shoes bumped into tall weeds with sturdy stems popping up from the ill-kept lawn. He rapped on the aluminum frame of the battered screen door with his knuckles. The click of a deadbolt unlocking followed.

As the back door opened, Ozzie's face appeared, framed by his dirty blond hair. The middle-aged man's skinny, short body came into full view after he pulled the door agape. He was dressed in his usual dark clothing. Ozzie took a second to peer around and then pushed the screen door aside. "Come in quick, Sheriff. Somebody will see you."

Jim followed Ozzie into the kitchen. "What have you got for me?"

Ozzie gestured toward a drip coffeemaker on the counter. "Want a cup of coffee first?"

"No, thanks."

Ozzie poured a cup of brew for himself. Jim figured Ozzie stayed up at night. The man's record proved he was a burglar by trade.

Ozzie put his cup on the kitchen table and sat. "What's my tip worth to you?"

"Fifty bucks?"

"I was thinkin' higher."

"Seventy-eight is all the folding money I have on me."

"Okay, but could you give me a bonus, if you make an arrest?"

"Yes. Who sold the drugs you claim killed Mark Spicer?"

Ozzie sipped his coffee and then leaned forward toward Jim. He spoke with a quiet voice as if to make sure nobody else heard him, although he lived alone. "Ethan Wood's been sellin' pills to Mrs. Carmen Spicer for three years."

Jim felt his brain go into high gear. "Are you implying Carmen killed her husband?" *I should've not said that*, Jim told himself.

"Hell if I know."

"What's Ethan's address?"

"I don't know, but his house is three blocks away on Eagle Way. It's the one wooden house on the block. His backyard's up against the interstate."

Jim scratched his scalp. "What's Ethan drive?"

"He don't have a car. He's got an old motorcycle."

"Thanks." Jim pulled out his fat leather wallet, dug out all his folding money, and offered it to Ozzie. He grabbed the cash, and his smile revealed the gap between two of his top front teeth.

"Much obliged, Sheriff."

Jim's phone rang. He saw the call was from Luke. "I gotta go, Ozzie." Jim hustled from the house.

* * *

JIM EXITED Ozzie's door on the west side of the duplex, walked around the corner, and got in his car. He touched the contact screen of his smartphone to call Luke back.

"Hi, Jim."

"What's up?"

"I spent all day with Carmen and learned a lot. She hired me as her bodyguard."

"Why?"

"Said she thinks someone murdered her husband and implied she could be next. She's scared shitless."

"You think she's still a suspect?"

"Maybe, maybe not, but she's a boozer and a druggie. The pupils in her eyes were constricted. I was movin' furniture all day for her. She's been moody, up and down, and irritable at times—all signs of an addict."

"She's quite impulsive to all of a sudden hire you to be her bodyguard."

Luke exhaled. "She also could've hired me cuz she's man crazy. Word is she's been sleepin' around."

"Don't tell Layla."

Luke sighed. "Yeah. I gotta figure out somethin' to tell her. Carmen wants me to stay in the mansion in the bedroom next to hers."

"Didn't you say the barn manager wanted you to sleep at least five days a week in Spicer's bunkhouse?"

"Yep."

"You told Layla?"

"I had to."

"Then I wouldn't tell her anything about your new sleeping arrangements."

"That's a given."

Jim figured now was the time to talk about Ethan the drug dealer. "I have news, too." He hesitated. "This case could wrap up fast."

"Good."

"You're correct about Carmen being an addict. I spoke with a snitch minutes ago. He fingered a drug pusher, Ethan Wood, who's been selling pills to Carmen for three years. She could've killed Mark for his money."

"My gut tells me she didn't."

Jim jostled his phone. "Still there's a possibility Carmen used drugs to kill Mark even if she didn't use her pills to do it."

Luke was silent for a second. "I'm startin' to think Carmen isn't a suspect. She's terrified unless she's a great actress. Plus she would've had to grind up a lot of oxycodone pills to get such an elevated concentration of fentanyl to spike Mark's beer."

Jim rolled his seat back and stretched his legs. "Even if Carmen's not guilty, Ethan should be able to tell us something useful. I'm in the Winburn neighborhood. He lives two blocks away."

"You gonna arrest him?"

"Yes, if he didn't skip town. Pushers know Dalton's Law requires people convicted of selling fentanyl to serve at least eighty-five percent of their sentences." Jim was thinking of his next steps as he spoke. "I'll coordinate with Lexington PD. But first, I'm gonna drive by Ethan's house and do a quick recon."

"Good idea to take in Ethan. But we shouldn't jump to conclusions about Carmen."

"True."

Luke cleared his throat. "We'll need to protect her whether or not she's guilty, though."

Jim admitted Luke had fine instincts, but he was human and wasn't perfect. *Was he on target about Carmen, or was he getting too close to her?* Mitch, the coroner, believed someone had spiked Mark's beer with powdered fentanyl, not powder from a bunch of ground-up fentanyl-laced oxy pills. The fatal dose had been too strong to come from even dozens of oxy pills.

Jim figured he needed to prove he was listening to Luke. "You could be dead-on about Carmen. If she put oxy powder in Mark's beer, it wouldn't have been such a super high dose as the lab techs found in his beer."

"I came to the same conclusion, Jim. I gotta go."

"Keep me posted."

# TWENTY-ONE

## AFTER DINNER, TUESDAY, AUGUST 6—LUKE'S RENTED FARM

LAYLA HAD CLEARED the dishes from the table and was loading the dishwasher. She wondered, *Why hasn't Luke called yet?* She withdrew her cell phone from her tight-fitting jeans and was just about to phone him when he unlocked the front door.

"I'm home."

Layla felt happiness spread across her body. "Aren't you supposed to stay in Spicer's bunkhouse tonight?"

"I got a new job at the farm." Luke sat at the empty kitchen dinette table.

Layla saw him blink when he sat next to her. Was he embarrassed about something—or did he feel guilty? "What's the job?"

Luke shifted in his chair. "Carmen asked me to be her bodyguard."

Layla straightened her back. "She afraid of something?"

Luke shrugged. "She's paranoid, but could be she's in real danger."

"Can you come home every night?"

"No. I've got to be on call at the farm in case somebody bothers her."

Layla squinted. "She make a pass at you?" Layla saw a red tinge form on Luke's tanned face.

Luke sighed. "Hiring me as a bodyguard ain't making a pass. She's upset. Thinks her husband was murdered and she could be next."

Layla peered into Luke's dark eyes. She again recalled Carmen's photo that appeared in the newspaper with an article about Mark's death. The woman was stunning. "Be careful, Luke. She may have killed Mark for his money."

"She has no reason to kill me." Luke paused. "I'm startin' to believe she didn't kill Mark. People involved with narcotics could harm her. She's a drinker and a druggie. Could be bipolar, too."

Layla's pulse pounded her temples. She touched the side of her head to try to calm down. "A killer could be living on Spicer Farm. It's a dangerous place."

"Investigation is part of my job."

Layla shook her head. "Going undercover is riskier than normal police work." Tears flowed from her eyes. "You're going to be a father, and all of a sudden you're marching off to work as Carmen's bodyguard." Layla wiped her wet cheeks with the side of her hand.

Luke slid his chair closer to her, put his arm around her shoulders, and hugged her. "Don't worry. Carmen's paranoid cuz she's a drug addict. Jim will make an arrest soon. This'll be over in a week."

Layla felt Luke's strong, warm caress, and she relaxed. "Sorry, Luke. When a woman gets pregnant, she can often become emotional. I was sensitive when I was carrying Angela." Layla knew that the amount of estrogen and progesterone in a pregnant woman's blood can make her moody during the first months of her pregnancy.

Luke kissed her lips. "I love you, Layla. I'll be more careful."

*I hope he doesn't get himself killed*, she thought, as she enjoyed the closeness and ardor of his embrace.

# TWENTY-TWO

## 6:15 P.M., TUESDAY, AUGUST 6—WINBURN NEIGHBORHOOD

JIM APPROACHED a mom-and-pop grocery store on the edge of Lexington's Winburn neighborhood to buy a sandwich and coffee.

*This workday won't be over for hours,* he thought. As he neared the screen door on the front of the building, he noticed an older man dressed in old-fashioned clothes. He was smoking a cigarette and sitting on a bench. The building's overhang blocked the rays of the sun. It was sinking lower in the western sky, and the man sat in deep shade.

Jim saw the guy's fingers shake as he sucked smoke from his fag. Glancing at the pupils of the man's eyes, Jim saw they were constricted. They should have been dilated open in the shadows under the store's wide eaves. *He's on drugs.*

The elderly fellow stared at Jim.

Jim wondered if the aged man had bought drugs from Ethan. "Sir, I heard a guy in this neighborhood can sell me oxy pills."

The man smiled, and his deep facial wrinkles grew pronounced on his wizened face. "His name's Ethan. You can't miss his beat-up house. It's a two-story wood home on Eagle Way near the interstate. The others are brick."

"Thanks." Jim was grateful for the info. He would quote the elderly man in an affidavit to establish probable cause to justify a search of Ethan's house. Jim would request a warrant to search the house as well as Ethan's person.

The middle-aged snitch, Ozzie, had told Jim that Ethan was selling illegal drugs. The old fellow's information corroborated Ozzie's tip.

Jim wanted to act fast. He'd have to fill out an electronic affidavit form on his cell phone, and forward the draft to the DA, who'd need to approve it. In turn, the DA would then send it to a judge to get a search warrant.

Even using modern, efficient electronic forms and procedures, Jim wasn't sure how soon he could search Ethan's house. Also, Jim needed to coordinate with Lexington PD. And, it was already after six p.m. Usually, search warrants were executed between six a.m. and ten p.m. He'd be lucky to get a warrant tonight. *But you never know,* he mused.

Jim withdrew seventy dollars from the ATM in the grocery store in tens and twenties. He also bought a roast beef sandwich and a cardboard cup of coffee. *I better get moving,* he thought.

\* \* \*

## 7:00 P.M., TUESDAY, AUGUST 6—WINBURN NEIGHBORHOOD

Jim stopped his car at the curb near an overgrown, eight-foot-tall hedge bordering the crumbling city sidewalk. Ethan's dwelling was behind the bushy barrier and towered over it. The drug dealer's two-story clapboard house had been light blue years ago, but half of its paint had flaked off to reveal bare, grayish wood.

The sound of flapping wings caught Jim's attention. He was surprised to see two gray pigeons land on the edge of Ethan's attic window and then flutter through its opening.

Pushing his way through a thin place in the hedge, Jim saw spots on a narrow brick walk adjacent to the house. *Motor oil dripped off something. The sidewalk's not wide enough for a car. Ethan's motorcycle must've been parked where the oil spots are.* Jim figured Ethan had ridden away.

When he peeked through two windows, Jim saw no lights on. The place was a mess inside.

Jim pushed his way back through the hedge and got in his car. He pulled out his phone and touched the county district attorney's name on its contact screen, Dick Troft. Jim pictured Dick, who stood five feet eight inches tall. The DA sported a white handlebar mustache. He was a politician—body and soul. He'd insisted Jim keep him up-to-date on the high-profile Spicer case.

Dick answered in his unique, cheery voice. "Hello, Jim. What's up?"

"I've got a solid lead in the Mark Spicer case. I need a search warrant for a Lexington drug dealer's house."

Jim imagined Dick's eyes lighting up. "What are the details?" His voice sounded high-pitched.

"The drug dealer, Ethan Wood, has sold drugs to Mrs. Carmen Spicer for three years, according to a confidential source. I also spoke with a man I met in the Winburn neighborhood who corroborated Ethan is a drug dealer."

Dick coughed. "See if you can get a written statement from at least one more person who swears Ethan Wood has been selling drugs."

"Okay." Jim remembered he had to coordinate with Lexington PD. "I'm going to phone LPD. I bet one of their officers can provide a statement. If so, would I have to track down the neighborhood man?"

"LPD testimony would work for me." Dick hesitated a second. "The Mark Spicer murder is our top case in the county."

Jim reckoned Dick would give the case high priority because Mark's slaying would be a hot news story when reporters learned of it. Dick often sought ways to get positive publicity because he was a politician who never stopped campaigning. Jim hesitated and then spoke. "How fast do you think we can move?"

"I'll get in touch with Judge Aspen. Can you search tonight before ten?"

Jim sighed. "It's late...I'd like to try for tomorrow morning."

"Okay."

* * *

## 8:15 P.M., TUESDAY, AUGUST 6—WINBURN NEIGHBORHOOD

Sitting in his car, Jim had been working for an hour writing a search warrant affidavit. Typing on the mini touchscreen keyboard most people used to compose text messages wasn't easy. Even under normal circumstances, writing an affidavit could take substantial time.

The document had to convince a judge there was a decent chance of finding specific evidence in Ethan's house or on his person. This would establish probable cause. Jim believed oxycodone pills laced with fentanyl would be in the house or on Ethan. Jim also asked for approval to search for fentanyl in powder or other concentrated forms because Mark had died of a massive overdose.

Earlier, Jim had phoned his Lexington Police Department contact, Detective Gus Schultz, and had gotten LPD's cooperation as well as a corroborating statement from Gus to include in the search warrant affidavit. Gus agreed it would be better to search Ethan's place Wednesday morning.

After emailing his affidavit to Dick, Jim called him fifteen minutes later.

"Hello, Jim. I received your affidavit and reviewed it."

"Is it okay?"

"It's fine. I'll let you know when a judge approves it."

Jim relaxed. "Thanks."

After Dick hung up, Jim decided to return to Ozzie's half duplex. *He may know where Ethan went on his motorcycle.* Would Ethan return home? If he did, he and his house would be searched.

\* \* \*

## 8:25 P.M., TUESDAY, AUGUST 6—WINBURN NEIGHBORHOOD

Jim was drowsy though he'd finished his cup of coffee. He walked to the back door of Ozzie's home. After knocking two times on the doorframe, he heard the muffled voice of the snitch from within the place. "Give me a minute."

Fifteen seconds later Ozzie opened the door. "You find Ethan?"

"He wasn't at home and neither was his bike."

"Odds are he's chasing ladies."

Jim focused on Ozzie's face. "Did you call him?"

Ozzie displayed a guilty face. "Why would I?"

Jim stepped forward. "Let me in. I stopped at an ATM."

"Okay."

The men moved to the kitchen table and sat.

Ozzie sighed and smiled. "What if I called him?"

"Where'd he go?"

"Will you pay me?"

Jim nodded.

"Said he'd hide in the woods behind Becker's Park. Told me he'll leave for Knoxville after the case goes cold."

Jim handed Ozzie a twenty and a ten.

"Thanks."

Jim rubbed his chin. He figured he'd check out the woods by the park tomorrow after the search of Ethan's house had been done. He recalled an abandoned half-burned-out house was in Becker's Park.

# TWENTY-THREE

BEFORE LEAVING on his motorcycle ride to the cabin, Ethan, the drug dealer, had smashed the SIM card he'd taken out of his phone and tossed both it and the mobile into a dumpster. Then he'd bought a burner phone for emergency use.

A half hour later he sat on a homemade stool in an abandoned cabin. The ramshackle structure stood in a thick wood behind Becker's Park, twenty miles from Lexington's city limits.

The park was underused, but every so often, visitors ate at the four picnic tables near the parking lot. County officials, short on money, mowed the grass near the tables, but nothing else. The rest of the area was overgrown with weeds and brushy bushes. Few people knew an abandoned cabin was a thousand yards away from the parking lot in a dense wood. Half of the log house had burned fifteen years ago.

Safe and comfortable, Ethan eased back against the cabin's rough wall. He recalled how, ten months ago, he'd begun to think of what he could do if the cops ever got on his tail. He'd decided to prepare the burned-out cabin as a refuge. His pal and drinking buddy, Malcolm, had a twenty-five-year-old minivan and agreed to help him stock the damaged cabin and make it livable.

Though Malcolm promised not to tell a soul about the hideout, Ethan couldn't trust Malcolm to keep quiet. When the man drank—and it was daily—he talked, often without thinking.

Ethan smiled when he recollected how he and Malcolm often carried a six-pack of beer with them and drank it after working on the log house. During the year, they'd made at least one trip a month to Becker's Park.

Ethan had the brilliant idea of using backpacks to tote cans of food and supplies to the hideout. Each time the men walked across the grassy expanse and woodland, they changed their route to the log house to avoid creating a path. A trampled track would've been an invitation for park visitors to find the hideout. To make it harder to see the little building, Ethan had planted vines around it. They thrived, covering the exterior logs with a leafy camouflage.

Ethan had put an olive-drab, rain-repellent tarp over the roof where the fire had burned a hole years ago. The men brought sleeping bags, candles, a propane camp stove, a whisk broom, toilet paper, and a coffee pot to the log shack to convert it into a cozy hideaway.

A natural spring was fifty feet away. Its water was clean and cold. An outhouse stood twenty feet from the cabin behind an impenetrable bush—not convenient, but well-hidden. The cabin even had a potbelly wood-burning stove. Ethan didn't need to light a fire in the middle of summer, but in winter, he'd done it. Of course, he'd built small fires with dry wood. They hadn't sent billowing smoke into the sky— an invitation for curious hikers or park visitors to investigate.

Earlier this day, he'd driven his motorcycle across the overgrown field and into the woods almost to the cabin. After manhandling his bike the final fifty feet to his hideout, he had hidden the motorcycle near the outhouse in a thicket of bushes.

If he were lucky, he'd ride the bike away from the park in

a week or two. To monitor whether or not the cops continued to search for him, Ethan had asked Malcolm to check his sources. Once the police quit combing the city for him, he'd skedaddle.

*I'll make a beeline for Knoxville. I'd be better off trying a new line of work, like working at a grocery store. I could sneak out food if I need it.*

Weary, Ethan slipped into his sleeping bag on the splintery floor. But worry crept into his mind.

*Is Malcolm going to keep quiet about the cabin?*

# TWENTY-FOUR

## 6:15 A.M., WEDNESDAY, AUGUST 7—SPICER MANSION

LUKE ARRIVED at the Spicer Farm minutes before sunrise. He parked his beat-up pickup in the far corner of the parking lot behind the mansion and carried a suitcase of clothes to the back door. Using one of two keys Carmen had given him, he unlocked the door at the same moment the sun popped into view, low in the eastern sky. Golden rays lit the mansion's entry.

The second key was for the bedroom Carmen had assigned him. Rolling his suitcase, Luke felt the corridor's luxurious carpet under his feet as he walked toward his room. Carmen's bedroom door was closed and locked.

As he stepped closer to his bedroom, Lilia, the maid, smiled and waved to him. "Carmen told me to expect you." Lilia brushed her hair aside. "She asked me to wake her when you arrived."

Luke nodded and stopped by his bedroom door.

Lilia took her cell phone from her apron pocket and touched the device's display.

Luke heard a phone ring in Carmen's room. "Lucas is in the hall." Lilia listened. "I'll tell him." She ended the call and caught Luke's attention. "I'll serve a full English breakfast in the dining room at six-thirty." She pointed at the dining room doorway.

"Sounds delicious." Luke wondered what food was in an English breakfast.

Lilia walked toward the kitchen, her hips swaying with each step.

Luke unlocked his bedroom, pulled his case inside, and began to put his clothes in an oaken dresser. After emptying the suitcase, he touched his diminutive, holstered pistol under his baggy work shirt. The weapon made him feel confident. It was a loyal friend. He felt his body relax, and then he left for the dining room.

Lilia was pouring steaming coffee. She pointed to a fancy chair. "Please be seated." She grinned. "After Carmen comes in, I'll bring breakfast."

Luke heard a sound behind him. He turned to see Carmen enter the room. She wore tight-fitting jeans and a short-sleeved, plaid Western shirt with metal snaps instead of buttons. "Good morning, Lucas." She appeared refreshed and alert.

"The same to you." He stood and pulled out her chair.

"You're a gentleman."

Luke noticed her eyes were normal—not dilated—as if she hadn't taken drugs that morning. Her speech was clear and succinct. He assumed she hadn't had a drink, either.

Lilia set plates loaded with food on the table. Luke smelled the bacon first, and then his eyes focused on scrambled eggs, fried tomatoes and mushrooms, buttered toast, baked beans, and a lump of sausage-like meat. He turned to Carmen. "What's this sausage called?"

"Black pudding."

Luke eyed it.

"It's common in the UK and Ireland. It's made of fat, onions, oatmeal, and cow's blood." She peered at his face. "Let me know if you like it."

After he had eaten everything else, Luke bit into the blood sausage, and then left the rest of it on his plate. He studied Carmen for a second as he gathered his thoughts. *I ain't gonna say a thing about black pudding.* Instead, he decided he'd talk about what bodyguards do.

At four in the morning, before he'd left for the Spicer Farm, he'd reviewed two bodyguard websites. "Carmen, okay if I talk about what a bodyguard does?"

"Yes."

"First, he's gotta assess the situation. We can figure out why you feel yur in danger. I'll write down a list of concerns."

"Then what?"

"We'll tour the house and farm to hunt for risky spots. We'll decide how to make you safer."

Carmen stood. "I'll get a tablet and a pen." She headed for her office.

\* \* \*

## 6:45 A.M., WEDNESDAY, AUGUST 7

Lilia stood in the kitchen near the stovetop. *I better call David right now.* He'd hired her, and she owed him her job. If she heard anything he might consider important, she passed the info to him. He paid her for it.

She held her phone to her ear after touching David's name on its screen.

"*Hola*, Lilia."

"Sorry to call before your breakfast, but I heard something interesting from Carmen."

"What?"

"She made Lucas her bodyguard."

"Why?" David's voice had risen.

"I don't know."

"She wants to screw him?"

Carmen whispered. "It wouldn't be a surprise."

\* \* \*

## 7:00 A.M., WEDNESDAY, AUGUST 7

Carmen moved close to Luke at the breakfast table. She held a ballpoint pen, and a yellow legal pad was on the tabletop. *She's gettin' too familiar*, Luke told himself. *Then again, she needs to trust me enough to tell me everything on her mind.*

He glanced at her eyes. "I've been trained as a security guard. I was in a boxing league, too. You can trust me to do a decent job guarding you."

The corners of Carmen's lips rose to form a subtle smile. "I trust you, or I wouldn't have given you the job."

Luke nodded. "What makes you think this farm's dangerous?"

Carmen sighed. "Promise you won't tell a soul what I'm about to say."

Luke felt a wave of excitement. "My lips are sealed."

He could smell her expensive perfume when she leaned forward. She spoke in a low voice. "Thousands of dollars in cash are in Mark's safe in small bills. It'll take hours to count it."

"Afraid someone will rob you?"

"Yes and…" She spoke in yet a quieter voice. "Mark sold expensive horses to Mateo, a rich Mexican sugarcane farmer. I think Mateo's laundering money."

"Are you positive?"

"It's obvious Mateo bought thoroughbreds to get rid of cash." Carmen paused. "Later, a wealthy oilman from Saudi Arabia bought the horses from Mateo."

Luke rubbed his chin. If it was true Mark had been helping a Mexican drug cartel to launder money, had Carmen known this from the start, or was she unaware of it until after Mark's death? Had her husband told her anything? He heard himself ask, "Do you think a drug cartel will kill you? Do you believe they killed Mark?"

"Yes and yes." She furrowed her brow and leaned even closer until Luke thought she'd bump his head. "I didn't know about the cash until after I found the combination for Mark's safe in his bank box."

"Shouldn't you call the police?"

She sat taller. "No. The cops will think I killed Mark." Carmen began to shake. Abruptly changing the subject, she said, "You said you go to meetings because you had a drinking problem."

"Yep." Luke frowned. *She was quick to trust me. Does she have an angle, or is she impulsive?*

Luke saw Carmen gulp. "You know I have a drinking problem. I'm hooked on pills, too."

"How do you get 'em?"

"From a dealer in Lexington." Carmen paused. "He sold me a bag of pills and left town. He thought the cops would arrest him for selling drugs to me which may've killed Mark."

"Don't you think the cops will find the pills you bought and accuse you of killing Mark?"

"I need them." Tears streamed down Carmen's face. "Keep quiet about this, okay?" She peered at him with her doe-like, brown eyes.

"Okay." Luke decided that after he and Carmen did a walk-through of the mansion and the farm, he'd call Jim to report what he'd learned.

Carmen blinked. "I need everybody to know you're my bodyguard. They'll think twice before making a move against me."

Luke sighed. "Wouldn't it be better for me to take a low profile?"

"No. I bet I read the same websites about bodyguards you did. One reason to have a guy like you is you're a visible deterrence. I told Lilia you're my bodyguard. Everybody on the farm must know by now."

# TWENTY-FIVE

DAVID SAT in his office and fingered his scrambler-equipped satellite phone. He asked himself, *Should I call Mateo? If I do, will he get mad?* David was obsessed with questions about Carmen and Lucas.

Why would she hire Lucas, a new stable hand, to be her bodyguard? Likely because Lucas was tough—a valid reason to hire him for protection. What was Carmen afraid of?

In his mind's eye, David pictured Carmen, a sexy woman who craved sexual intercourse. Did she want sex so soon after Mark had died? From personal experience, David knew she was sex-crazy. Had she hired Lucas to screw her?

Did Carmen realize Mark had been laundering Mateo's drug money? If she did, was she scared? The odds were, yes. Mark had claimed he never informed her about the farm's finances and contracts. But she must've found close to a million bucks in greenbacks in his safe. Though Carmen was a paranoid junkie and as hot as a feline in heat, she wasn't stupid.

Earlier, David had tried calling Ethan's number three times. Ethan hadn't answered. Had the Lexington drug pusher realized Carmen suspected Mark of laundering money? She had been buying pills from Ethan for three years. According to him, she'd never hinted she believed drugs were being routed through the farm or cash was being laundered. If she had learned the pigeons carried illegal drugs, David wondered if she would have dared to ask him for pills. She'd had sex with him. It was conceivable she'd trust him to deliver drugs to her free of charge.

David took a deep breath and tapped Mateo's icon on the satellite phone.

"*Hola*, David. How's business at the farm?" The two men spoke in Spanish.

"First excuse me, Boss, for calling, but as you can imagine, after Mark died the situation here has been in flux."

"What changed?"

"Carmen may have figured out our business alliance with Mark."

David heard Mateo exhale. "It was bound to happen."

"She was upset when Mark died." David paused. "And she's often high on drugs and acts without thinking. But most upsetting, she's promoted a new hire stable mucker, Lucas Blanco, to be her bodyguard, and perhaps her lover, too."

"What?" David heard Mateo's voice rise. "Years ago, you told me she was hot and man crazy, and she even had relations with you."

"*Si*, Boss. She'll have sex with any man she's attracted to. After she has had a man, she drops him and finds another."

"Lucas is lucky today, but later he'll be back to mucking stalls." Mateo laughed. "I should make a trip to Kentucky to find out if she'll want to play with me."

"She is *muy bella*, Boss."

"Why not rekindle your relationship with her?" Mateo snickered. "Marry her, and our problems will be solved. *Nuestro Club*'s drugstore and laundry business would continue as usual."

"I would if I could, Boss, but she is fickle." David inhaled and tried to relax. "Boss, Terry bumped into Lucas. Terry believes he felt a pistol under the work shirt Lucas was wearing."

"Hmm. Lucas could be a *Los Hermanos* spy."

David knew that the drug cartel, *Los Hermanos*, based in Bogotá, was the most powerful illegal drug syndicate in Colombia. The Colombians were always working to expand their reach across the Western Hemisphere.

The leader of *Los Hermanos* was a blood-thirsty man by the name of Ricardo Cortez. He was often accompanied by his aide, Jamie—a stocky man with steel-gray, wiry hair. Jaime was ruthless, too.

David didn't want to tell Mateo what to do. Instead, David asked a question. "Will you check out Lucas, Boss?"

"At once. If he's with *Los Hermanos*, he's using an alias."

David cleared his throat. "Lucas speaks in English with no accent. Terry tried to talk with him in Spanish, but he refused. Lucas said his mother's Mexican, but she didn't teach him Spanish. She thought he'd blend in better in the US."

"He could be Colombian with a mother from Bogotá or an American thug Jamie hired." Mateo coughed. "We have many pictures of *Hermanos* members on the computer. Send me a pic of Lucas."

"I'll email you his driver's license photo."

"Watch him." Mateo paused. "If we're lucky, we'll learn he's just an American gigolo."

David gulped and then asked, "What should we do about Carmen?"

"Convince her to agree to the same deal Mark had. If she doesn't, we'll take other actions."

"Yes, Boss."

Mateo disconnected.

David called Terry's cell phone. *Terry needs to be careful with Lucas*, David thought. Terry's phone went to voicemail. David left his office to search for Terry to order him to monitor Lucas.

# TWENTY-SIX

## 11:15 A.M., WEDNESDAY, AUGUST 7—SPICER HORSE BARN

AFTER LUKE and Carmen had toured the mansion and farm to examine the property for vulnerabilities, they stood outside the rear entrance of the main horse barn. Carmen peered down the line of stalls. "I ride my mare, Sweetie, almost daily."

"You could be attacked when you ride." Luke wondered if she rode on a regular schedule.

Carmen cut his thoughts short. "You should ride with me. Take Sammy, Mark's stallion."

"Okay." Luke wondered if it was far-fetched to think an assassin might plant an explosive in a saddlebag. "I could check Sweetie every day."

"Why?"

"To make certain nobody's put a chemical or a burr on the tack to make Sweetie buck."

Carmen glanced at her vehicle parked near the barn. "Somebody could tamper with my SUV, too."

"I'll check it." Luke figured he could use a mirror taped to a broken rake handle to search underneath Carmen's SUV for a bomb. Cutting a brake line was a tactic an enemy could use, but losing her brakes wouldn't necessarily lead to

Carmen's death. On the other hand, a powerful explosion would kill a person in the vast majority of cases.

"Will you check my car daily?"

"Yes, but I'll vary when I do it." Luke reckoned it was smart to avoid checking on a schedule. An assassin would study his and Carmen's routines and pick a strategic time to strike. Even if paranoia and drug addiction had increased her fright, her on-target hunch that Mark had been murdered convinced Luke her fear of assassination was reasonable.

Carmen gestured at her SUV. "Anything special I should do with my car?"

He viewed the garage on the edge of the parking lot. "Always park in your garage and lock it. Anyone else have a garage key?"

"David does."

"I'll get you a heavy-duty padlock at a hardware store."

Carmen blinked. "I'd like to go with you."

"Okay. We'll get the finest lock Farmer's Hardware's got."

Carmen peeked into the barn at Sweetie's stall. "Get acquainted with Sweetie and Sammy while I go to my office to see if anyone phoned."

Carmen walked at a fast pace toward the mansion.

From the corner of his eye, Luke thought he saw someone step behind bales of hay in the middle of the barn.

* * *

## 11:25 A.M., WEDNESDAY, AUGUST 7

As Luke reached the center of the horse barn, he neared a stack of hay bales. As he passed the pile, he heard a noise. It sounded like a foot dragging across the layer of hay on the floor. Or had someone behind the bales swept up spilled hay?

Luke walked to Sweetie, Carmen's mare, and began to examine the horse's equipment—the bridle, bit, reins, harness, collar, halter, saddle and saddle pad, cinch, stirrups, and lead rope.

A slurred voice in a Mexican accent boomed behind Luke. "What the hell you doin', Lucas?"

Luke turned and saw Terry, who stepped closer to him. The man's breath reeked of alcohol. Luke studied him. "Carmen asked me to check her horse and its tack."

With fire in his eyes, Terry glared at Luke. "You been sniffing around Carmen, huh? She gonna screw you?"

Luke eased a breath from his mouth. "If you ain't heard, she hired me to be her bodyguard."

"I got the next claim on her, *amigo*." Terry took an aggressive step forward. His massive, six-foot-tall body collided with Luke. "Stay away from her, gigolo." He spit out a wad of gum.

"I already got a girlfriend." Luke had made his voice as calm as he could. He didn't want to fight the man. It would draw undue attention to himself and his job to protect Carmen. She'd told the maid he was her bodyguard, and by now, everyone at Spicer Farm knew it, including Terry.

Terry pushed Luke. Luke stepped back. Terry sneered. "You're a yellow-bellied coward." He shoved Luke again.

Luke reckoned he'd better defuse the situation, but how? Under normal circumstances, Terry was hostile. But today he was bellicose. Luke held up his palm. "No need to rile up the horses, Terry."

At once the arrogant Latino threw a roundhouse right-handed punch at Luke. Luke dodged the blow, grabbed Terry's right wrist, and pulled the wrist in the direction it was flying. The man's momentum carried his muscle-bound body forward. He stumbled and fell flat on the floor with a thud. Dust rose around him. He pushed himself up on his knees. Luke could smell the brute's sour breath.

Terry's neck and face were red under his deep tan. He appeared more embarrassed than hurt. As he rose to his feet, he came close to tripping. He turned. "You bastard." He charged Luke.

Luke leaped aside. Terry caught himself, or he would've

fallen again. The man grabbed a mucking rake and swung it at Luke, who evaded the speeding stable tool. Luke heard it whistle as it came within two inches of his chest.

Luke felt his pulse pound.

*I had enough of this crap.*

He grabbed the rake handle and wrenched it from the bull-like man. Luke tossed the tool across the stable's central passageway out of Terry's reach.

"I'm going to beat the shit out of you." Terry threw a wild punch at Luke.

In a defensive stand, Luke deflected the blow with his left forearm. He powered a right-hand punch at Terry, jolting the man's jaw as if a mule had kicked it. Terry's knees buckled like they were made of rubber. He was unconscious before he hit the floor with a heavy thump.

Luke spied a bucket of water near a stall. He picked it up and tossed the cold liquid on Terry's head.

Terry's eyes opened, and he ran his fingers across his jaw. They were red with blood. Luke frowned at the defeated man. "Leave before I hit you again."

Terry glared at Luke. The muscular Latino crawled away toward the exit near David's office.

Luke watched as Terry used a vertical beam to pull himself up. "I'm gonna get you. You won't see it coming." He staggered from the barn.

Luke noticed the wad of gum Terry had spit onto the barn's floor.

*At least I'll get somethin' useful outta the fight.*

He withdrew an evidence bag from his back pocket and used it to pick up and then store Terry's gum.

# TWENTY-SEVEN

LUKE STEPPED out of the barn and leaned against its sun-warmed, outside wall. His knuckles hurt after he'd slammed them into Terry's jaw. Stretching his right arm above him, he flexed his fingers four times. His pain subsided.

Luke reached into his jeans and pulled out his phone.

*Lucky it didn't get broke in the fight.*

He touched Jim's name on the cell's contact list.

"Hi, Luke. Learn anything significant?"

He paused and considered what to say first. "Carmen said she found cash in Mark's safe. It was a lot—enough to take her hours to count." Luke flexed his bruised knuckles. "Carmen thinks Mark was laundering money for a rich Mexican, Mateo."

"Why does she believe that?"

"Mateo paid cash to Mark for pricey thoroughbreds. Later, Mateo sold the same horses to a rich Saudi oil man. I have a hunch the Arab wired clean money to Mateo to pay for the animals."

"The cash could be drug money."

"Carmen's scared shitless. Thinks the Mexicans killed

Mark, and she's next." Luke figured it was time to tell Jim about Carmen's drug addiction. "She said she buys pills from her pusher who's from Lexington. He told her he was leaving town cuz the police could be after him for selling the drugs that killed Mark."

The faint sound of men talking came through Luke's phone. Then Jim spoke. "I'm at a Lexington pusher's house. We got a warrant. An informant said Ethan Wood's been selling drugs to Carmen for three years."

"Find anything?"

"A mess. His motorcycle's gone."

Luke wondered how many pills Carmen had bought from Ethan after Mark died. "Do you plan to search the Spicer Farm for Carmen's drugs?"

Jim paused. "What do you think?"

"I'd wait."

"Why?"

"A massive dose of fentanyl killed Mark." Luke switched his phone to his left hand. His fist was hurting. "Unless Carmen bought pure fentanyl powder and spiked Mark's beer with it, she didn't do it. Odds are she bought typical oxycodone pills from Ethan. They have fentanyl in them, but it's a small amount compared to what Mitch found in Mark's body and beer mug."

Jim bumped his phone. "Who do you suspect at the farm?"

"Could'a been David or one of his employees." Luke took a deep breath. "One of them, Terry, took a swing at me. He'd heard Carmen hired me as a bodyguard. The way he talked, he's hot to get in her panties. He was as buzzed as a dog after it'd lapped up a gallon of beer."

"You okay?"

"My knuckles are sore."

Jim sneezed. "Allergies." The sound of Jim blowing his nose came through the phone's internal speaker. "I got a tip Ethan's hiding in an old cabin in the woods at Becker's Park. I'm leaving for the park after I finish here."

"If he talks, he could clear Carmen."

"He could also tell us if the Mexicans are laundering money and piping drugs into Eastern Kentucky." Jim sounded like he had hay fever. "Keep in touch. I gotta get back to work here."

# TWENTY-EIGHT

A FIGURE DRESSED in a camouflaged outfit moved in silence through the underbrush toward a decrepit cabin hidden under a wall of vines. The sneak could smell a smokeless fire burning in the abode's potbelly stove. Had Ethan eaten lunch? Would he soon visit the outhouse?

The man crept closer to the outbuilding and sat on a log concealed by bushes. The fallen tree was a mere twenty feet from the entrance of the privy. With a tranquilizer rifle at the ready, the prowler settled down to wait for Ethan to emerge from the log house. With a snicker, the hunter thought, *Everybody has to go to the bathroom. Will he pee in the bushes or use the outhouse?*

Fifteen minutes passed. The cabin door creaked.

The assassin smiled. His heartbeat sped up. A pleasurable, exciting feeling—the same anticipation a deer hunter feels a moment before killing a prize buck—coursed through the stalker's body.

Ethan emerged from the log house.

A cascade of thoughts ping-ponged within the killer's brain.

*A quadruple dose of horse tranquilizer will do the trick. Ethan should be unconscious in seconds.*

The amount of "Tranq" needed to knock out an animal was based on the brute's weight. Three to ten or more minutes have to pass before the anesthetic would knock out a steer, bear, or gorilla. Because it was hard to get the dosage right, tranquilizer guns weren't usually used to take down people. Not enough tranquilizer, and a victim would not keel over. A slight bit more Tranq, and death would result.

Ethan weighed close to 175 pounds. A horse can weigh from 1,500 pounds up to a ton. Based on his weight, Ethan would be injected with about ten times the tranquilizer needed to knock out a horse.

Though the killer hadn't tested Tranq on a human being, he hoped Ethan would collapse at once, as always happened in Hollywood movies. But they were fantasy, not reality. *Ethan better fall fast, or I'll have to use my blackjack.*

Whether the powerful drug merely knocked Ethan out or killed him didn't matter. A twenty-two caliber round smashing through his right temple into his brain would make his death appear to be a suicide.

The killer had heard horse tranquilizer had been found in seven percent of the bodies of American drug overdose victims. If an autopsy showed Tranq in Ethan's body, it wouldn't appear suspicious because he was a drug dealer, and he could've been using his product.

The murderer was happy horse tranquilizer was not a controlled substance. The clear liquid veterinary version was easy to get. Not an opioid, it would slow breathing and heartbeat, and lower blood pressure. These changes and the suppression of the central nervous system could kill.

An added plus was the pupils in Ethan's eyes would constrict, and he would appear to have had an opioid over-dose. If the killer had to flee before shooting Ethan, chances are responding medical personnel would treat Ethan with Narcan. It wouldn't work. The killer realized the vast majority of medical people didn't know about Tranq or how to test for it.

The tranquilizer rifle's sight was zeroed in on Ethan, who walked at a slow pace toward the outhouse. The killer's air rifle was powered by a cigar-sized metal cylinder containing compressed carbon dioxide gas. When the rifle's trigger was pulled, the gas would drive the Tranq dart from the barrel.

The executioner squeezed the weapon's trigger. A metal dart zipped through the air and struck Ethan's throat. He slapped at his neck. The projectile fell away. He stumbled. He fell. Blood streamed from a puncture wound.

The killer whispered, "Darn! This weapon fired high." But still, he was satisfied the dart had hit his prey. The hunter emerged from the bushes, smiling.

Ethan's body shook for two minutes and then was still. His lifeless eyes stared vacantly at the sky.

The killer neared Ethan's body, kneeled, and set a backpack down. Digging into it, the criminal took out a bottle of water, a box of tissue, a thermos containing ice, a plastic garbage bag, and a small tub of styptic powder—the kind veterinarians use to stop bleeding from minor cuts on cats and dogs.

Wearing blue nitrile gloves, the felon dabbed the puncture wound with a tissue and then tossed styptic powder on the puncture, causing the blood to clot. Next, the culprit poured ice from the thermos into a plastic sandwich bag, sealed it, and held it against the puncture wound. The killer hoped the ice would reduce bruising where the dart had struck Ethan's throat.

The criminal withdrew a twenty-two-caliber pistol from the light backpack. Still kneeling next to Ethan's body, the slayer put the weapon's muzzle against Ethan's right temple and squeezed the trigger. A loud pop echoed. The bitter smell of spent, smokeless gunpowder mixed with the odor of Ethan's bowel movement.

Next, the murderer unloaded the handgun and pushed Ethan's limp fingers on the loose bullets. The perp then reloaded the pistol with the same bullets. After picking up the brass from the spent round, he again used Ethan's fingers to put a print on the casing and dropped it close to Ethan's right hand.

After removing a fake suicide note from a sandwich bag, the rogue pressed Ethan's fingers onto the message and set it aside under a rock. The shooter then placed the pistol in Ethan's limp hand.

Except for the pistol, the bullet casing, and the note, the killer collected what he'd brought to the shooting scene and dropped it in his garbage bag. Finally, he tacked the suicide note to the outside of the cabin and snuck away.

# TWENTY-NINE

JOSE MARTINEZ, who helped Terry take care of Mateo's pigeons, saw a half-dozen of the birds fly through the horse barn's hay doorway. They had returned from Lexington before they normally did. Jose thought he'd seen two of the birds with pouches of drugs still attached to their legs.

Jose moved his short, stocky body at power-walk speed toward the rear door of the huge Spicer horse barn. After rushing up the wooden plank stairs to the pigeon coops in the loft, he examined the pigeons.

He ran his hands through his hair. "Shit." All the birds still carried their pouches of fentanyl-laced oxycodone pills. Ethan hadn't removed the drugs like he was supposed to. Even worse, the pigeons were poking around searching for seeds. They hadn't eaten.

They normally ate at Ethan's Lexington house and then returned to roost and sleep in the barn.

*David will be mad*, Jose thought. He remembered two prior incidents when Ethan had gotten drunk the night before and had overslept, neglecting the pigeons. David had chewed him out on those occasions. The Lexington drug pusher had been more dependable in the last year and a half. Had he gotten dead drunk once again?

Jose withdrew his phone from his hip pocket. He touched David's name.

"*Hola, Jose*. What's going on?"

"All of the birds returned from Lexington. They still had pouches on their legs."

"Goddamn it. I'll call Ethan." David paused. "Put the birds in a cage and feed them. I don't want them to go back to Lexington if something's wrong."

# THIRTY

DAVID COULDN'T STOP FUMING when he thought about his pigeons flying back to the Spicer Farm from Ethan's place. They still carried pouches jammed with illegal pills. Where the hell was Ethan?

"Son of a bitch." David spoke out loud though nobody else was in his office. The more he wondered about the situation, the angrier he became. What if the cops had nabbed Ethan? Was he dead drunk again? Had he had a heart attack and died? Had someone robbed him?

David grabbed his burner cell phone and once again tapped in Ethan's cell number. The phone rang ten times. David waited five minutes and tried Ethan's number for a final time with the same result.

"Damn." *Somebody needs to check Ethan's house.*

David searched his desk drawer and found Ethan's extra house key. He'd demanded it after Ethan had screwed up more than a year ago, and the pigeons had returned with their pouches full of drugs.

Grabbing his landline telephone handset, David tapped in Bruno Chavez's cell number. Bruno was tall, strong, and loyal.

"*Hola*, Boss."

"Ethan's messed up again. The birds returned hungry with their pouches loaded with pills. I need you to drive to Ethan's house to find him. If you locate him, slap his face and sober him up." He paused and fingered Ethan's house key. "Stop at my office to pick up Ethan's house key."

"Okay. What if he's not around?"

"Check the neighborhood. Find the SOB. Call me when you do."

*　*　*

## 2:10 P.M., WEDNESDAY, AUGUST 7

Bruno, a tall man, got into a Spicer Farm company car and pushed the driver's seat as far back as it would go. He pressed the accelerator too hard. The tires squealed. He sped toward Lexington. When he entered the Winburn neighborhood, he slowed. Two blocks from Ethan's house, he saw flashing police lights.

"Goddamn," he muttered.

He lifted his foot off the accelerator when he was two blocks from Ethan's dilapidated house. He slowed to a stop at the curb, reached in his glove box, and removed compact binoculars.

Peering through the field glasses, Bruno saw police swarming around Ethan's place. A half-dozen squad cars and a step van labeled "Crime Scene Investigation" had parked near Ethan's house.

Bruno noticed more of the home's paint had flaked off since he'd seen the place a year ago. Not wishing to catch the attention of the police, he tossed the binoculars on the front passenger seat and turned on his car. Within seconds he'd turned around.

After stopping in a fast-food restaurant's parking lot, he snatched his mobile phone with his meaty hand. "Hello, David. It's Bruno."

"You sound out of breath."

"Ethan's place is crawling with cops."

"Shit. They see you?"

"No."

"Wait a while and go back. If the cops are gone, ask around the neighborhood to find out if anybody knows what happened."

"Okay, but isn't it risky?"

David sighed. "You got a point. I'll call a guy who can find out if they arrested Ethan."

"Should I come back now?"

"Yeah." David paused. "Hope Ethan doesn't rat on us. When you get back, let's discuss who'll replace him. You'll have to drive pills to an alternate location until we can train the pigeons to fly there."

"See you soon." Bruno hung up. He wondered if Ethan had left the city, or if he was in the cops' hands and ready to squeal.

# THIRTY-ONE

LUKE'S CURIOSITY peaked when he saw a pigeon fly to the hayloft doorway near the top of the Spicer horse barn. The bluish-gray bird had black wing markings and whitish underwings. He thought he'd seen bands attached to its legs. Did the bird carry a pouch?

After Luke surveyed his surroundings and saw no one near, he entered the barn and climbed the wooden steps to the hayloft. He saw two dozen pigeons in open cages.

A dovelike bird fluttered into a cage and perched on a wooden rod. A colored band was attached to its left leg and a numbered band was on its right one.

Trying not to scare the pigeon, Luke eased toward its cage. He crouched and peered at the fowl. He reckoned it was a "homer." He'd heard homing pigeons always returned to the first place they had flown from when they were juveniles. Their home locations are burned into their memories. If a bird is taken to a distant place—as far as four hundred miles away—the pigeon will fly back to its home coop.

Luke had once seen the beginning of a homing pigeon race when 100 birds had been released in Louisville. The first bird to return to its home in Lexington won the contest. A "pigeon man" had explained the foot bands contained radio frequency identification chips.

A computer recorded the time each pigeon left to fly back to its home coop. Another computer checked the birds in. The speed and distances flown by all the birds were entered into a computer program to determine the winner and runners-up. Depending on wind and other factors, the pigeons flew from forty to eighty miles per hour.

A question arose in Luke's mind. *Could these racing club pigeons also carry drugs?* He'd earlier read an article about inmates who'd smuggled narcotics into a prison using carrier pigeons. *I gotta ask Carmen about the birds.*

# THIRTY-TWO

MATEO SAT in his luxurious office five miles from Tijuana, Mexico. He smiled and felt warm in the sunshine beaming through the wide windows into the air-conditioned room.

He had ordered his office building, which also included his luxury apartment, to be constructed in the countryside. His drug money had bought him a palace. Fountains stood in the courtyard. A landscape artist had planted trees in pleasing places at the edges of his expansive plot of land.

He felt secure and at ease in his domain. Bodyguards patrolled the perimeter fence. Willing and capable, his crew of personal soldiers protected his profitable business.

As he was drinking his sweetened and cream-infused coffee and enjoying every sip of it, sharp knocks sounded on the frame of his office door.

He glanced toward the knocks. A rail-thin young man with an untrimmed beard and unruly hair waited.

"Come in, my young professor."

Mateo called the youthful man "Professor" because he was a computer expert. He'd graduated at the top of his class at the National Polytechnic Institute of Mexico. Mateo paid the boyish man better than any legitimate company would have.

Mateo smiled. "What have you learned about Lucas Blanco?"

"We have a match for Señor Lucas Blanco's picture in the *Los Hermanos* database."

Mateo stood. "Lucas is a Bogota cartel member?"

"He is. His real name, according to our records, is Joseph Murphy. He is a *gringo* by birth, but he is employed by *Los Hermanos* as an enforcer."

The young "Professor" appeared nervous to Mateo. "Have a seat. You did a great job. Have a cup of coffee." Mateo pointed at a silver coffee urn.

"Thank you, Boss."

Mateo sat. "I must take action."

# THIRTY-THREE

LUKE CLIMBED down the wooden steps leading from the hayloft to the ground level of the horse barn. As he left it, he spotted Carmen. "Carmen, we need to talk." He nodded at his truck, and they walked to it.

He unlocked the passenger door and motioned for her to get inside. She focused on him. "What's up?"

He pointed at the hayloft door. "A pigeon flew into the loft. I saw a band on the pigeon's leg, so I climbed up to the loft to check the bird."

Carmen focused her brown eyes on Luke. "Did I tell you Mateo and David race pigeons?"

"They race 'em?"

"Yes." Carmen leaned close to Luke. He could feel her body heat. "Mark told me Mateo had started a pigeon racing club. He joked racing pigeons was like racing horses but cheaper."

Luke furrowed his brow. "How long have they been doing this?"

"At least three years. I often see birds with pouches. Mark said the pouches are for messages."

Was Carmen playing dumb? Luke peered into her doe-like eyes. "It's obvious the Mexicans are smuggling drugs with the birds. Illegal narcotic pills can fit in those pouches."

Carmen sighed. "After Mark died, I began to wonder if the pigeons were carrying things besides messages."

Luke again gazed at the hayloft door. "Who's in charge of the pigeons?"

"Jose and Terry."

"They could've poisoned Mark." Luke paused. "'Specially if they handled drugs."

As Carmen slid closer to Luke, she touched his shoulder. "I'm scared."

"I'll watch those two guys."

She gave him a quick hug. "Thanks."

Luke figured she was trying to get closer to him. It was important to keep her in his confidence. But he couldn't let her get enthralled with him. According to her reputation, she went after any man who appealed to her. No doubt she had her sights on him. He would have to be careful how he dealt with her.

Luke unlatched the truck's driver's side door. "We should get out soon 'cuz people might see us and wonder what we're up to. Gossip's gotta be the main entertainment on this farm."

# THIRTY-FOUR

## 2:50 P.M., WEDNESDAY, AUGUST 7

SHERIFF JIM PIKE and two of his deputies had decided to stop for a bite at Rocky's Burgers near Becker's Park. They were on their way to the park to search for Ethan, the drug dealer.

When the burger joint's automatic doors swung outward, Jim saw Steve, the owner of Kobold Farm, a well-known thoroughbred trainer. He sat in a booth with a steak sandwich in his hand. Jim had spoken with Steve a half-dozen times during the previous three years.

Jim glanced at his deputies and grinned. "Could y'all order a burger, fries, and a soda for me, please? I'll be back."

Jim approached Steve. "Hi, Steve. Isn't Kobold Farm close to Becker's Park?"

Steve set his half-eaten steak sandwich on his plate. "Yep, Sheriff. It's not used a lot, but it's a nice place to visit."

Jim smiled. "Mind if I sit while my buddies order my burger?"

"Take a load off."

Jim sat across from Steve. "I was thinking Becker's Park would be a nice place to have our police picnic. People say it's not crowded."

Steve shrugged. "It's overgrown, but four picnic tables are near the parking lot if you don't have too many guests. I suppose you could bring folding tables and chairs if you needed to seat a bigger crowd."

Jim cocked his head. "I should drive to the park and analyze it before we commit."

Steve sipped his soda and set it down. "I suggest you ask the county to cut the grass. It's two feet tall. And a fire-damaged cabin is in the woods. They ought to knock it down."

Jim leaned on his palm with his elbow propped on the table. "Ever see illegal activity around in the park?"

"People say a Lexington drug pusher hikes in the park every so often. He carries a pack."

Jim opened his eyes wider and grinned. "If he's around when we visit, I bet he'll leave fast."

A movement in Jim's side vision caught his attention. He turned and saw one of his deputies waving at him while holding a takeout bag. "My buddies are waiting. Thanks for the info, Steve."

# THIRTY-FIVE

## 2:55 P.M., WEDNESDAY, AUGUST 7—SPICER FARM

AFTER THROWING trash from the back of his truck into the dumpster by the parking lot, Luke heard whistling. It was coming from behind the bunkhouse. The whistler was warbling an oldies tune.

Ernie, the redheaded stable hand, came around the corner, stopped whistling, and halted near Luke. "I saw Carmen get out of the truck. I was watching you both through the window."

"She was askin' security questions."

"Yeah, sure." Ernie laughed. "Has she screwed you yet?"

"I got a girlfriend already."

Ernie pulled a tin from his jeans pocket. After unsnapping the metal container, he put a lump of chewing tobacco into his mouth. He paused. "I bet Carmen will lure you into her bed. But your girlfriend has nothing to worry about. Carmen doesn't stick with one guy for months or years."

Luke smiled. "Could be rumors about Carmen got out of hand."

"I already told you she's been in bed with David." Ernie displayed a mocking grin. "She even got in bed with Terry once. He was drunk and bragged about it."

"Oh?"

"Yeah, and they say she slept with the owner of the Kobold Farm when Mark was away on business."

"Nothing's going to happen between me and Carmen."

Ernie slapped Luke on the back. "Don't worry. You'll be fine even if you have to take back your old mucker job after she dumps you." He spit out tobacco juice. "I like you, and I'm in charge of tending the horses. David will listen to me and keep you."

"Thanks, Ernie. At least I got job security—unless the two Mexicans who take care of the pigeons try to get me fired."

Ernie exhaled. "It's a shame about those guys. The pigeons are on the top of their to-do list, even though there's lots of fancy thoroughbreds to take care of."

Luke leaned closer. "Thanks fur your support."

The men parted. Luke wondered what Carmen would do next. Would she make an overt pass at him? If so, how would he handle it?

# THIRTY-SIX

## 3:05 P.M., WEDNESDAY, AUGUST 7

SHERIFF JIM PIKE and his two deputies, Phil and Jerome, stopped their vehicles in Becker's Park near four picnic tables. Jim got out of his SUV and stretched his legs and arms. He eyed his deputies.

"The county park manager told me the cabin's about nine hundred yards that way." Jim pointed. The shack was supposedly hidden in the dense woods in line with a towering pine tree. "When we get close, keep out of sight. I'll decide how we'll approach it after we spot it."

The three men crossed into the overgrown field, which was 500 yards across. Like Steve Kobold had said, the grass was two feet tall and thick. When they reached the edge of the woods, the men moved with stealth. Jim stopped. "I think it's beyond the tallest tree." He gestured with his head. The trio set off, pushing underbrush aside until they reached a clear area short of a canopy of trees.

Jim saw an unusual cluster of vines covering three or four trees. Taking care not to step on dead branches and leaves, the men moved in silence toward the vines with their pistols drawn.

Concealed behind the vegetation, they crept around the

vines. Jim saw an outhouse and the back of the cabin. A chill ran down his spine. A man's body was lying near the privy. Jim signaled his men to remain quiet. They approached with caution. Jim peered into the cabin. No one was inside. He turned and squinted as he gazed at the dead man's face. "It appears to be Ethan."

Phil focused on the body and the flies buzzing around it. The man's eyes were open and staring up at the canopy of trees. A bloody bullet hole was in the victim's right temple. The corpse gripped a pistol in a lifeless hand.

Deputy Jerome Sanders gestured at the cabin. "A paper's on the wall." Taking care not to step on footprints or potential evidence, he moved closer to the shack. "It's a suicide note."

Jim read it. "Mark Spicer was a friend. I'm sorry I sold him a defective batch of pills that killed him. I can't live with myself. Please express my sorrow to his wife, Carmen. I have no family. No one will miss me. Goodbye, Ethan Wood."

Logic told Jim the note was a fake. Why would a man hide to avoid capture and then kill himself? Why not commit suicide in his own house? Would "defective pills" contain enough fentanyl to result in the extreme concentration of it found in Mark's body?

Jim's second deputy, Phil Ortega, squinted as he studied the pistol from a distance. "It's a .22 caliber Ruger."

Jim surveyed the area. "Okay, men, we need to secure the scene. I'm going to call this in while you two set up barriers." He regarded his two men. "Jerome, go back to the lot and block the driveway with your cruiser. Get out a clipboard and paper. Start a sign-in, sign-out sheet."

Jim next trained his eyes on Phil. "Go back and grab evidence bags and markers, shoe covers, nitrile gloves, and a roll of crime scene tape. Come back and mark the core crime scene."

After the men had left, Jim slipped his cell phone from his hip pocket and dialed the station. He heard the phone ring on the end of the line.

"Sergeant Baker, Sheriff's Department."

"This is Jim. We found a body in Becker's Park. Send all the folks you can spare to help secure the scene. Make sure Alice arrives soon and tell her to drive the larger crime scene truck here."

Next, Jim called Mitch, the coroner. He answered after two rings. "Did you find another body?"

"Yes. You must be clairvoyant. How soon can you get to Becker's Park? We found the body of Ethan Wood, a drug dealer, by a cabin in the woods. It could've been suicide, but something's fishy about the scene."

"I'm leaving now, Jim." He paused. "Is the cute blond on the scene—the crime scene investigator?"

"Alice is coming."

* * *

## 3:40 P.M., WEDNESDAY, AUGUST 7—BECKER'S PARK

The sheriff's senior crime scene investigator, Alice Strom, arrived in her truck fifteen minutes after Jim's call. Jim watched as she drove the CSI step van across the field.

He wondered, *Where's she going to stop?* She was guiding her vehicle up to where the tree line began. Avoiding low-hanging tree branches, she inched into the woods and parked a hundred yards from the cabin.

Petite and agile, she hopped down from the van with alacrity. Her braided blond pigtails bobbed as she approached Jim, who stood outside of the yellow crime scene tape. "Where's the body?"

Jim pointed. "Behind the vines and cabin, before the privy."

Alice nodded. "We all should be wearing nitrile gloves and footies in the core crime scene and the command area, too." She glanced around her. "Could someone set up a second ring of tape farther out to mark the command area?"

Jim smiled. "Yes, ma'am." He and his deputies would stay in the command area until Alice had completed her work in the core area where the body was.

Alice grinned. "I better get going."

Ricky Barnes, another deputy, watched as she left. "She's a beauty, ain't she?"

Jim sighed. "Let's stick to business." He handed a roll of yellow crime scene tape to Ricky. "You heard the lady. Create a command area."

Six minutes later Alice returned and walked to Jim. "Blood splattered on dried leaves near the victim. One drop of blood seems out of place, considering the wound is in the right temple. The drop's darker than the rest of the blood."

Jim wrinkled his brow. "Are you hinting a separate person's blood is near the body?"

"Yes." She held up two evidence bags. "I took blood samples. A DNA test should tell us a lot."

From behind him, Jim heard the sounds of people walking through the woods. He turned. Mitch, the coroner, and his assistants approached, carrying their equipment. Mitch had a slight limp. Jim snorted. "Hey, Mitch, you should have gotten a ride with Alice. She managed to drive her step van close to the scene."

Mitch cocked his head. "My eyesight has declined. I could've hit a tree branch." He took two deep breaths as he glanced at Alice. "Please show me where the deceased is, dear."

"Follow me."

"Don't walk too fast, Alice. I'm not a spring chicken anymore."

\* \* \*

### 3:55 P.M., WEDNESDAY, AUGUST 7—BECKER'S PARK

Mitch felt winded. *I'm getting too old for this job,* he told himself as he followed Alice around the vine-covered trees.

She stopped short of the yellow crime scene tape circling the area around the body and took six yellow tent stakes from her back pocket. She glanced back at Mitch. "I'll mark an entry path for you."

Mitch smiled. *She's on the ball, unlike Wilbert.* Mitch sighed when he recalled how Wilbert had destroyed vital evidence at a crime scene a year before he'd retired.

Alice turned toward Mitch. "You can come in past the tape."

Mitch approached the deceased man, who lay flat on the ground near the outhouse. As Mitch neared the corpse, he noticed a dot on the dead man's neck. After kneeling near the body, Mitch saw a barely perceptible bruise beginning to form around the spot. He bit his lip. *Could the spot be a puncture wound?*

Mitch heard someone approach from behind him. He turned and saw Jim near the yellow caution tape. "What do you see, Mitch?"

"A puncture wound on the neck. A faint bluish bruise is around it." Mitch stood and glanced at Jim. "I wonder if he was stabbed with a needle."

Jim scratched his head. "Was it suicide or homicide?"

In his early seventies, Mitch's spindly legs wobbled. "I have to complete the autopsy before I can give you an answer." He rubbed his gray, scraggly mustache. "I'll take a blood sample to see if I can find suspicious substances in the bloodstream. Could be this man was killed with a chemical. Someone could've shot him after he was dead."

Jim sighed. "We found a note tacked to the cabin. It could've been planted. This man was a drug dealer, and the note claims he killed himself because he sold a substandard batch of drugs to Mark Spicer."

"So, Mark's murder and this death are connected." Mitch whistled. "I suppose the autopsy of this gent is at the top of your list."

"Yep."

Mitch signaled to his two men. "Let's get this stiff to the morgue." He nodded at Jim. "I should have answers soon. I'll call you."

# THIRTY-SEVEN

MITCH STOOD in the morgue by Ethan's body. Mitch had taken a sample of the dead man's blood and found it contained a lethal dose of Tranq, a horse sedative. A common drug in horse country, farmers used it to knock out animals without killing them. Tranq was not a controlled substance. It was easy to buy.

Air rifles were used to shoot tranquilizer darts at animals. Mitch figured the killer used such a rifle to shoot a dart into Ethan's neck. Mitch reasoned the murderer didn't care if Ethan died from a Tranq overdose or not because a bullet would kill him if the dose of horse tranquilizer didn't.

Mitch reminded himself, *Plenty of air rifles are in horse country.*

Tracking the killer would be difficult even if he'd been bold enough to buy Tranq, an air rifle, and darts. Or he could've stolen what he needed. Many horse farms had a supply of Tranq in their barns as well as rifles to shoot the Tranq darts.

After grabbing his cell phone, Mitch touched Jim's name on the phone's display. He could hear the phone ring.

"Hi, Mitch. Got autopsy results?"

"Yep. It was murder. I found Tranq, a sedative to knock out horses, in Ethan's blood. The puncture wound in his neck was from a Tranq dart shot from an air rifle." Mitch glanced at Ethan's body and his throat. "We're lucky the bruise showed up around the puncture wound. I don't know why the bruise wasn't much larger."

Jim's phone made a noise as if his beard had scratched it. "You think you would've ruled it suicide if it weren't for the bruise and puncture wound?"

"Yep. Otherwise, I wouldn't have tested for Tranq."

Jim cleared his throat. "I also have a development to report. Ethan was left-handed. He would've shot himself in his left temple. It's obvious the perp killed Ethan to cover up Mark's murder."

Mitch narrowed his eyes. "I don't know if our friendly DA is going to like what a mess this is."

"On the other hand, he could like it because it'll be a major story."

# THIRTY-EIGHT

## 5:00 P.M., WEDNESDAY, AUGUST 7—SPICER FARM

DAVID RELAXED IN HIS OFFICE, pulled out his cell phone, and decided to check what the security camera in the pigeon coop area had recorded.

After accessing the camera application on his phone, David at once saw a video recording of Luke entering the hayloft near the coops and staring at the pigeons.

"*Jesus Cristo*," David said out loud. Then in silence, he told himself, *First, Carmen hires Lucas as a bodyguard. Already he's examining the pigeons. Lucky the guys took the drug pouches off the birds.*

David had to figure out a way to fire Luke. But how? Lucas worked directly for Carmen as her bodyguard. Was she already screwing him?

It was time to call Mateo to find out if he'd learned anything about Lucas's background. At the least, Mateo needed to know about Ethan. He was missing, and a replacement dealer had to be recruited.

David unlocked his desk drawer and removed his secure satellite phone. He touched Mateo's name on its contact list.

\* \* \*

## 5:07 P.M., WEDNESDAY, AUGUST 7—SPICER FARM

David held his ear against his encrypted satellite phone. He could hear it ringing Mateo's number.

"*Hola*, David, I've been meaning to call you. I have distressing information about Lucas."

David felt his throat constrict and he struggled to get his words out. "I'm glad I'm not bothering you, Boss. I must talk about Lucas, too. I'm worried because I saw him on a security video. He was examining our pigeons in the barn loft. Lucky he didn't see any with pouches attached to their legs."

David heard Mateo handling his phone. "Your report adds to my concern about Lucas." Mateo exhaled quickly. "We believe he is a member of *Los Hermanos*, the Colombian cartel. We have to deal with him."

David felt less cowed since his hunch about Lucas had been valid. Lucas indeed was someone to watch. "How did you find out Lucas is a *Los Hermanos* member?"

"Do you remember the skinny young man I hired who is a hotshot computer expert?"

David envisioned a thin man who resembled a teenager with a messy beard and unkempt hair. "The one you call Professor?"

"Yes. He wrote a facial recognition program. He matched Lucas's driver's license picture with the image of a man in our database of *Los Hermanos* people. This man's name is Joseph Murphy, a *gringo*. He's a *Los Hermanos* enforcer."

David now felt confident. "Boss, are you positive Lucas is Joseph Murphy?"

"We are not a hundred percent positive, but Lucas has been poking around the pigeons. And Carmen hired him to be her bodyguard. It's time for us to remove him from Spicer Farm. We can't take a chance with him."

David's mind raced at supersonic speed as he thought about Lucas's possible motives. It was conceivable *Los Hermanos* sent Lucas to spy on Mateo's operations in the Lexington area. The drug trade in Louisville and Lexington was lucrative. *Los Hermanos* were aggressive, and they often fought with other groups to take over their territories.

David heard himself say, "What will Carmen say when we remove Lucas from the scene?"

"She won't know what happened if he disappears. I'll send specialists to take care of the problem. I'll let them decide how to do it. If Lucas had an accident, Carmen would not complain to us."

"When will this happen, Boss?"

"I'll send two men on the jet today. I'll give them passwords, which I'll send to you so you'll know they are our guys. They will work fast." Mateo paused. "I have to line this up. Goodbye and thank you for calling."

# THIRTY-NINE

## 7:00 P.M., WEDNESDAY, AUGUST 7—SPICER FARM

LUKE PEERED at a mirror he'd duct-taped to a broken rake handle. It showed him the undercarriage of Carmen's SUV. He didn't see a bomb. Still, he was beginning to think her fears of assassination were justified.

Next, he lifted the vehicle's hood and examined the engine compartment. When he snapped the hood closed, his cell phone rang. Carmen was calling.

"Hello, Carmen. Everything okay?"

"I have a problem with the drain in my bedroom sink." She sounded sleepy. "Could you come and help me?"

"Yep."

As Luke walked to the mansion, he began to consider what motives Mark's acquaintances could have had to kill him.

*I'll ask Carmen if Mark dealt with people who didn't like him, perhaps one or more of the Mexicans.* Luke could also grill her about Mark's history. She must know a lot about him she had yet to mention.

When Luke entered Carmen's bedroom, he saw her standing by the sink. It was filled to the brim with water. She turned to face him.

He smiled. "This will be easy to fix. I'll put a pail under the j-trap, take it off, and clean it."

"Thanks, Lucas." She slurred her words. "You'll find a bucket and a wrench in the closet down the hall on the left."

Luke figured she'd been drinking. Or had she taken oxycodone? Then he spotted a half empty bottle of white wine on the end table near her bed. He bit his lip and left the room to find the closet. In it he found a pail, the wrench, rags, a roll of paper towels, and a wire coat hanger. "Perfect," he whispered.

When he returned to Carmen's bedroom, she was sitting on a chair near the sink. She cocked her head. "You must think I'm nuts to believe Mark was murdered." Her words sounded unclear, smeared. "Everybody else says an accidental overdose killed him."

Luke kneeled near the sink. "No, yur sane. I'd be scared, too, if I learned Mexicans were smuggling drugs into my barn usin' pigeons."

Luke placed the bucket under the j-trap, grabbed an adjustable wrench, and began to loosen the slip-joint nuts holding the trap in place. Water seeped from the joints and dripped into the pail.

Carmen moved her chair closer to Luke to see close up what he was doing. She slurred, "I'm trying to think of people who could've killed Mark. Those are the ones you must keep tabs on." Her drunken words were indistinct.

"It's a good idea to figure out who could be after you." Luke dumped crud from the j-trap, emptying the gook into the pail of water. Then he bent the coat hanger into a V-shape and reamed out the inside of the trap.

Carmen was so high she couldn't hide what she thought. She squinted. "One of our stable hands quit before David hired you." Her voice was unsteady. "He kept staring at me in a strange way like he meant to do me harm. Kobold Farm hired him."

Luke put the j-trap back in place and tightened the slip-joint nuts. "It's a stroke of luck he quit, cuz afterward David hired me."

Carmen caught sight of Luke's eyes. "The guy who quit argued with Mark before our big party, but I don't know why they were fighting."

"I'll keep him in mind. Remember his name?"

"Josh. I don't know his surname."

"Did Mark have enemies?"

"One guy was a competitor." She gestured in the direction of the neighboring Kobold Farm. "The owner of the farm east of us, Steve, was a low-key rival because he's a horse trainer."

"Did they argue?"

"I don't know." She paused to get up and grab her bottle of wine and a water glass. "Steve and my husband had been close friends during high school. But their friendship ended when Mark married his first wife, who happened to be Steve's high school girlfriend."

Luke focused on Carmen's words. "Was Steve bitter toward Mark after the marriage?"

"Afterward they didn't socialize with each other, except during annual farm parties."

"Did Steve go to the party where Mark died?"

"Yes, as did many other horse farm owners and the Lexington social elite." Carmen took a sip of wine. "The farm hands were allowed to mingle in a roped-off area of the lawn."

"Did you notice drug use?"

Carmen shook her head no. "But my dealer, Ethan, showed up." She sighed. "I had invited him."

"Could he have sold drugs to Mark?"

Carmen flushed. "No. I told Ethan not to sell at my party." Her voice was unsteady. "Ethan dressed nicely. I was surprised how different he appeared. He normally dresses in jeans and a work shirt. I gave him money to rent a suit."

"You're close to Ethan?"

"I've known him for three years. I feel sorry for him. If he hadn't become a dealer, he would've married and had a better life."

"You sure Mark never tried drugs? It must've been easy

for him to get them if he was laundering money for the Mexicans."

Carmen shook her head. "I was stupid. I had no idea about the money, drugs, and the Mexicans. Mark kept it all hidden from me."

"Anything else you noticed during the party?"

Carmen sipped her wine. "I thought it was weird David and Ethan were having an extended conversation. Now it makes sense."

Luke wiped his hands on a clean rag. "You think David and the other Mexicans are laundering money?"

Carmen was unsteady, though she was sitting on her chair. "Yeah, but David wouldn't have killed Mark. They were friends."

"But what if Mateo got in a dispute with Mark?"

Carmen bowed her head. Her face was pale. "I don't know. I'm scared, and I don't know how to get out of it."

Luke stood and picked up the bucket of filthy water. "I'll get rid of this dirty water."

"Come back soon." Her body shook.

"Be back in a minute."

# FORTY

MATEO SAT on a garden chair under his pergola with a vodka cocktail in his hand. He set the drink on his patio table and eased back against a pillow.

Complications at Spicer Farm were on his mind.

*I have to control the situation. Since Mark is dead, why not take out Carmen, too?*

Mateo's investigators had reported both Mark and Carmen had no living relatives. Also, the farm owed back taxes.

Before matters got worse, Mateo figured he had to act. The farm was a fine asset because he could launder bundles of cash when he bought and sold horses. Besides, it was a fine location from which to distribute product to Lexington and Louisville. He hoped to expand his business by adding cities, including Cincinnati.

The idea of killing women was repulsive to Mateo, but one of his astute lawyers had pointed out the *Nuestro Club* cartel could buy the farm at a discount if Carmen were dead. The property tax people would sell her farm at auction to collect the back taxes. He would bid whatever it would take to win the Spicer Farm. His money laundering and drug distribution business could then continue unhindered.

He fingered his encrypted satellite phone which rested on the table near his drink. All at once, he decided he should eliminate Carmen. Though a beautiful woman, she was defective, with bipolar tendencies. She was too impulsive, unstable, and flighty to become a valuable partner like Mark had been.

Terry, his main pigeon tender, had reported back from the farm two days ago that a sizable propane tank sat outside the mansion, near Carmen's bedroom. Terry had suggested if the tank ever exploded, it could destroy her bedroom and kill her.

After Terry's report, Mateo had begun to reflect on the possibility of hiring someone to place a bomb on the propane tank. Who better to do it than Tokyo Joe? Of course, Tokyo had been working for the Bogota bunch, *Los Hermanos*, the Colombian cartel, a *Nuestro Club* rival.

Would Tokyo take the job? Was he a loyal member of *Los Hermanos* or a contractor? One way to find out was to give him a call.

Mateo's private investigators had found the little-known number for Tokyo. Mateo had entered it into his satellite phone's contact list a day ago. He stopped playing with his telephone and touched Tokyo's contact number on the phone's screen.

Within three rings a man answered. "Who's calling? How did you get this number?"

"This is Mateo of *Nuestro Club*, a Mexican cartel. I have a job for you if you want to take it."

"Are you calling on an encrypted line?"

"Yes, Tokyo." Mateo paused. "I got your number because my investigators are the best. We know all about you. You have a great reputation. I learned you did a job for *Los Hermanos* by placing a bomb on the Alaska-bound cruise ship. I assume you're a contractor, not a member of *Los Hermanos*."

"I do independent contract work. What's the job?"

"We need a bomb placed on a propane tank outside a bedroom on a horse farm near Lexington, Kentucky. It must appear the propane tank exploded by accident. The objective is to kill a person in the bedroom, which is near the propane tank."

"When would you like the job done?"

"As soon as possible. My man, Terry, can give you the details. He'll call you. We realize you may be out of the country or have other obligations at the moment."

"You're in luck. I'm in Cincinnati, not far from Lexington." He spoke fast. "I could do the job as soon as late tonight. It wouldn't take long to drive to Lexington."

"What is your fee?"

"Two hundred and fifty thousand American dollars. Wire fifty K to my bank account as a down payment. When I get it, we're in business."

"Fine, Tokyo. Give me your wiring instructions. I will send fifty thou at once."

"We have a deal."

# FORTY-ONE

DAVID'S ENCRYPTED satellite phone rang. Mateo was calling.

"*Hola*, Mateo."

"I've made an important decision. I decided to buy Spicer Farm."

David squinted. "Will Carmen sell it?"

"She could, but we have a different option." Mateo hesitated. "We've researched Mark's and Carmen's backgrounds. Neither have heirs. We're going to take her out. Our lawyers believe we can buy the farm for cheap."

David felt a jolt of anger spiral through his body. "Boss, why are we stooping so low to kill a woman? We could make her a partner, as we did with Mark."

"We need absolute control of the farm. The Lexington area is a fruitful market for our drugs, and the farm is the top money laundering scheme we've come up with."

"But, Boss, she's beautiful."

"Your judgment is clouded because you screwed her, but I've decided. We've hired Tokyo Joe, a bomb expert."

"Didn't he place the explosives on the cruise ship for the

Colombians—*Los Hermanos*—during the hijacking? Would he tell the Colombians?"

"He can keep a secret and works for the highest bidder."

"What about Lucas, or whatever his name is?"

"The two men who'll deal with Lucas are in the air."

David felt a squeezing in his throat. "A bomb will kill Carmen?"

"*Si*, it will be done at night when she sleeps."

"I wish I could change your mind about Carmen."

"When it's over and done, you'll forget her." Mateo disconnected his phone.

David wondered, *Did Mateo send a killer to murder Mark during his party? Had Mateo planned to kill both Mark and Carmen weeks ago?*

# FORTY-TWO

LUKE DUMPED the pail of dirty water in the janitor's closet sink and washed his hands.

Within three minutes, he re-entered Carmen's bedroom. She had been drunk when he'd left. Had her tongue loosened even more? If he was lucky, he could learn additional information related to Mark's murder.

After closing the bedroom door behind him, he didn't see her. Her bathroom door was closed. It creaked and then opened. Carmen stood in the doorway in the nude. Then she stepped onto the soft deluxe rug on her bedroom floor.

Luke gulped.

"Lucas, hold me. I'm scared." She held her arms wide as if to welcome his embrace.

He moved a step toward her and stopped. "Carmen, I told you before I have a girlfriend. She's pregnant."

Carmen sat on her bed. "Don't worry. I won't tell if you won't." Her slurred words were slow coming from her mouth.

Luke figured he should leave fast, yet he didn't want to upset her. He needed to keep his job to continue investigating suspects. There was plenty to worry about. His undercover operation. The possibility somebody intended to kill her.

He crossed his arms. "I can't do this with you. Yur a beautiful woman. But I've made a pledge to my girlfriend. She's going to have a baby." He wondered, *Will Carmen fire me?*

Carmen slipped under the covers on her bed. "Leave me."

Luke took a step backward. "I'll still be your guard. I'll help you get through your time of grief. I'm a friend." He observed her. *Is she gonna kick me off the farm?*

Tears dripped from her eyes and dribbled down her face. She tucked her blanket under her neck and wiped her teardrops aside. "I still want you to be my protector. You're a loyal man. I accept you as a friend. But please leave."

"Okay." Luke left the room.

# FORTY-THREE

LUKE SAT HALF asleep on a garden chair on the mansion's covered porch. The air was muggy though a steady rain had driven away the day's blistering heat. He didn't want to be in his bedroom next to Carmen's room. He feared she'd try to seduce him again if he stayed inside.

The vivid image of her alluring, nude body appeared in his mind's eye as it often had during the last few hours. Yet, Luke had managed to deflect her blatant sexual advances while not offending her. He didn't want to blow his cover. Still, it had taken all of his self-control not to bed her. As the naked Carmen had reached out to embrace him, thoughts of his pregnant girlfriend, Layla, had kept him faithful.

He smiled when he imagined what life would be like as a father. Would he be an adequate dad? His father had not been a good influence. A silent man, he'd spent his life working, drinking, or drunk. But how could Luke complain? He, too, was an alcoholic, but he was recovering—attending LifeRing sessions with alcohol and drug abusers. As an expectant father, he was dead set not to fall off the wagon.

Carmen was sleeping off her drunkenness in her bedroom. Luke was certain she wouldn't find him on the porch, even if she awoke and prowled the mansion seeking his company.

Luke began to doze. A warm breeze and the sound of heavy raindrops hitting the porch roof lulled him into a light, fitful sleep, even though his chair was not comfortable.

* * *

## 2:45 A.M., THURSDAY, AUGUST 8—HARDWOOD LANE, NEAR SPICER FARM

Professional bomber Tokyo Joe, now a contractor for the Mexican cartel, *Nuestro Club*, neared the end of his drive from Cincinnati to the Lexington area. The trip had been uneventful, but the weather had turned rainy when he got closer to Lexington. He drove through random downpours. Lightning flashed and thunder rumbled as he neared the Spicer Farm on Hardwood Lane, a blacktop country road.

Tokyo was glad the Mexican cartel's man, Terry, had emailed him a map of the farm, a dozen pictures of the Spicer mansion, and photographs of the propane tank he was to blow up. It weighed twenty pounds when full of propane. The goal of the explosion was to kill a woman who slept in a bedroom near the tank.

Tokyo figured his task would be easy. Hidden behind bushes and five feet from the exterior wall of the bedroom, the tank was in a great spot to cause severe damage when it detonated. He'd decided to place a tiny amount of C-4 explosive and a cell phone detonator on the nose of the tank. It pointed at the house where the woman's bed was.

Tokyo reckoned the C-4 explosion would fracture the tank. Propane gas would spew against the building's wall and mix with air. Heat from the explosion would ignite the gas. The fireball would destroy the wall and much of the mansion, and incinerate the unlucky lady.

Never one to have nightmares, Tokyo regarded the bombings he carried out as a moneymaking hobby. He never stayed to view the damage he'd done to property, people, pets, or livestock. With no images of maimed corpses and body parts stored in his brain, nightmares never plagued him.

He wouldn't need much C-4 explosive. All it had to do was to breech the propane tank and spark the gas to explode. Tokyo seldom set off such a minor blast, but he was convinced it would sound like thunder, even from a short distance.

Tokyo was glad it continued to rain, lightning flashed, and thunder rumbled.

While Tokyo followed a bend in the road, his GPS device spoke. "Destination is on the right in 200 yards." Spotlights lit the Spicer Farm's gateway.

As Tokyo approached it, he slowed, stared down the gravel driveway, and saw the distant mansion, an enormous barn, and smaller buildings. A light atop a tall pole lit the parking lot near the mansion and the barn. He was pleased the side of the expensive home where the propane tank sat was hidden in darkness. He felt at home and protected by the blackness of night.

After cruising past the driveway, he pulled his rental car off the road and parked behind bushes, near the farm's fence, 150 yards from the main gate.

Rain pattered on the roof of the car while he slipped on his mini night vision goggles. After pulling the hood of his waterproof jacket over his head and putting on nitrile gloves, he got out of his vehicle, lifted his trunk lid, and grabbed a gym bag. It held a meager amount of C-4; a detonator; a cell phone, which would act as a remote trigger; black electrical tape; and tools.

Tokyo kicked a horizontal fence board loose and stepped through the gap he'd created. He was quiet as he moved over the lush grass, though his shoes were getting soaked and made squishing sounds as he walked. He stayed hidden in the blackest shadows. He was sweating under his jacket because the rain was warm and the night felt sticky.

His view through the goggles made the night seem like day. Gazing at darker places, he kept his eyes aimed away from the bright light on the pole. In minutes, he stood in the shadows of the mansion's wall. He spotted the rake Terry had placed on the exterior of the mansion to mark the target's bedroom.

After locating the propane tank hidden in the bushes, he took out his small tin snips, but they slipped from his wet nitrile gloves and hit the propane tank with a clang.

"Shit," he whispered.

He listened for four or five seconds but heard nothing except rain and distant thunder. Then he peered down at the tank, and his trained hands and fingers stuck the putty-like explosive on the tank, wired up the detonator, and taped the cell phone trigger into place.

* * *

LUKE'S EYES had been closed for ten minutes and he was enjoying a restful sleep when a metallic sound awakened him.

Had someone banged a wrench against a steel object? The noise had come from around the mansion's corner, in the deep shadows outside of Carmen's bedroom. Scanning for danger, Luke stood and crept with stealth toward the sound.

After reaching the building's corner, Luke peeked around it toward Carmen's bedroom window and the twenty-pound propane tank fifteen feet from it. All of a sudden, he heard squishy footsteps coming from the dark shadows near the tank. Concealed by inky darkness, he edged around the corner and peered toward the baffling noise.

* * *

AFTER FINISHING THE SETUP, Tokyo heard what sounded like footfalls in the spongy, wet grass. He turned. Through his night vision goggles, he saw a tall, strong man coming around the corner of the mansion.

Tokyo's heart started to race.

*Don't panic*, he told himself. *Be quiet and slow.* Moving through the darkest places he could find, he retreated toward his car.

\* \* \*

THE PARKING LOT floodlight atop a twenty-foot pole blinded Luke when he moved out of the shadows along the mansion. After his eyes recovered, he saw the silhouette of a man trotting away into the darkness.

The wind howled like a lone wolf, and the rain came down hard. Like a camera flash, lightning illuminated the fleeing figure who wore a hooded rain jacket. The crash of thunder had sounded almost at the same time.

Luke was tempted to chase the man, but his gut told him no. What had the stranger been doing around Carmen's bedroom window? The propane tank was fifteen feet from the window and five feet from the outer wall of the building. Was the prowler on a mission to detonate the tank? Luke took two steps toward the tank and considered, *Am I as paranoid as Carmen?*

He reached into his pocket, pulled his penlight out, and switched it on. A putty-like material was pasted on the tank, and a cell phone was taped to the metal body of the steel container. Blood rushed to his face. His heart galloped like a horse sprinting toward the finish line.

*The putty's C-4 explosive.*

Luke's heart pounded faster. He gasped. With both hands, he grabbed at the putty-like material, wires, electrical tape, and the cell phone and yanked. He sprinted toward the fishpond.

His muscles straining, he hurled the tangle of wires, cell phone, and the explosive toward the pond. A fraction of a second later, as he dove behind a concrete retaining wall near the water's edge, the C-4 exploded, its blast muffled by the pond's water. A dirty spray, globs of mud, and blades of Kentucky bluegrass flew up and over the wall, pelting Luke.

After waiting ten seconds, he stood. His breathing began

to return to normal, and his heartbeat slowed. But his ears were ringing.

*The muffled explosion must have sounded like far-off thunder to anybody inside.*

As luck would have it, he saw a flash in the distance and afterward heard a weak crash of thunder.

Soaked by muddy pond water, Luke stood on his toes and peered over the concrete retaining wall. Far away, on the shoulder of the winding road, he saw a dark sedan screech away. "Must be the bomber," he mumbled.

Rain poured from the sky and washed the mud and blades of grass from Luke and his clothing. A bolt of lightning flashed and hit a stand of trees across the road. In a micro-instant, the thunderous sonic boom created by the lightning strike assaulted his ears.

*That thunder's a hell of a lot louder than a minor C-4 detonation.* Now he was certain nobody on the farm had guessed a bomb had exploded because the blast had occurred under a muffling layer of pond water.

Luke reckoned the C-4 had exploded when it first began to sink into the pond. He knew cell phones could work to a maximum depth of a foot under the water's surface. Radio waves could only go through water a short distance.

It was unlucky Luke hadn't thrown the bundle into the water sooner. Then it would've sunk to the muddy bottom of the pond, and the fleeing bomber couldn't have triggered the blast. If the C-4 and cell phone had survived underneath the water, Luke figured he could've found them. But the explosion had destroyed useful evidence, though bits of the phone might still yield clues.

Luke decompressed.

*I gotta call Jim. A chopper or a cruiser could track the getaway car. But it's got to be far gone.*

As Luke withdrew his cell phone from his soaked pocket, the odor of ozone created by the lightning drifted to him. It smelled like a mixture of chlorine and burning electric wires.

\* \* \*

## 3:05 A.M., THURSDAY, AUGUST 8–SPICER MANSION

Luke still heard a slight ringing in his ears. He figured the muffled explosion under the pond's water had been loud enough to cause it.

On his phone's contact list, Luke touched Jim's name. The phone rang nine times.

Jim answered with a groggy voice. "Luke, you have an emergency?"

"Somebody rigged a propane tank with C-4 and tried to blow up Carmen's bedroom with her in it."

"Holy Christ. Anybody hurt?"

"No. I pulled the C-4 off and threw it into a pond a second before it exploded. I dove behind a concrete wall."

"Need help?"

"You could send a squad car to Hardwood Road to search for a dark sedan speeding north."

"Any suspects?"

"A man, medium height in a black hooded jacket." Luke sighed.

"Wait on the line. I'll radio the sergeant on duty."

"Don't tell anybody about it yet. The explosion sounded like a distant lightning strike."

"Okay. Our man can arrest the guy for reckless driving."

Luke heard Jim set his phone down. After walking to the patio cover, while waiting for Jim to resume their conversation, Luke sat on a dry lawn chair. He wiped rainwater from his face.

He wondered if parts of the cell phone, which had triggered the explosion, would have survived. How could he recover its debris from the pond at night? After the sun rose, farm hands would see him mucking around in the pond, if he tried to find phone remnants then.

At first, he couldn't think of an excuse for searching in the pond. Then a thought struck him. After dawn, he could say he'd dropped his high school class ring in the pond.

His mind shifted gears. What was he going to tell Carmen about the attempt on her life? He should take her to a hotel. Anyway, everybody at the farm thought she was trying to bed him.

A rustling noise came through his mobile's earpiece, and Luke heard Jim grab his cell phone. "Is your cover blown?"

"No. The explosion blended in with the thunderstorm. No one noticed the blast but me."

"Then I won't send the troops to the farm yet."

Luke was relieved. Sending a crowd of officers could blow his cover. The explosion hadn't aroused anyone. He figured David and his Mexican team had no reason to suspect him.

Jim made a yawning sound. "We'll be lucky if our squad car catches the perp. An on-ramp to the freeway is two miles north of Spicer Farm."

Luke was sleep-deprived, but his mind was busy. "I'll take Carmen to a hotel after sunrise."

"Do it."

"Once I figure out what hotel she'll be in, could you set up a plainclothes detail to go there and make sure somebody doesn't try to kill her?"

"I'll check into it."

Luke yawned. "The surveillance team should only act if they see bad guys are closing in on Carmen."

"Agreed."

Luke rubbed his eyes. "I should be able to take her to a hotel without much controversy cuz people at the farm think Carmen wants to go to bed with me. They won't be suspicious if I drive her away unless one of them planted the C-4."

"What will you tell Carmen?"

"That someone placed a bomb on the propane tank. As her bodyguard, my advice is for her to spend a day or two in a hotel room."

"Will she call 911?"

"No way. She's scared shitless we'll charge her with murdering her husband."

Jim coughed. "Mark's murderer may have decided to do her in, too."

Like a chess player, Luke planned ahead, picturing alternate outcomes. He thought, *Odds are the Mexicans are cartel members*. It was certain they were laundering drug money. A Mexican cartel could've murdered Mark to shut him up, settle a grievance, or take control of his farm. It was possible the Mexicans planned to kill Carmen because she was the sole owner of the farm or knew about their illegal doings.

Luke was ashamed he'd been silent for ten seconds. "Sorry, Jim. I was mulling over what you said. A Mexican drug cartel could've killed Mark cuz he was involved with them but got them PO'd. One possibility is they want to get Carmen out of the way, too. Afterward, they could buy the farm."

Jim sighed. "I'm debating if I should pull you out and raid the place. I bet we'll find plenty of drugs and money."

"Yeah, but will we find evidence to prove who killed Mark?" Luke was mindful of the fact that the DA's top priority was to solve Mark's murder. Mark had been a famous thoroughbred trainer and a member of Lexington's elite. Dick the DA wanted all the publicity he could muster. Luke didn't like politics dictating how an investigation should go, but the DA was a politician through and through.

Jim rubbed his phone against his beard, making a sandpapering sound. "You think I should keep you in place?"

"Yep. The Mexicans think I'm a gigolo, fishin' to get money outta Carmen. With your permission, I'll try to join them to find out what they're up to. I could flash something at them to make me pass for a crook. Firearms with filed-off serial numbers or ghost guns would do."

Jim exhaled. "Okay, try it. We have two or three ghost guns in the evidence room." He paused. "How's the weather where you are?"

"It stopped raining. A cold front blew through. The sky's clearing."

"I'll call the highway patrol to request a chopper to fly over the freeway to search for a speeding sedan."

"Okay, Jim. Call back. I got ideas to bounce off you."

"Okay." Jim hung up.

# FORTY-FOUR

## 3:15 A.M., THURSDAY, AUGUST 8—SPICER MANSION

AFTER JIM DISCONNECTED, Luke set his phone on vibrate. Then he walked to the pond's edge to search for explosion debris. He aimed his penlight at the edge of the pond and into its murky water. At first, he couldn't see anything unusual except a dead fish floating on the surface. Then, swinging the flashlight's beam across the water, he saw at least two dozen lifeless fish bobbing on the waves. The C-4 detonation had killed countless bluegill, catfish, and largemouth bass. Luke figured Mark had certainly stocked the pond.

The wind was cool. A front had blown through. The storm had dumped at least an inch of rain on the land, and the air wasn't sticky anymore. Luke was grateful the thunder and the pond's water had masked the muffled C-4 explosion. If they hadn't, David and the other farm hands would have gone outside to investigate the detonation.

Luke guessed the bomber had not been someone from the farm because the culprit had escaped by car. Then again, he could've worked on the farm but fled anyway. Luke figured he'd ask around to find out if any farm hands were absent. But he realized he couldn't conduct a full investigation like a normal detective would. If he did, he'd arouse suspicion by asking too many questions.

Luke rubbed his hair. It was still wet from the storm and splashed pond water. After wiping his hand on the leg of his trousers, he returned to the porch to await Jim's call and to think of a way to have the propane tank removed. He could say he had smelled gas and then call a repairman to take the tank away to be fixed.

Luke recalled Jim's cousin, Jasper, owned a propane distribution company. Could Jasper be called in? Jim could send a bomb squad guy with Jasper to be his "helper." Luke could pretend to lose his class ring in the pond. Luke, Jasper, and the bomb squad guy could mimic searching for the ring. The explosives expert could use a fish net to lift cell phone parts from the water.

Another idea occurred to Luke. He could ask Jim to call Rita Reynolds, a high school classmate of theirs from years ago. She was a rising star in the FBI. Luke was confident Rita could persuade a bomb squad expert from the Federal Bureau of Alcohol, Tobacco, Firearms, and Explosives (ATF) to investigate the pond.

Rita wouldn't hesitate to help because the holler was where she'd grown up, and Luke and she had known each other for years. But would she request a full-blown federal task force to go after the Mexicans? They had to be responsible for most of Lexington's illegal drug distribution.

*Federal task forces are bureaucratic. But a plus is the feds have lots of people and resources.*

Luke's cell phone vibrated. Jim was calling back. *Should I suggest Jim call Rita?*

\* \* \*

## 3:25 A.M., THURSDAY, AUGUST 8—SPICER MANSION

Luke answered Jim's call. "Is a squad car on the way?"

"Yeah, and since the storm is over, the highway patrol

launched a long-range drone with an infrared camera to scout the freeway."

"That's positive." Luke paused. "I have ideas we should discuss."

"Shoot."

In less than four seconds, Luke planned what he was going to say. He needed to get Carmen to leave the farm and also have the propane tank removed. He also wanted a bomb squad specialist to search for debris from the explosion. Should he ask Jim to call in the feds via Rita, the FBI agent? Luke took a deep breath. "We need to search the pond for bomb parts."

Luke envisioned Jim shaking his head. Jim sighed. "How are we going to send the bomb squad in and not upset the Mexicans and not blow your cover?"

Luke shifted in the wrought iron chair on the porch. "Ask your cousin, Jasper, to drive his propane service truck here to take away the tank. I'll say I smelled gas. Jasper would bring a bomb squad guy who could pose as his helper."

Jim coughed. "I think I could get Jasper to do it. He's a man of few words. He'll keep his mouth shut." Jim took a moment before he continued. "How can a bomb squad guy search the pond and the area near it without being noticed?"

Luke explained his lost ring idea. During the search for Luke's class ring, the bomb expert would look for explosion debris. Luke coughed. "Jasper would happen to have a fish net in the truck."

"I like the plan. I'll ask Lexington PD to lend us their explosives expert."

Luke fingered the penlight in his pocket. "What about the ATF?"

"You know someone at the ATF?"

Luke was still debating with himself if he should suggest Jim call Rita to ask for help from the FBI, ATF, and DEA. He closed his eyes and tried to predict what could happen if the feds joined the investigation. They'd take it over. Jim would have to coordinate with the feds. Luke sucked air into his lungs. "I'm thinkin' you could call Rita Reynolds. She could get us an ATF bomb expert. They're top-notch, and they won't slip up and leak to the press."

"Our friend Dick, the DA, will be afraid the feds will claim all the glory if they're called in. He always wants press coverage to focus on himself."

Jim heaved a sigh. "I'll call Rita. Let's hope she won't get angry when I wake her."

Luke felt a chill course through his body. He'd had an adrenaline rush ever since he'd found the C-4 stuck on the propane tank. The high had made it easy for him to ignore danger. Until this moment, it hadn't hit him how close he'd come to being blown to bits.

He saw a mental picture of Layla. He imagined her pregnant and emotional, having learned of his death. He was to become a father. He saw her alone with no one to help with the newborn baby, his child-to-be. He must be cautious.

Jim's voice pulled Luke away from his reverie. "Still there, Luke?"

"What you said made me realize how close I came to meetin' my maker."

"Understood." Jim paused for five seconds. "Your undercover information-gathering gig isn't safe anymore."

Luke nodded. "I gotta stay alert."

"I'm going to set up a task force—our deputies, Lexington PD, and the state police at least. We'll monitor you. If you get in trouble, we'll roll in and pull you out." Jim paused a beat. "I'll call Rita."

Luke flushed, though the breeze blowing across the porch was cool. He guessed that as more people learned about the inquiry, the greater the chance the news media would expose the investigation. "After you call Rita, can you let me know if she can get an ATF bomb squad guy?"

"Yes. I'll call her now."

# FORTY-FIVE

ON A WEEK OF LEAVE, FBI agent Rita Reynolds was deep in dreams enjoying her sleep in the guest bed in her mother's home in the holler.

She'd put her mobile phone on the bedside table. A shrill ring jarred her awake. She wondered, *Who's calling at this hour?* She sat up and rubbed her eyes. Leaning on an elbow, she grabbed the phone. Its screen showed Jim Pike's name. "Hello, Jim. It's kinda late."

"Sorry. Luke had a close call, but he's not hurt. A propane bomb almost did him in."

Rita sat up straight. "What happened?"

"He spotted a propane tank with C-4 on it and threw the explosive in a pond. The bomb detonated, but Luke hit the ground behind a wall. The sound of the blast mixed in with the thunderstorm. Nobody noticed the explosion."

Rita exhaled. "Where'd it happen?"

"On a horse farm, the Spicer place. Carmen Spicer was the target. She wasn't hurt and neither was anybody else."

"I read about the OD death of Mark Spicer, the horse trainer."

"It was murder." Jim paused a moment. "Mark had

twenty times the fentanyl in his system than a normal OD victim would have. We're keeping it quiet." Rita could hear Jim take a quick breath. "We need your help. Could you get an ATF bomb squad guy to check out Spicer Farm's pond for evidence?"

"Yes. I'll call my ATF contact immediately." She gazed at her clock. "If we're lucky, ATF could respond this morning."

Jim coughed. "There's a problem. Luke's working undercover as a stable hand investigating Mark's murder. We believe money laundering and drug trafficking are happening at the farm."

"How do you suggest we proceed?" Concerned for Luke's safety, Rita admitted to herself she still loved Luke even though he was living with Layla.

Jim's voice interrupted Rita's musings. "...and I decided to take Luke's advice and ask my cousin, Jasper, to pick up the propane tank. He has a propane supply company. The bomb squad guy can ride in Jasper's truck and pose as his helper."

"How can he search the pond and not arouse suspicion?"

"Luke's gonna claim he lost his class ring in the water."

Rita smiled. "He's always one step ahead of the rest of us." She got out of bed, still holding the phone next to her ear. "I better hang up and call my ATF buddy."

"Before you go, Rita, I've got one more request. Luke's planning to take Carmen to a hotel to keep her safe for a few days. Could you request a surveillance detail to keep an eye on her there?"

"I can set it up. Carmen won't know an FBI team is there at the hotel unless somebody makes a move to take her out. Just let me know where she'll be staying."

"I will as soon as Luke tells me. Thanks for everything, Rita."

"No problem."

"Let's regroup after you line up the ATF guy. I'll fill you in about the rest of the investigation then."

"Call you soon." Rita hung up.

# FORTY-SIX

## 7:30 A.M., THURSDAY, AUGUST 8—SOMEWHERE IN TENNESSEE

THE RISING sun was low in the eastern sky when Tokyo Joe found a cheap motel in Tennessee. He paid cash for a room. As he carried his suitcase into the fleabag lodging, a sick feeling spread in his stomach. It was necessary to phone Mateo ASAP to report he'd blown his mission at the Spicer Farm. He hated failure. Reputation is everything. Who was the guy who'd ripped the C-4 from the propane tank? Tokyo thought he'd seen him someplace before, but where and when?

While running to his car, Tokyo had glanced backward and saw the tall man rip the C-4 bomb from the propane tank and scramble toward the farm's pond.

Tokyo had stopped fleeing and rushed to activate the cell phone trigger. The bomb exploded at almost the same instant the man threw it into the water. It was dumb luck the blast had occurred at all below the pond's surface.

Tokyo was glad the explosion had destroyed evidence, including the cell phone; the detonator; the electrical tape; and the wiring. As luck would have it, the thunderstorm had masked the detonation.

It was unfortunate the man had dived behind the

retaining wall and survived. But if he'd been killed, the cops would've swarmed the place. They could've now been hot on Tokyo's trail.

Tokyo's temples felt like a drummer was beating them. He collapsed onto the bed's worn blanket and held his hands against the sides of his head. After five minutes, the pounding inside his skull subsided.

He breathed in and out and felt calmer. He reminded himself he'd worn his night vision goggles, and they included an internal, high-resolution digital camera with a motor drive. He had two dozen sharp images of the man who'd ripped the bomb from the propane tank. Tokyo removed the memory chip from the goggles' camera. Next, he grabbed his scrambler cell phone and tapped in Mateo's number.

It was past four-thirty a.m. outside of Tijuana, Mexico, where Mateo's compound and luxury apartment were. Tokyo's mouth was dry. He dreaded waking the head of a Mexican drug cartel in the wee hours of the morning. Mateo's phone rang eight times.

"Tokyo, why the fuck are you calling at this hour?" Mateo spoke in English with a pronounced Mexican accent.

Tokyo came close to peeing in his pants. "Sorry, Mateo, but I thought you ought to know the mission at Spicer Farm failed."

"What?"

"A tall man was outside the house in the shadows. He pulled my device apart and threw the C-4 in a pond. It exploded."

"Did he die?"

"No."

"Are the cops after you?"

"It was around three a.m., and a thunderstorm was hitting the area. The explosion blended in with the noise of thunder. I left fast and got on the freeway. I haven't seen a cop since then."

Mateo sighed. "I'll have to rethink my options."

Tokyo gulped. He found it hard to keep speaking, but he

did. "I'll refund your money. And I will make another attempt. But I'll need to wait until…"

"Don't bother. I have other plans." Mateo paused. "Calm down, Tokyo. You made an excellent attempt. Do you have a description of the man?"

"I have two dozen pictures of him. I've got an IR camera in my night vision goggles. I'll text the pix to you."

"When?"

"In five or ten minutes. After I copy the images to my scrambler phone, I'll send them."

Tokyo could hear Mateo breathing easier and his voice seemed calmer. "Here's my email address…"

# FORTY-SEVEN

*THE PLAN'S WORKING OUT*, Luke thought. Seconds ago he'd talked with Jim again on the phone. Jim had reported his cousin, Jasper, had agreed to drive one of his company's trucks to the Spicer Farm to remove the propane tank. Jim also said Rita had worked out a deal with the ATF. A special agent who was an explosives expert would meet Jasper at his propane distribution company. Jasper had said he and the agent could arrive at the farm as early as eight-thirty a.m.

Luke wondered if the ATF guy would find useful evidence. Would he locate mangled parts of the cell phone, wires, or electrical tape? Still, the bomber may have taken care not to leave evidence. Chances are he had worn gloves and cleaned the bomb parts with alcohol or bleach.

Thoughts of his close brush with death sobered Luke. In less than a year he would be a father. Was taking another chance in this investigation worth it? Did he have nine lives like a cat? He'd already had at least three close encounters with the Grim Reaper since he had become a deputy sheriff.

Luke withdrew his cell phone from his hip pocket and touched Layla's name on his contact list.

"Hi, Luke. How are you?" Layla sounded happy. She had the rich, sweet voice of a singer.

"I'm fine." Luke tried to disguise his anxiety. "This investigation should end soon." He realized he'd made his voice sound too reassuring. Layla was perceptive.

Layla breathed into the phone. "You sound under the weather."

"I'm tired." Luke's words were sincere. "I called cuz I miss you."

"I ache for you, too." Layla paused. "I want to hold you and kiss you. I need you." She sniffled. "My hormones are acting up. Being pregnant causes changes."

Luke sighed. "I could use a hug, too."

"Something wrong?" Layla's voice seemed softer to him.

Luke peered vacantly at the pond beyond the retaining wall. "I'm bored. I'd prefer kissing you."

"I can tell when something's up, darling. Be safe."

*I'm gonna lie*, Luke thought, and he felt guilty. "Don't worry. I'm tired because the thunderstorm kept me up last night."

"Me, too. You're always on my mind."

Luke sucked air into his lungs and glanced at his watch. Jasper and the bomb squad guy could arrive in a half hour. "I gotta go. Love you darlin'."

"Bye. Hugs and kisses."

Luke put his phone in his pocket and resolved not to take risky chances. But he had a gut feeling his situation was going to get worse fast.

# FORTY-EIGHT

*GODDAMN LUCAS STOPPED THE HIT.* Mateo sat in his three-bedroom luxury apartment. It was part of his palatial office complex, which stood five miles from downtown Tijuana.

*I'm steaming mad, and I have to calm myself.* His forehead flushed while he continued to think about the failed attempt to kill Carmen.

Following Tokyo Joe's phone call, Mateo had rousted his young computer expert, Professor, from a deep sleep. Then the drug lord had ordered the young man to analyze the digital pictures of the stranger who'd foiled Tokyo's assassination attempt on Carmen.

The pictures Tokyo had taken were excellent. Professor identified the man as Joseph Murphy, a.k.a. Lucas Blanco, a *gringo* enforcer for *Los Hermanos*, the most powerful of Colombia's drug cartels.

Were the aggressive Colombians planning to invade Mateo's territory in Lexington and Louisville? Mateo believed that was the case. He'd already sent two hit men, *sicarios*, to murder Lucas. They were now in Kentucky, planning how to kill him and make his death appear accidental. He wished they had done the job sooner, but Mateo reminded himself he'd ordered the two *sicarios* to take their time, plan well, and not be sloppy.

Mateo felt his brain boil. He believed Murphy, or Lucas, as he was known on the Spicer Farm, was on a mission to convince Carmen to make an alliance with the Colombians. *Los Hermanos* probably wanted Lucas to protect Carmen while they worked out a deal with her now that her husband, Mark, was dead.

Mateo drummed his fingers on his desk. *Los Hermanos* must be negotiating terms with Carmen. Why hadn't he taken David's advice to make a proposal to Carmen? David was spot-on. Carmen wasn't stupid, and she was beautiful in a dramatic way even if she was an addict. Of course, they hadn't expected *Los Hermanos* to send a spy disguised as a stable hand to the Spicer Farm. It was lucky Professor had unmasked Lucas.

After reaching in his desk drawer, Mateo snatched his encrypted satellite phone. He'd order David to tell Carmen who Lucas was and to begin to bargain with her. Afterward, he'd call the two *sicarios* and tell them to move with speed to take out Lucas.

Mateo touched David's name on his satellite phone's contact list.

"*Hola*, Mateo."

"Tokyo failed last night to take out Carmen. But you are right about her. We'll make a deal with her. Lucas will be gone soon."

"I'm glad you changed your mind about Carmen, Boss."

"Treat her well, and she could become yours." Mateo paused. "I have a different plan…"

# FORTY-NINE

LUKE FOUND Carmen in the dining room holding a cup of tea and sitting at the heavy oak table. Her eyes sparkled though she'd been drunk the night before. She wore a low-cut top and short shorts and appeared to be refreshed. He wondered, *Why didn't she have a hangover?*

Did she remember she'd shown her bare body to him?

He sighed. *How am I gonna tell her she had been seconds away from death, and I came close to being blown into hamburger meat?*

Would she call the police? Or would she follow his directions and go to a hotel?

She set her teacup down and zeroed in on his eyes. "I'm sorry about last night. I drank a lot. I'm like two people, reckless when I've had too many, and ladylike when sober."

"I understand. I'm glad you're up and about this morning cuz I got somethin' important to say." Luke sat next to her and marveled at how radiant her skin was, despite the fact she abused her body.

She furrowed her brow. "You aren't going to abandon me, I hope."

"No. I'm still yur bodyguard." Luke poured a cup of coffee. He sipped the brew, gathering his thoughts. He set his cup down on his saucer with a clink and peered into Carmen's liquid eyes. "During the thunderstorm, I was outside on the porch, and I heard odd noises near your bedroom window. I investigated and saw a man leaving…"

"A peeping Tom?"

"Worse. He wired your fireplace propane tank to explode."

Carmen cocked her head. "What?"

"I pulled a bomb off the tank and threw it into the pond. The bomb blew up after it hit the water. The thunderstorm and pond water masked the explosion. Nobody but me and the bomber knows what happened."

"What'll we do?"

"I'm gonna tell David I smelled gas, and I'll have the propane tank hauled away."

"Because they missed killing me, doesn't mean they're done."

Luke sighed. "True."

Carmen's body began to quake like the leaves on an aspen tree in a strong breeze. "Have you called the police?"

Luke observed her. "Not yet."

"Don't."

"Why not?"

"The cops will think I killed Mark to get the farm and his money."

Luke wondered if Jim would decide to raid the farm that very day. Evidence of money laundering and drug trafficking would be easy to find on the Spicer place. A clue or two could allow the DA to charge one of the Mexicans with Mark's murder. But Luke didn't have solid evidence related to Mark's demise, except he'd died of a super high overdose.

*As innocent as Carmen seems, she could've killed Mark. But who tried to kill her?*

Luke heard himself ask Carmen, "Why not go on vacation for a week? I can take you to a nice hotel. You could pay in cash and use an alias."

Carmen's shaking became less severe. "Okay."

"Pack a bag. I'll sneak you away in my truck after the propane tank is taken away."

Luke's mobile phone vibrated. He glanced at a text from Jasper. "We've arrived."

Luke caught Carmen's attention. "The truck's here for the propane tank. I'll be back soon."

Carmen nodded.

\* \* \*

## 8:30 A.M., EASTERN DAYLIGHT TIME, THURSDAY, AUGUST 8— SPICER FISHPOND

Luke exited the rear doorway of the mansion and saw a flatbed truck with orange stake fencing around the outer edge of its wooden bed. The vehicle moved at a slow speed on the driveway. Racks held propane tanks of mismatched sizes. A toll-free number and "Propane" were painted in orange letters on the sides of the white truck.

Luke heard gravel in the driveway crunch as the truck neared him and then stopped.

David approached Luke. "What's going on?"

With his class ring visible on his left hand, Luke pointed toward the bushes where the propane tank was. "I smelled gas. I called a propane company to fix it."

David's body language showed he was irritated. "I'm in charge of operations on this farm. You should consult me before making a call for service."

Luke sighed. "Sorry, David. If I'd seen you, I would've told you. But when you smell gas, you shouldn't put off calling." Luke studied David's face for his reaction. His eyelids flickered.

David was staring at the truck when two men got out and slammed its doors. "Are they going to fix the leak on site?"

Luke shrugged. "They said they need to take it to their shop."

David watched as the men approached. "Since you called them, work with them. I got paperwork to do." David turned and stomped toward the barn.

Luke removed his ring and put it in his hip pocket. He glanced toward the truck and recognized Jasper, owner of the propane company and Jim's cousin. He was thin, tall, and anorexic in appearance. The man was missing a top front tooth. Jasper and a second man walked to Luke and stopped.

Jasper squinted and said in a low voice, "Jim told me about it. I'll keep quiet."

Luke nodded.

The second man, the undercover ATF explosives expert, moved closer to Luke. "I'm Tom." He winked and grasped Luke's hand. Luke felt a piece of paper in Tom's gloved palm. He smiled. "My cell number's on the paper."

"Thanks, Tom." Luke slipped the paper in his back blue jeans pocket. "I'll mosey over to the pond and pretend to drop my class ring in it as we planned."

His back to the barn, Tom gave Luke a thumbs-up sign.

Luke fingered a stone he'd put in his watch pocket.

Tom grinned. "I'll get the dolly."

"The tank's behind those bushes." Luke pointed at the shrubbery.

Jasper had tools in his rear pocket. "I'll be over by the tank." He pulled an adjustable wrench from his pocket and walked away.

Luke went to the edge of the pond beyond the concrete retaining wall where he'd tossed the C-4 explosive in the water. He noticed something was missing. No dead fish were in sight. Hours before dozens of fish had been floating on the surface of the large pond.

Luke spied a boat on the far side of the water. A fishing net leaned against a post next to an oversized bucket. Someone had gathered the dead fish and disposed of them, but who? Luke turned around and caught sight of the barn. The outside door nearest David's office opened. David emerged and gawked at Luke.

*This is my chance*, Luke thought. He stretched his hands over the water and dropped the stone. It splashed. Luke kneeled and thrust a hand into the water as if he were trying to find his ring.

Tom had rolled the propane dolly to the shrubs, and Jasper had unbolted the tank from its base. Luke waved at them. "I dropped my ring in the water. You guys have anything I can use to fish for it?"

Jasper and Tom walked toward Luke. Curious, David also neared him. Jasper stopped near Luke, who was on his knees on the edge of the pond not far from where the C-4 and the cell phone had exploded.

Luke eyed Jasper. "I lost my class ring."

Usually quiet, Jasper spoke with a loud voice. "My fishin' gear's in the truck. I bet a net would help." He turned and walked toward the truck.

Meanwhile, David stopped twenty feet away. Luke thought Jasper had sounded like a high school actor reading his lines. But English was David's second language, and he might not have noticed Jasper's rote-like speech.

Jasper returned with a long-handled fishing net. Tom stepped up to him. "Boss, I can do it."

Luke pointed at the place he thought the C-4 had detonated. "I think this is where my ring went in. When I stretched, it flung out in the deep section."

Tom dipped the net into the water and started to fish for bomb residue.

David mumbled, turned, and returned to the horse barn.

Tom spent twenty minutes dragging the net across the bottom of the pond. He found parts of the phone, wire, and ragged pieces of electrical tape. Out of sight, he slipped them into a bag. Then he walked to the truck with the sack and the net. Luke slipped his class ring back on his finger. Would the ATF find latent fingerprints on the tape, or DNA? Experts could figure out a great deal about the phone—or could they?

As Tom pushed the propane tank on the dolly toward the truck, Luke smiled. "Thanks, fellas."

Luke thought, *I gotta get Carmen to a hotel.*

# FIFTY

DAVID'S HEAD WAS POUNDING. He sat in his chair behind his desk and tried to calm himself and think. No doubt Lucas was Joseph Murphy, an enforcer employed by the Bogota drug cartel, *Los Hermanos*. Mateo had told David that Lucas had tossed Tokyo Joe's bomb into the pond. The excuse Lucas gave to search the water where the bomb had gone off was obvious. Was Lucas a policeman?

David focused on his office wall, trying to figure out what to do next. If Lucas was indeed with law enforcement, Mateo would have to withdraw all his employees from the farm and cover their tracks. They would need to stop all operations in the greater Lexington and Louisville areas.

They'd have to figure out a new method and another place to launder money and distribute drugs. In effect, the local cops would make it easy for *Los Hermanos* to take over Mateo's turf.

David lit a cigarette. It wasn't often he smoked. After taking a deep drag, he settled back in his chair.

*Los Hermanos wouldn't dare to start operations so soon after we left Kentucky...or would they?*

Nervous, David worried Mateo would not like receiving

another phone call. Yet David's intuition and alarm told him to call.

With shaking hands and sweat beading on his forehead, David tapped Mateo's name on his encrypted phone.

"*Hola*, David. What's happening?"

"Boss, I'm calling to keep you informed of developments. Lucas has had a man take away the propane tank. Another man with him searched the water. He seemed to be trying to find bomb fragments." David swallowed and felt his throat compress. "Could Lucas be a cop?"

"No. If anything, *Los Hermanos* were gathering evidence to use against us. They may use the parts to convince Carmen we tried to kill her." He paused. "We've confirmed Lucas is Joseph Murphy."

David sighed. "I had a gut feeling he was too smart to be a stable mucker."

Mateo laughed. "Don't fret, my friend. I've asked our recently hired Kentucky private investigator to check out the local cops and Lucas—or Joseph—whatever his name is."

"When will the new PI arrive?"

"Tomorrow Victor Vargas, who goes by VV, will be in the area and stay in Lexington. His office is in Louisville."

At least the boss was doing something to check out Lucas. But David's stomach acid began to travel up his throat. He swallowed spit to try to dilute the burning fluid. "Thank you for your support, Boss," David mumbled. He gritted his teeth to fight back his heartburn.

"You'll feel better after VV investigates the police. *Los Hermanos* are a greater threat to us than the cops are. I bet Lucas already offered Carmen a deal with the Colombians." Mateo paused and slurped coffee. "As soon as you can, take Carmen aside and make a deal with her. Offer her a bigger take than Mark got. If it doesn't work, go higher."

"Will do, Boss."

Mateo hung up.

# FIFTY-ONE

LUKE WATCHED as the propane truck left the farm and turned onto Hardwood Lane. His brain was busy, and he'd made a snap decision to take Carmen to the brand-new Bluegrass Luxury Hotel. It stood at the side of the freeway fifteen minutes away.

Luke took his cell phone from his hip pocket and touched Jim's name on the device's screen.

"Luke, is everything going to plan?"

"Yep, the propane truck left just now, and Tom snagged bits of bomb evidence."

"Good. What hotel will you take Carmen to?"

"The Bluegrass Luxury Hotel."

"I'll tell Rita. She'll send an FBI surveillance team to keep tabs on Carmen."

"That's good news."

"Keep in contact. I need to call Rita ASAP." Jim hung up.

Luke believed he'd made the correct decision to drive Carmen to the hotel in his well-worn, gasoline-powered pickup truck. Her SUV was too easy to recognize. He opened the creaking door of his pickup and fired up the engine. As it was apt to do, it sputtered and stopped. He restarted and gunned it. Gray smoke spewed from the ancient truck's exhaust pipe. The smell of toxic fumes dissipated after the truck ran for a minute.

He pulled the vehicle behind the tool shack by the parking lot and killed the engine. It sputtered to a stop. After meeting Carmen in her bedroom, he planned to wait until no one was in sight, and then escort her from the mansion to his vehicle. She could duck down until he'd driven a half mile from the farm on Hardwood Lane toward the exit to the freeway.

At a quick pace, he crossed the parking lot and headed toward the rear door of the mansion. When he grasped the doorknob and began to twist it, he asked himself, *What about her suitcase?* He'd have to carry it in full view. What else could he do?

As he walked on the expensive carpet in the mansion's hallway, he wondered what would happen if someone saw them leave.

*It won't matter.* The farm's employees thought she was having sex with him.

He tapped on Carmen's door. "Can I come in?"

"Yes."

Carmen was in her bra and panties. He blushed. "Sorry."

"No worries. Pretend I'm at the lake in a bikini." She grabbed a pair of knee-high nylons and slipped them on.

"Once you're dressed are you ready to go?"

She stepped into tight-fitting, expensive slacks. "Yes. Where are you taking me?"

"The Bluegrass Luxury Hotel. They opened for business three weeks ago."

"I've heard of it. I hope nobody recognizes me." She put on a silk blouse.

"If you stay in yur room and order from room service, you should be fine." Luke saw her suitcase was packed.

Carmen slipped on a pair of sunglasses with outsized lenses. "When I check in, I'll wear these and a blond wig I put in the suitcase."

"You have cash?"

"Plenty."

"Let's go." Luke picked up her suitcase and grasped her hand.

\* \* \*

## 9:40 A.M., THURSDAY, AUGUST 8—SPICER MANSION

Lilia was polishing the wooden conference table in the mansion's meeting room. The odor of furniture wax made her feel like she was a maid working in a royal palace. Spicer Farm management required everything to be kept spotless and in top working order. The floors were clean—vacuumed on a strict schedule. The bathrooms were scrubbed daily.

Paid well, thanks to David's support, Lilia was happy, but tired today. She set her rag on the table. She sat on a heavy oak chair and peered out at the green land behind the buildings.

Her hearing became more acute when the rear entrance door clicked shut. A crimson blur registered in the corner of her eye. Turning her head, she saw Lucas rush toward the parking lot with a red suitcase. He pulled Carmen behind him.

"She's going away with him," she whispered in Spanish. Was the pair about to commit a mortal sin? If they did, she hoped Lucas would repent. He must know Carmen had been married. Did the church consider it a mortal sin if Lucas made love to Carmen, a lost soul? She'd committed adultery. No one could save her. She'd never go to heaven.

But for Lucas, it was a separate matter. He could be saved if he could resist. If he did fall under Carmen's spell, Lilia prayed Lucas would confess and repent. He was worth saving. He seemed like a fine man, even if David didn't think he was.

*I must call David to let him know Carmen is sneaking away.* Lilia removed her phone from her apron pocket.

# FIFTY-TWO

CARMEN RESTED on the fancy desk chair in her hotel room on the top floor of the fifteen-story building. The remnants of her lunch were on a hardwood tray atop a walnut desk. She held a glass of fine red wine and gazed out the window at the scene far below her.

Horse farms were on both sides of the freeway. She could make out grazing thoroughbreds. Most were a rich brown, and they seemed like tiny toy horses.

*I wish I were outside in the sunshine and fresh air.*

Instead of gulping, she sipped her wine. The bottle of cabernet sauvignon was close to full. It tempted her. She admitted wine was enjoyable, but she had decided to reduce her alcoholic intake.

*If I can drink less each day, I'll be better off.*

She imagined going to a LifeRing meeting with Lucas. He'd explained it was like an Alcoholics Anonymous meeting.

*I should do it…*

Her mobile phone rang.

She checked the device's display. David was calling. "Hello, David. Didn't anyone tell you I'm on vacation?"

"Sorry. No." David eased out a breath. "Let's talk about Lucas. He isn't who he says he is."

"What?"

"His real name is Joseph Murphy. He works for a Colombian drug cartel, *Los Hermanos.*"

"I don't believe it." Carmen felt her pulse pound.

Her gut warned her David was lying. Lucas didn't act like a drug pusher. He seemed to be the opposite. He'd said he was attending LifeRing meetings to keep sober, and he claimed he met many drug addicts who went to the meetings. The way he talked about how drug abusers struggled to beat their addictions made her think he was truthful. Of course, he could be lying. Some people were first-rate liars, but Lucas was upfront.

As these thoughts zipped through her head, David's deep voice returned her to the present. "We've confirmed it. His picture and details about him are in our organization's database. It includes information about competitors."

Carmen shrugged. She bit her lip and felt her face heat up like she was near a stoked fire. "I know you had a deal with Mark. How else would he get bundles of cash in small bills?" She wondered what else she should say to David, if anything. She'd been caught flat-footed—hadn't had time to work out what to do or how to act.

She figured this day would come, a time she'd have to deal with the Mexicans. She had no excuse to delay, or did she?

David kept talking. "Mateo has asked me to bargain with you." Carmen had noticed David's tone.

*Is he agitated? No, he's anxious.* Carmen paused and then spoke. "What are you offering?"

"The same deal we made with Mark, but we'll increase your percentage."

Carmen pushed her toes down into the soft carpet. "I'll think about it." She paused. Who'd tried to kill her? The Mexican cartel or a separate group or person? Should she bring up the bombing? "What would my percentage be?"

"You and I will examine Mark's past horse sales to Mateo. We'll increase your take by eight percent."

"I still need time to consider your offer."

"This is a proposition you can't refuse."

Carmen huffed. "You'll kill me, if I don't agree? Someone tried to murder me last night with a bomb." She wondered why she'd been brash and brought up the attempt on her life. But her words had come out of her mouth as if they had minds of their own.

"A bomb? What are you talking about?"

Carmen realized she'd laid the bombing issue on the table, and she was obligated to provide details. "The noise of the explosion must've mixed with the thunderstorm sounds."

"Explosion?"

"Lucas found explosive putty and wires looped around the propane tank near my bedroom. He ripped them off and threw them into the pond. The putty exploded."

"He made it up. The thunderstorm was an excuse." David waited for a second. "You didn't see any damage, did you?"

Carmen wondered what else she should say about the bomb. What if the Mexicans had done it? Were they behind Mark's death? No doubt the Mexican cartel was smuggling drugs; had supplied them to Ethan, her dealer; and had laundered money with the help of Mark. Had Mark gotten them angry enough to kill him? *But Mark and David seemed to have been friends. David tried to save Mark by using Narcan.*

She pictured Mateo. He was slick and sleazy. True, they'd met years ago, but people don't change after they've become adults. Were Mateo's main interests money and power? She guessed he was the drug lord in charge of the Mexican drug cartel. If she made a deal with him, it would be a compact with an evil man. Instinct cautioned her not to trust him. But what else could she do? Calling the cops was out of the question. If the Mexicans had killed Mark, they'd figure out a way to frame her.

*Yeah, I'm paranoid. But I have a reason to be scared—no,*

*cautious. Someone murdered Mark. Did the smiling snake, Mateo, hire someone to kill me?*

Carmen felt bold. "How do you know a small explosion didn't go off underwater in the pond? The water would've muted the blast, and the sound of it would've mixed with the thunder. Lucas told me."

"Don't believe him." David sounded annoyed. "I have proof about Lucas. Our private investigator, Mr. Victor Vargas, will be in Lexington today. VV can show you Lucas's picture from our *Los Hermanos* information file."

"I'm on vacation. I don't want to cut it short."

"VV could meet you at a place of your choosing. It will take little time."

"Give me VV's cell phone number. I'll call him."

On the spur of the moment, Carmen decided she could put on her blond wig and sunglasses and take a taxi to Charlie's Café to meet VV. It was often packed with customers. Once there, she'd remove her wig and glasses in the ladies' room.

David gave her VV's number. He sounded happy she'd agreed to meet the PI. Then David's tone changed. "Don't call the police. We have evidence you've been buying drugs you could've used to kill Mark. We'll give proof to the authorities, if necessary."

A jolt of fear hit her like an electric shock. She steadied herself and breathed in and out. "I don't plan to call the cops." She reckoned she had no choice but to work with the Mexican cartel.

"I'm glad you decided not to cause havoc." David paused. "The reason Lucas tried to frighten you with the bomb story is because *Los Hermanos* want to make a deal with you. Have they made an offer?"

Carmen wondered if she should lie, and say yes. But it could trigger the Mexicans to kill her if they thought she'd made a bargain with the Colombian cartel. "No."

"Don't be surprised if Lucas approaches you to work with *Los Hermanos*." David's voice had been gruff. But then he continued in a warm, reassuring voice. "My advice is to decline the Colombian offer. We will offer you a bigger percentage than they will. We'll protect you."

Carmen sighed. "I don't think Lucas will make an offer because he isn't who you think he is." She felt her heart pound. "But I'll meet VV and examine your evidence. Good-bye, David." She hung up.

* * *

## 4:10 P.M., THURSDAY, AUGUST 8—LEXINGTON

Carmen wore her blond wig and oversized sunglasses when she left her hotel by way of its back entrance and the building's loading dock.

Carmen didn't realize she'd evaded her FBI surveillance detail. One of its team members was in the men's room, and the second agent was sitting in the lobby near the main entrance of the hotel.

Carmen hailed a cab. Within twenty minutes, it stopped around the corner from Charlie's Café. She wore red slacks, hoping the private investigator, VV, could spot her with ease in the café.

She carried a paper shopping bag she'd gotten from the hotel's gift shop. The large sack held a second set of clothes.

A flush of adventure excited her. Warmed by the late afternoon sun, she felt beads of sweat course down her back. She examined the foot traffic on the busy corner. No one seemed suspicious. A street vendor sold magazines, and a food truck was parked near the curb, but no one was loitering.

She wondered, *Am I stupid to do this?*

Lucas had warned her not to leave the hotel. Either he was a tremendous liar when he had told her about the bomb, or he'd spoken the truth. Too bad she couldn't go to the police.

The odor of sizzling hamburgers and reheated hot dogs drifted her way from the food truck. Her stomach rumbled with hunger, but she resisted their appeal and turned the corner. The exterior of Charlie's Café was green, and its front window was wide and tall.

Before sitting down, she walked to the rear of the café, entered the ladies' room, and put her wig and sunglasses in her shopping bag. As she left the restroom, she glanced into the kitchen and saw an exit sign above a door on the far wall.

She stepped into the kitchen and caught a chef's attention. "Excuse me."

"Yes, ma'am?"

"I'm going to meet with my boyfriend to break up. May I exit through the back door?"

The man smiled. "Of course. It opens to the alley. Go left, and you'll see the bus station." She'd planned to go to the taxi stand at the station after the meeting.

She sat in a booth by the front window and ordered a coffee. Then she pulled her mobile phone from her purse and tapped in the PI's number.

"Hello." A man's baritone voice boomed into her ear.

"Mr. Vargas. This is Carmen."

"I was told you might phone. Feel free to call me VV."

"Can you meet me at Charlie's Café, VV?"

"Yes. It's a five-minute walk from my hotel."

"I'm sitting by the window and wearing red slacks."

"I've seen your picture. See you in ten minutes."

VV hung up.

* * *

## 4:50 P.M., THURSDAY, AUGUST 8—DOWNTOWN LEXINGTON

Carmen sipped her coffee and kept watch from the front window of Charlie's Café. Unsure if she could recognize VV from the pedestrians who walked by, she trusted her instincts.

As she waited, she became nervous and jumpy.

*I shouldn't have ordered coffee.*

She pushed her porcelain cup to the side. VV was at least

five minutes late. She peered out the window again and saw a short man with a beer belly. He wore navy-blue slacks and a ratty tropical sports jacket, tan in color.

He held a cigarette, put it to his lips, and sucked smoke into his lungs. He glanced upward, doubtless at the café's sign. Then he made eye contact with Carmen. She held up her hand. He forced a smile onto his serious face. After a final, quick drag on his smoke, he dropped the butt on the sidewalk, and crushed the cigarette stub under his shoe.

Carmen saw a spark fly into the air from near his loafers and extinguish. She sized up the unkempt man. His oily, mussed hair was jet black. His nose was fat and his eyebrows were bushy. He smiled, and she noticed his teeth were yellowed.

The front door slapped shut as he entered the coffee house.

Carmen felt his eyes inspect her. It was as if he had x-ray vision and could see beneath her clothes.

He tilted his eyes downward, and they lingered on her red slacks. He grinned. "Carmen, I'm VV. May I sit?"

Carmen nodded. *I've got to be calm.*

VV plopped into the booth across from her. "Let's get down to business." His jowls vibrated. He extracted a business-size envelope from the inside breast pocket of his sports jacket. A pistol was in a holster under his armpit. He slid the packet across the tabletop. "This is for you."

Carmen pulled the envelope toward her, lifted the unsealed flap, and took out its documents. On top was a Houston Police Department mugshot of Lucas. It seemed to be his picture, but it was captioned Joseph J. Murphy. The rest of the papers were arrest records. She glared at VV. "How do I know you didn't fake this?"

"You can find the same documents online. Use your phone. Many websites have the same info. Or you could go to Houston and check it out in person. They're public records."

Carmen grabbed her smartphone and found a website with access to Houston PD arrest records. She opened the site and paid a fee with her credit card. In seconds she saw the same mugshot and information VV had given her. She felt her face go pale. "Can I keep this?"

"Yes." VV smoothed his oily hair. "David asked me to advise you to fire this guy."

"I'll think about it."

VV stood and coughed. He leaned on the table. Carmen figured the man was a heavy smoker. He then stood straighter. "Call me any time for help. If you make a deal with Mateo, I'll be working for you, too." He weakly waved. "Gotta go."

Carmen watched him leave. Once outside, he lit a cigarette and walked away. He went in the opposite direction from the bus station.

After leaving cash on the table, Carmen carried her bag to the restroom to change clothes and don her sunglasses and wig.

# FIFTY-THREE

## 6:15 P.M., THURSDAY, AUGUST 8—BLUEGRASS LUXURY HOTEL

FAMISHED, Carmen ordered dinner from room service—a steak, mashed potatoes, and vegetables. Switching on the local evening TV news, she sat on her bed to wait for her food. She regarded her bottle of red wine, stood, and grabbed a water glass.

*Damn, I could use a drink to calm my nerves.*

The bottle felt familiar in her hand as she poured a generous amount of cabernet sauvignon into the tumbler.

The purplish red wine tasted great, but at once she felt guilty. She'd vowed to reduce her drinking and go to a Life-Ring meeting. She hoped Lucas would take her.

*Oh, yeah. Lucas. Is he a fraud? A gangster? A thug?*

Wine flowed down her throat, warming it. She felt better but still ashamed.

"I should call Lucas," she said out loud. She took her cell phone from her purse, set the instrument down, and reconsidered whether or not to call him.

As she was thinking, she heard a TV anchorman reading a crime story.

*Soon he could be talking about me.* She muted the television and then shut it off.

A tapping sounded on her door. "Room service."

She set the glass of wine on the desk and peered through the peephole. A young man in a white jacket stood by a shiny dinner cart. Carmen saw plates covered with metallic lids. The odor of steak and mashed potatoes entered her room through the crack under her door.

She wondered if the man could be a killer. But her hunger prevailed over her fear, and she unlocked the deadbolt.

The cart squealed as the man rolled Carmen's dinner into the room. Relieved, she tipped the young man well.

"Thanks, ma'am."

The steak was tasty, and the warm mashed potatoes, soaked with gravy, diluted the wine in her stomach. She was happy the meal had improved her mood.

She frowned at her tumbler of wine, stood, grabbed it, walked to the bathroom sink, and poured the blood red liquid down the drain.

*Why'd I dump it?*

Then she recalled she still had half a bottle of wine left should she change her mind about drinking.

Afraid to call the police, scared of Mateo, and uncertain about Luke, she began to read a paperback romance novel, but her mind wandered.

*If Lucas was a man named Joseph Murphy, was Lucas's girlfriend, Layla, a made-up person? Would he ever be interested in me?*

Carmen fingered her cell phone, then touched "Lucas" on her contact list.

"Hi, Carmen. You okay?"

Carmen was furious he'd asked if she was okay. "No, not since I learned who you are."

"What?"

"You're Joseph Murphy, an American member of *Los Hermanos*, a Colombian drug cartel."

"It's not true."

"I have your Houston Police mugshot and your criminal record." Her heart beat fast like that of a bird or a puppy. She felt warm tears drip down her face. Her nose became congested.

"It's gotta be a fake. They can do it with a computer and a photo program."

Carmen tried to stop weeping, but it was useless. She was aware Lucas could hear her crying. "I searched the Houston Police website. Anybody can see mugshots and criminal records online."

She grabbed a tissue from her purse and tried to dry her tears. She wiped her nose, but she knew she'd still sound stuffed up when she spoke. Her chin wouldn't stop shaking no matter how hard she tried to stop it.

She could hear Luke breathing hard. "Who fed you this crap?" His voice was harsh.

"I met with Mateo's private eye, Victor Vargas."

"Where are you now?"

"Back in my hotel room."

"Did Vargas meet you there?"

"No, I went to Charlie's Café, and he met me there. He has no idea where I'm staying."

Luke was silent for a moment. "If you think I'm crooked, why not call the police?"

Carmen breathed hard. "Because they'll think I killed Mark. And the Mexicans implied they'd kill me if I don't make a deal to launder drug money like Mark did."

"I'm still your bodyguard. Don't trust the Mexicans. Stay put in the hotel, 'til I figure what to do next."

Carmen huffed. "Who am I supposed to believe? You work for a Colombian drug cartel. Will you offer me a better deal than the Mexicans did?"

"I don't know how the Mexicans faked my mugshot, but I swear I'm not workin' for any drug cartel."

"You're lying." She blew her nose. "Does the girlfriend of yours exist?"

"Yes."

Carmen ended the call. She lay under the covers and cried herself to sleep.

# FIFTY-FOUR

LUKE WAS SITTING on his bedroom floor in the mansion, leaning against the wall. He was wondering how Carmen had evaded FBI surveillance. He focused on his cell phone beside him on the carpet.

If the Mexicans thought he belonged to *Los Hermanos, a* Colombian cartel, why not embrace the idea? Could he claim he'd double-crossed the Colombians, and they were gunning for him? He could ask to join the Mexican cartel. Even if the Mexicans believed him, would they try to kill him?

First, he'd try to convince Carmen to keep him as a bodyguard.

Luke called Jim.

"Anything to report, Luke?"

"The Mexicans think I work for a Colombian drug cartel."

"What?"

"Carmen said Mateo's PI, Victor Vargas, gave her a mugshot of me. It's the picture of a guy who looks like me, Joseph Murphy. The PI claims I'm a member of *Los Hermanos,* a Bogota cartel, and I'm spying on the Mexicans."

"How did the PI get past the FBI team?"

Luke shrugged. "He didn't. Carmen managed to leave the hotel without being seen, and she met Vargas in a café. She must've put on her wig and big sunglasses and slipped past the FBI agents."

"Artificial intelligence software could've created the mugshot."

"Carmen said she found the same picture and arrest records on Houston PD's website."

"What's the name on the mugshot?"

"Joseph Murphy."

"I'll check the Houston PD site." Luke heard Jim typing on his computer keyboard. "I'm staring at the mugshot of a guy who could be your brother if you had one."

"You gotta be kidding."

"The picture resembles you, but it's not an exact match." Jim bumped his phone, jarring Luke's ear. "HPD could know where this guy is. If we luck out, he's in jail." Jim paused. "I may have to pull you out. The Mexicans will be after you."

Luke strained to figure out what to say next. "Carmen said the Mexicans offered her a deal to launder money."

Jim was silent for two seconds. "We'll raid the farm ASAP."

Luke wondered if Dick the DA would argue against a raid when there wasn't a solid lead related to Mark's murder. The task force had probable cause, but it was related to drugs and money laundering. Solving Mark's murder would be a vote-getting bonanza for Dick. "Jim, you think you should powwow with our friendly DA, Dick?"

"I have to."

"What will he say if we raid Spicer Farm and don't arrest anybody for Mark's killin'?"

"I don't like how Dick uses politics to tweak investigations." Luke heard Jim cough. "How close are you to finding anything useful about the murder?"

"I don't have a solid clue who killed Mark."

Jim was silent, and then he spoke. "You up to trying to infiltrate a Mexican cartel?"

"Yep." Luke wondered if he'd spoken too soon.

"How could you gain their confidence?"

Luke licked his lips. "Like I suggested before, I could flash illegal guns at David."

"It could work."

"I'll ask Carmen to convince the Mexicans to let her keep me as her bodyguard. She could tell 'em I want to switch outta the Colombian cartel to the Mexican one."

"It's worth a shot." Jim paused. "Tom, the ATF bomb squad guy, called me an hour ago. Said they found Tokyo Joe's fingerprint on a fragment of the cell phone Tom fished from the pond."

Luke sat up straight against the wall. "Tokyo's the same guy who put the bombs on the cruise ship for the Colombian cartel."

Jim sucked air into his lungs. "*Los Hermanos* could've hired Tokyo to kill Carmen."

"Why would they?" Did the Colombians wish to eliminate Carmen to disrupt the Mexican cartel's laundering operation, cause chaos, and take over the illegal drug trade in Kentucky?

Jim remained silent for a while. "Okay, see if you can convince Carmen to ask the Mexicans to keep you as her Mexican cartel bodyguard. But get out fast if you get in trouble."

"Yes, sir."

"Report back ASAP about what develops. I gotta go." Jim hung up.

# FIFTY-FIVE

## 2:30 A.M., FRIDAY, AUGUST 9—SPICER FARM PARKING LOT

TWO *SICARIOS*, Mexican assassins, had worked for *Nuestro Club* and Mateo since they'd been teenagers in the slums of Tijuana.

Jorge, the older of the two hitmen, had answered Mateo's recent call. He remembered Mateo's exact words. "Wait to kill him until I say so. Then make it seem like *Los Hermanos* did it."

"How can I make it have the appearance of a Colombian hit?"

"Hang the body from a bridge. Write a message on a white blanket and attach it to the body."

"What should it say?"

"Death to those who double-cross *Los Hermanos*."

Jorge had felt uneasy about hanging a body from a bridge. He was unfamiliar with Kentucky and the ways of its people. "What if no bridge is nearby?"

"Put the sheet by the body. Take precautions so it doesn't blow away."

"*Si*, Boss."

Now Jorge, a ruthless killer, and his younger teenaged partner, Alonzo, stood in the shadows of the Spicer horse barn. Alonzo was on his first mission and was an apprentice being trained by Jorge.

When Mateo had hired the two men days ago, he'd told Jorge to kill Lucas and make it appear to be an accident. But Mateo had changed his mind. Now they were to murder the man and make it plain his death was no accident. But where to do it? Jorge had figured one option would be to attack the man in a secluded place.

Jorge decided to plant a tracker on Lucas's truck. He felt the device in his pocket. With it, they could see where Lucas drove. Did he always take certain routes? David had said Lucas could have a girlfriend on a farm nearby.

Jorge turned to his buddy. "Watch for people. If someone approaches, whistle like a bird."

Jorge didn't like to walk through the pool of dazzling light flooding the parking lot. Then again, the parking area was by the bunkhouse where he and his partner-in-crime stayed. It wouldn't be unusual for them to be there.

Jorge eased into the lit area and strolled as if he were on his way to the bunkhouse. He stopped in the shadow behind Lucas's beat-up truck. Jorge surveyed the area and saw no one. Lying on the gravel, he felt it bite into his back as he slid under the truck and placed the magnetic tracker. He stood and walked toward the bunkhouse. Alonzo followed him.

"We can track him with our phones," Jorge whispered.

Alonzo held the bunkhouse door ajar. "You positive the tracker will work?"

"I used it twice before. Watch, and you will learn."

# FIFTY-SIX

## 10:00 A.M., FRIDAY, AUGUST 9—BLUEGRASS LUXURY HOTEL

HER EYES PUFFY, Carmen woke after a fitful night of dozing and crying. She peered at her face in her hotel room mirror. *I must control my emotions.* She wept for another minute, but her distress was less intense than it had been the night before.

*What am I going to do?*

She felt depression invade her entire self. After turning on the warm water in the bathtub, she tossed her nightgown aside and stepped into the soothing water. After leaning back, she relaxed and closed her eyes. Her feelings of anxiety and despair began to evaporate as she peered into the blackness beneath her eyelids. She felt as if she were floating on a warm, tropical ocean.

After five minutes, she began to think of her options.

*One: Call the cops. No.*

*Two: Make a deal with the Mexicans. Iffy.*

*Three: Work with the Colombians, Los Hermanos. Only if Lucas makes an offer.*

*Four: Flee and change my name. No. My cash wouldn't last. The cops would search for me. They'd find me and accuse me of murdering Mark.*

Should she join the Mexicans? If she did, she'd have a pact with evil and become a member of an illegal enterprise, a criminal. She moved her hands under the warm bath water. It was starting to cool. She stood, water dripping from her body.

As she dried herself under the ceiling heat lamp, she felt stronger.

*I'm going to take charge and do something. I can't mope in this hotel room any longer.*

In minutes she put her makeup on, dressed, placed her blond wig on her head, and grabbed her oversized sunglasses. Next, she tossed her other clothes into her suitcase and added her bathroom items. She snapped the case shut.

"The hell with hiding," she whispered. *I'm going to eat breakfast in the hotel restaurant. Then I'll take a cab to the farm and fire Lucas.*

\* \* \*

## 10:35 A.M., FRIDAY, AUGUST 9—SPICER FARM

The morning was turning hot, and Kentucky's legendary humidity drove Luke inside the mansion. He sat in the kitchen where he watched Lilia, the maid, mixing cake batter.

Luke held a tumbler of ginger ale and ice Lilia had given him. She turned and gazed at Luke. "When's Carmen coming back from vacation?"

"I don't know." Luke reckoned Lilia was passing information to David. The two of them often chatted. Once, from a distance, Luke had seen Lilia glance at him as she spoke rapid-fire Spanish with David. She'd blinked and turned her head away when she'd noticed Luke staring back. He figured his hunch about her was sound.

Lilia held her bowl of batter and poured it into a cake pan. "Carmen left in a hurry. Didn't tell me in advance."

"Hasn't she always been unpredictable?" Luke figured

everyone on the farm wondered why Carmen had left the farm with him in his truck. Rumors must be circulating. And people must've been asking why he'd returned without her.

Lilia shrugged. "She often acts on the spur of the moment, but she always tells me before."

Luke heard the kitchen door creak behind him. He turned. Carmen stood in the doorway.

"Lucas, we need to talk."

Luke felt blood rush to his temples. "You said you were gonna be on vacation for days."

Luke saw Carmen tap her foot twice on the kitchen floor tiles. Her eyes flashed like a stop sign at a busy four-way intersection. "Let's talk someplace else."

* * *

CARMEN HALTED by her office door and searched for her key in the biggest side pocket of her purse. She felt Lucas's eyes focused on the back of her head.

*Why am I taking him into my office instead of a place where people can see the both of us?* After all, Lucas was a dangerous criminal, a member of a Colombian drug cartel.

When she grabbed her key chain, she felt clumsy and shaky. She unlocked the door. "Come in."

"How'd you come back?" Luke followed her into the room.

"By taxi."

"Why didn't you stay put? Somebody tried to kill you with a bomb."

"You invented the bomb story."

"I damn near died to save you."

Carmen noticed an artery throbbing in Lucas's throat, and his face was red.

*He's a damn fine actor, talented enough to join the Lexington Players.*

It was unfortunate she had no choice but to expose him. She unsnapped her purse and found the business-size envelope VV had given her. "Let's sit at my desk where I can set these papers down."

Luke bit his lip and eased onto the chair closest to her desk.

Carmen leaned back in her leather chair. Her body relaxed. She felt as if she were taking steps to better her situation. She sat straighter, lifted the envelope flap, and slid Lucas's mugshot to him. Afterward, she pushed the arrest records in his direction. "You're fired. Get the hell off this farm. I never want to see you again."

Luke sighed. "I can explain..."

"Joseph Murphy, I should call the police and turn you in, but I won't."

"You gotta listen to me."

* * *

LUKE FIGURED he had little chance of saving his undercover role at the farm. For a fleeting two seconds, he felt like quitting the investigation. Carmen had fired him, and he was soon to be a father. Why take a chance and get killed? He'd come within moments of dying when he'd ripped the C-4 explosive from Carmen's propane tank.

"Carmen, you figured it out. I'm a member of *Los Hermanos*, but they're plannin' to kill me. I blew a job, an important one..."

"I'm glad I'm letting you go. Otherwise, the Colombians would show up here sooner or later."

Luke was unsure what to say next, but he figured it wouldn't matter. "I've got experience dealin' with evil people. You still need a bodyguard even if the Mexicans make a deal with you. Remember what happened to Mark."

Carmen's eyelashes flickered. "The Mexicans say you're a threat. Why would they want you to be my bodyguard?"

"I can give them info about *Los Hermanos*. And I'll ask to join the Mexicans." He paused. "The drug business is risky. You need me."

She observed him. He felt like her eyes were lasers

cutting into his brain. She furrowed her brow. "I could plead with David. But don't get your hopes up."

"Thank you, Carmen." Luke tried to grin, but his weak smile ended in a second. *I made a mistake. At best the Mexicans will tell me to skedaddle. Worst is they do me.*

Carmen stood. "I'll find David and see what he says." She patted Luke's shoulder. "Stay put. Lock the door."

Luke nodded.

# FIFTY-SEVEN

DAVID WAS ALONE in his office smoking a Cuban cigar. He liked the taste of its tobacco. Letting the smoke linger in his mouth, he felt its flavor increase. Buzzed, he brought the Havana up to his nose. He liked its smell.

A tap, tap, tap sounded on his closed office door. *It's Carmen.* Her knock was distinctive. Lilia had phoned to warn him Carmen had returned. "Come in." David set his cigar on his ashtray and stood.

Carmen strode into the office and halted near him. "We need to talk business."

"Have a seat."

David watched her sit. He felt his pulse increase. She was stunning. Images of her nude in his bed invaded his thoughts. It was fortunate Mateo had stopped thinking of killing her.

Carmen settled in her chair. "VV saw me and gave me Lucas's mugshot and arrest records."

"Fire Lucas, but don't call the cops. They'd investigate the farm."

Carmen crossed her legs. Was she being defensive or assertive?

Her brow wrinkled. "I don't see how I can avoid going

into business with you guys. But the drug business is dangerous. I need a bodyguard."

David picked up his cigar and puffed it to keep it burning. "We'll get you a top-quality man."

Carmen spied a bottle of wine on David's shelf. "Could I have a glass of wine?"

David stood and poured red wine for her and himself.

*She's nervous. But she'll be a loyal partner once she settles down.*

After sipping her wine, she set her glass on David's desktop. "I was about to fire Lucas when he told me something which will interest you and Mateo."

David leaned forward. "What?"

"He admitted he's with *Los Hermanos* but said they want to kill him."

"He made it up like he fabricated the bomb story."

"I trust him."

"We don't."

"He wants to join your cartel. And he said he could give you and Mateo intelligence about the Colombians."

David figured Carmen was afraid of joining Mateo's enterprise. She was hesitant and had a crush on Lucas. But it wouldn't continue forever. She jumped from one man's bed into another in quick succession. It wouldn't hurt to call Mateo and confer. He had a need to know what was happening. "I'll phone Mateo. I'll let you know what he decides."

Carmen smiled. "Thank you." She stood. "Call me when you get an answer."

"Of course." David gestured at Carmen's chair. "Sit down and relax. I have developments you'll be interested to hear about."

Carmen sat. "I'm all ears."

"It's about Fast Guy…"

# FIFTY-EIGHT

DAVID WATCHED as Carmen left his office. She was worth saving. Would Mateo demand she be disposed of since she seemed to be joining forces with Lucas, a former member of the Colombian cartel?

*I can argue she'll be agreeable to taking our deal if we allow Lucas to continue as her guardian. But is he indeed being hunted by Los Hermanos? Or is he their spy, claiming to be on their hit list?*

Peering from his window, David saw Carmen hustling toward the mansion.

*Where is Lucas?* David had yet to see him that morning. *I better call Mateo.*

After unhooking his keychain from his belt, David chose the key for his locked desk drawer. In seconds he had his encrypted satellite phone in his hand. His fingers hovered over Mateo's name on the device's display. David set his jaw and tapped the call icon. He tried to relax.

"*Hola*, David."

"Boss, I have an unexpected development."

"What?" Mateo sounded irritated.

"Lucas confessed he's a former member of *Los Hermanos*, but he's asked to join us."

"Why?"

"He said the Colombians want to kill him."

David could hear Mateo breathing, then letting out air. "Could be a trick."

"Yes, Boss, but what if he's telling the truth?"

"I doubt it, but I'll ask VV to check with his contacts in Bogota."

David's throat felt dry. "Carmen wants to keep him as a bodyguard."

"Why?"

"She trusts him. I believe she's screwing him."

"What does it matter? Is she going to sign on with us, or do we have to remove her from the scene?"

"I think she'll soon join *Nuestro Club* if Lucas continues as her bodyguard." David held his breath, waiting for Mateo to reply.

"You were right before about Carmen." Mateo paused. "Even if Lucas is a spy, he can't learn much more about us. Tell her Lucas can be her bodyguard."

"Should I inform her now or after VV reports back?"

"At once. I'll tell our *sicarios* to hold off killing Lucas until you get Carmen on board."

"Then what?"

"He'll die. It'll seem to be an accident."

David sighed. *I must get Carmen to join us.* His stomach began to bother him. "Boss, what if he's on the Colombian's hit list?"

"We'll do him in anyway. The police will figure *Los Hermanos* did it. Once in our club, Carmen will be okay if she thinks the Colombians did it. She'll find another man to bed."

David steeled himself. "I'm glad we don't have to dispose of Carmen. The police would investigate."

"True. The other line's ringing." Mateo disconnected.

# FIFTY-NINE

LUKE STOOD in Carmen's office next to her desk. The click of a deadbolt made a sharp sound. Luke felt himself jump. As he turned his head toward the door, it swung ajar. Carmen entered, smiling. "David's calling Mateo about you. He may agree you can continue working for me."

Luke surmised it was a slim chance. "Does David know I'm in your office?"

"No." Carmen sat at her desk and relaxed. "David will call with an answer."

"When?" Luke sat on a chair near the desk.

"Soon, I think." Carmen took her cell phone from her purse and laid it on the desktop.

Luke wondered what the odds were he'd be able to stay undercover. He reckoned chances were less than one in ten. "I'll be surprised if Mateo agrees to keep me on."

Carmen reached behind her toward her bookcase, grabbed a pillow, and put it behind her back. "Ye of little faith. He's going to say yes because *Nuestro Club* needs me to launder money. They want me to agree without a hassle. I made it clear I need protection, and you're my man."

"I never heard of *Nuestro Club*."

"I didn't either until a few days ago. It's the name of Mateo's cartel. Mark never told me about it."

Carmen's phone chimed. "Hello, David." She nodded and grinned. "I'll tell him. Okay. Bye." She zeroed in on Luke's eyes. "Mateo agreed you can join *Nuestro Club*."

"I didn't expect that." Luke felt elated for a brief three seconds. But his inner voice warned, *This gig could go on forever. What's Layla gonna say?* He gulped and stood.

Carmen got up and gave him a bear hug. "You don't have to worry about *Los Hermanos* anymore." She pulled away from him but still held his shoulders. "Should I still call you Lucas?"

"Yep, I got a fake birth certificate. I don't want people to find out I'm Joseph Murphy, 'specially the *Los Hermanos* crowd."

"Okay, Lucas." Carmen tilted her head, stood on her toes, and kissed Luke on his lips. "I'm glad you're my bodyguard. I get jumpy when I think of the jam I'm in. I can't call the police when two rival drug cartels could turn on me."

Luke closed his eyes and then reopened them. "You'll be fine." But his inner voice was speaking. *I should've got out of this assignment when I had the chance. I gotta be around when my child's born.*

"You okay, Lucas?"

"Yep, just stunned." He eased down on the office sofa. "I never figured they'd agree."

Luke's sixth sense advised him he was in trouble. He needed to keep his eyes open and be prepared to defend himself. He figured the *Nuestro Club* cartel was biding its time, waiting for a time and place to get rid of him.

Carmen turned her leather chair to face him. "I've something to tell you about an expensive horse we have."

"Which horse?"

"Fast Guy. Mateo owns him. David bought him from me for Mateo without my knowledge. David said a man was going to deliver two million dollars in cash to me in a suitcase next week. The Arab, Ali, is going to buy Fast Guy from Mateo. Where should I put the money?"

Luke rubbed his beard. "I'd put the cash where Mark kept it, in the old safe." *I gotta call Jim about this.*

Carmen patted Luke's shoulder. "I'm going to pay you a nice bonus."

"Thanks. Lock it up in the safe. I got no place to keep it. I won't start a bank account with it cuz somebody will talk if I walk in with a bundle of cash."

Carmen gazed at him. "Let me know when you need money. I'll keep track and subtract it from your bonus."

"Thanks."

Carmen leaned forward. "Do you have any idea how I can spend the Fast Guy money without arousing suspicion?"

"David could help you figure it out."

Luke wondered if Mateo had hired Tokyo Joe to kill Carmen with the bomb. True, Tokyo had worked for the Bogota cartel, *Los Hermanos.* But he could work for anyone willing to pay. He may have calculated no one would learn he'd attached C-4 explosives to Carmen's propane tank. In most circumstances, nobody would guess a propane explosion had been triggered by a bomb. It would've been considered a disastrous accident in which Carmen burned to death.

With Carmen gone, would the Mexican cartel, *Nuestro Club,* buy the farm?

*Chances are Nuestro Club killed Mark, but a rival cartel could've killed him, too.*

Would an enemy cartel have killed Mark and later bombed the mansion to incinerate Carmen? Would their goal be to disrupt *Nuestro Club*'s operation?

# SIXTY

LUKE WANDERED from the mansion and searched for a safe place where he could make a phone call.

*The pickup could be bugged.* He sighed. *Am I gettin' as paranoid as Carmen?*

He paused to think.

*No, I'm not fearful enough.*

A glob of C-4 explosive had damn near blasted him into ground beef, and the *Nuestro Club* Mexican drug cartel believed a rival Colombian criminal enterprise had employed him as a special agent.

He was positive the Mexicans didn't trust him. He figured they were putting out feelers to learn if the Colombian *Los Hermanos* cartel was indeed planning to assassinate him—or his look-alike, Joseph Murphy.

Although Carmen was unstable and fearful, at least she was watching her back. Someone had tried to kill her. She was dealing with ruthless criminals who didn't hesitate to commit murder.

Luke walked to a grove of trees and sat on a clump of soft grass behind an oak. "They ain't wired this tree," he whispered to himself, and laughed at the fact he'd lowered his voice.

He withdrew his mobile phone and touched Jim's name on the device.

"Luke. Any progress?"

"Mateo bought one of Mark's thoroughbreds, Fast Guy, for two million dollars without Carmen knowing about it. A man is supposed to deliver the cash in a suitcase."

"The feds will be happy when they find out."

"How big is the task force?"

Jim hesitated. "It's substantial. It includes the FBI, DEA, Lexington PD, and the sheriff's department, but don't worry. If you get in trouble we'll parachute people in if we have to."

All of a sudden Luke felt better. He pictured Layla very pregnant with his child. He'd better stay alive. The kid would need a dad.

So what if Mark's murder wasn't solved? The federal task force would make an important drug bust, arrest a bunch of criminals, and Dick would still get credit. "I'm glad you and Rita set up the task force. My situation's iffy."

"What's going on?"

"Carmen begged Mateo to hire me as her bodyguard. He did. I think they did it to make it easier to convince her to launder money."

"Don't be surprised if we raid the place soon."

"Okay, but I wanna put in a good word for Carmen. It's like she's facing a grizzly bear attack, a sheer cliff, and drug-pushin' murderers all at once. She hasn't committed to the Mexican cartel yet. And she's scared shitless of calling the sheriff's department. Thinks we're gonna toss her in jail for Mark's murder."

"Your gut tells you she's innocent?"

"Yep."

"Dick will have the opposite opinion. He wants a scalp, even if Carmen's a nice-looking young thing. She's an addict and had access to lots of pills. She bought drugs from Ethan. He's dead, and she's alive. Dick will try to prosecute her for Mark's murder."

Luke narrowed his eyes. "My instincts ain't usually wrong. She's innocent." He paused and began to think fast. What if the existence of the federal task force leaks? If the *Nuestro Club* Mexicans heard about it, they could conclude he was with law enforcement. Or they could guess Joseph Murphy had been undercover, checking out the Colombian cartel's business in Houston. Yeah, it was far-fetched, but making himself appear to be a real criminal was of the utmost importance. His idea of flashing illegal firearms at David "by mistake" could work.

Jim asked, "Anything else?"

"Yep. Remember how we talked about letting David get a peek at illegal firearms?"

"Yes. I found two ghost guns in the evidence cage."

Luke grinned and peered at the blue sky. "When can I git them?"

"Tonight."

"Can you meet me at my house? I'll park my truck in the barn. We can put the weapons in my truck's toolbox. I don't want Layla to see 'em." Luke saw Layla in his mind's eye and felt at ease.

"What time?"

"Let's have supper at five-thirty at my place. I'll call Layla and confirm it with her."

"She's a fine cook."

Luke felt hungry thinking of Layla's cooking. "I'll call you back after I call her."

\* \* \*

## 11:50 A.M., FRIDAY, AUGUST 9

The wall-mounted telephone rang in Layla's kitchen at Luke's rented farm. The intense ringing was jarring compared to the cricket noise her cell phone emitted when it alerted her to a call. To stop the irritating sound of the obsolete touch-tone device, she rushed to answer it.

She grabbed the handset. "Hello."

"It's me." She heard Luke's familiar voice and felt calmer.

"Darling, how's it going?"

"Fine. Could you set another place at the table for dinner tonight? Jim would like to visit."

Layla felt fortunate because she'd planned a fine meal for Luke.

*It's lucky I bought a four-pound leg of lamb.*

She had prepared *au gratin* potatoes in a slow cooker to go with mixed vegetables. "I've got a good-and-plenty layout planned, enough to feed a squad."

"I'm glad you don't have to cook extra."

"It's leg of lamb." Layla knew it was his favorite dish.

"A second ago my mouth started waterin'."

"You guys gonna discuss business?"

"Yes, but we'll also chat and enjoy a night away from the investigation."

Layla wondered how many days Mark's murder probe would go on. Had Luke and Jim hit a dead end? Would Luke get back on a normal schedule? "Is the Spicer Farm investigation close to the end?"

"I'm hoping." Layla heard him breathe faster. "After it's over, should we announce we're going to be parents?"

Layla's heart fluttered.

*Does Luke want to marry me? He does want this baby.* Her silent words were joyful. "I'd like to tell the world." She felt proud. "Let's tell Jim first."

"I agree."

"I can't wait to tell him." A possible result of the announcement occurred to Layla. Then Jim might take extra steps to keep Luke out of harm's way.

She heard Luke breathing. He sounded relaxed. "Do you want to bring up the baby topic?"

"Yes, dear."

"See you soon." His voice was strong and confident. "I love you, and need to feel you in my arms."

"Me, too." Layla made a kissing noise.

After their call ended, Layla regarded the spacious country kitchen with its pots, pans, and cooking tools hanging from the walls. She scanned the sturdy oven and cooktop, as well as the canisters of sugar, flour, tea, and coffee. The kitchen, the house, the farm, the land, and the wildlife were all part of a healthy rural environment where her newborn could thrive. *This beats Louisville public housing.* Her heart was happy.

# SIXTY-ONE

LUKE COULD SMELL STRAW, dirt, and motor oil inside the sturdy barn on Ford's farm, which he rented. He'd parked his decades-old Dodge Ram pickup inside the red farm building.

*I don't need Layla seein' me and Jim hiding illegal guns in my toolbox*, he mused.

When Luke viewed his truck inside the barn, he realized it matched the atmosphere of the century-old structure. He felt as if he'd traveled back in time. After a moment of thought, he snapped back to reality.

*I gotta set up the toolbox.*

He left the wide barn door ajar. Through the crack, he would be able to see Jim arrive in his sheriff's SUV.

Luke stepped to his truck and unlocked the padlock on his crossover toolbox. It spanned the pickup's bed behind the rear window. He peered into the box.

*The ghost guns will fit in easy enough.*

When he leaned down and peered inside the box, he scanned his jumble of rusted tools and then he noticed a burned-out taillight he'd replaced years ago.

"This is what I need."

He grabbed the bulb and a screwdriver. In less than a minute he'd removed the left taillight lens cover and its working bulb. He installed the burned-out bulb and put the good bulb in the toolbox.

Luke planned to park his truck close to Spicer's horse barn tomorrow. After David left his office, Luke would start to talk with him and mention the truck's taillight was out.

*Then I'll open the toolbox. David will see the guns, and I'll close it real quick.*

Luke reckoned it didn't matter whether David pretended not to see the illegal weapons, or if he asked about them. Either way, he'd think Luke was a criminal, not a law enforcement officer.

Luke heard gravel crunching in the driveway outside of the barn door. He turned. Jim's SUV stopped, and he got out of his vehicle carrying a cloth laundry bag.

Jim pushed the barn door open and came in. "I have two ghost guns."

Luke opened the bag and peered inside. "Let's hide 'em now."

As Luke put the illegal weapons into the toolbox, Jim took five pictures with his mobile phone. He returned the device to his hip pocket. "In case somebody asks, these pictures are proof you're doing this like we planned."

Luke locked the toolbox. "Let's see what Layla's cooked. I believe it's leg of lamb."

\* \* \*

JIM HAD VISITED Ford's rambling farmhouse many times over the years. Tonight, he glanced into the additions, nooks, and crannies of the home as he followed Luke inside.

Jim recalled old man Ford had added to the house little by little. It was sad he'd died of a heart attack. He was "good people," industrious and friendly.

Ford's house had taken on his good-natured personality. Luke was lucky Mrs. Ford had rented him the place. He was growing hemp, taking advantage of the new market for its fiber.

Luke led Jim into the dining room. The aroma of roasted lamb greeted Jim. "Smells delicious, Luke."

"Layla's a great cook."

Behind him, Jim heard footsteps on the carpet. He turned. Layla was carrying a platter of *au gratin* potatoes.

"Thanks for coming, Jim." Layla was alluring in a summer dress. "Luke and I love to have company visit."

"I'm grateful you and Luke invited me." He paused. "Having a meal with y'all will uplift my spirits."

Layla beamed and set the plate of potatoes on the dining room table near the sliced lamb. Mixed vegetables, fresh bread, butter, jam, and apple pie sat nearby. Jim felt his stomach juices flowing.

Layla caught Jim's eye and then glanced at Luke. She was as happy as a student on the final day of school. "Y'all can grab plates and serve yourselves."

Six-year-old Angela entered the room. "It smells tasty, Maw."

Layla took Angela's hand. "Come and meet Sheriff Pike, dear."

Jim felt warm inside.

*The girl's a charmer.*

Jim bent down. "I'm pleased to meet you, Angela." He shook her young hand.

"I'm pleased to meet you, too, Sheriff."

"You can call me Jim."

Angela's eyes sparkled. "Yes, sir."

Jim sensed Layla wanted Angela to call him by his last name, but he felt as if he were part of Luke's family. He and Luke had been friends, well-nigh brothers, since childhood.

Layla led Angela to the serving plates and helped her choose food while the men waited in line.

After they'd begun to eat, Jim noticed Layla—an upbeat woman—was even happier than normal. When they were eating dessert, Layla tapped her spoon against her water glass. "I have an announcement." She glanced from person to person at the table. "Angela will have a baby brother or sister in less than a year."

"Maw, you're going to have a baby?"

"Yes, darling. You'll have fun playing with your brother or sister after the baby becomes a toddler."

Jim felt a blush form on his face. "Congratulations to all of you." He felt happy for Luke. Becoming a family man should make Luke's life better.

*Should I take him off the undercover assignment? I'll sleep on it. I'll check with Luke after he flashes the ghost guns near David.*

# SIXTY-TWO

LUKE HAD INFORMED Layla he was scheduled to work that afternoon at the Spicer Farm, even though it was the weekend. He stopped his Dodge Ram pickup truck in a parking space close to the rear door of the Spicer Farm horse barn. He recalled David often left his office at noon to get a thermos of coffee from the bunkhouse dining area.

Luke unlocked his crossover toolbox. After removing the left taillight lens cover and the burned-out bulb, he leaned against the truck, toying with the burned-out bulb. He'd left his screwdriver on the truck bed above the exposed taillight socket and waited.

*Am I layin' my life on the line to help Dick git reelected?*

The task force would find ample evidence of drug dealing, smuggling, and money laundering if Jim raided the horse farm today. If the task force delayed taking action, *Nuestro Club* Mexican cartel members might learn they were in the crosshairs of law enforcement.

The rear door of the barn slammed.

Luke turned and saw David approaching. Luke squatted near the exposed taillight socket and glanced at David, who stopped near the truck.

Luke stood and faced David. "I gotta change this burned-out bulb. Otherwise, cops could stop me."

"We don't need police snooping around the farm."

Luke walked toward his toolbox. "I think I got a spare in here someplace." When David came closer, Luke lifted the steel box lid. Two ghost guns with their purple plastic parts came into view. Within two seconds, Luke closed the lid as if he didn't want David to see the illegal weapons.

David stopped, wide-eyed. "Don't try to hide them, Lucas."

Luke shrugged. "I'm planning to sell 'em soon as I can in Lexington."

"Better dump them. We're gonna pay you plenty to protect Carmen."

"Okay, but we still got to discuss salary." Luke thought, *He took the bait. He won't believe I'm a cop.*

"I'll ask Mateo what he thinks your pay should be. We take care of our own."

Luke nodded, and David continued toward the bunkhouse. *They better take care of me as a friend, not an enemy.*

\* \* \*

LUKE REINSTALLED the working bulb in the taillight socket and replaced the lens cover.

*I gotta call Jim.*

Luke walked past the barn behind a row of tall bushes.

*If the Mexicans think I'm a veteran criminal, will they welcome me?* He doubted it, but at least they'd think twice about coming after him.

He patted the miniature 9mm SCCY pistol and holster under his loose-hanging shirt. He felt confident and figured he could also take his Smith & Wesson pistol out of his truck if things began to look iffy. He'd stowed the weapon in a toolbox and put it in a paper bag under a layer of garbage.

He grabbed his mobile phone and touched Jim's name on its display.

He heard Jim's voice. "Hi, Luke."

"I flashed the guns. No doubt David believes I'm a brother in crime."

"First class work. I'll swing out tonight to your place at seven to pick up the guns. Okay?"

"Yep. Meet you in the barn."

# SIXTY-THREE

DAVID STOOD near the fifty-cup coffee brewer. As he filled his thermos, he planned what he'd tell Mateo about Lucas. He'd start by saying Lucas would be an ideal fit for *Nuestro Club* if he could be trusted. Would Mateo agree?

If Lucas took David's advice and dumped the ghost guns in a lake or a garbage can, it could help prove he'd be loyal.

When David walked toward the barn and his office, he noticed Lucas was gone. A crook, would Lucas sell the illegal firearms instead of tossing them into a lake?

David went into his office and poured a cup of coffee.

*I should call Mateo and get it over with.* He fumbled with his keyring and selected the correct key. *I must calm down.*

He unlocked the desk drawer where he kept his satellite phone.

It was afternoon in Kentucky and about ten a.m. in Tijuana. Mateo would be up and about unless he was screwing one of his whores.

David viewed his steaming cup of coffee.

*Better hold off drinking it. I'm jittery as it is.*

He tapped Mateo's number into the encrypted satellite phone.

"David, you're calling at a decent hour for once."

"My apologies for my previous emergency calls. This is a routine report about Lucas."

"Go ahead."

"He unlatched his truck toolbox, and I saw two ghost guns. He's not a cop. I asked him to dump them."

"Sounds reasonable."

"If the cops find him killed, they'll search the farm and ask questions."

Mateo exhaled. "I'll call off the hit until after he gets rid of the guns. Demand to see his toolbox tomorrow. After Carmen agrees to our terms, Lucas's death will appear to be accidental."

"*Si*, Boss."

Mateo hung up.

David felt his shoulders relax.

*I'm glad I didn't say Lucas is a good fit.*

# SIXTY-FOUR

## EARLY EVENING, SATURDAY, AUGUST 10

TWO S*ICARIOS*, Mexican assassins, Jorge and Alonzo, sat in their black rented van. They had hidden the vehicle behind a bush on a Hardwood Lane turnout. From their concealed location, Jorge monitored the Spicer Farm's entrance and driveway. Although Jorge was sweaty, he was as calm as a hunter in a blind watching for prey.

Jorge lifted a pair of compact binoculars to his eyes. He viewed the bunkhouse door. "I see Lucas. Get ready to tail him at a distance."

Alonzo turned on the van's engine. "All set."

"Wait 'til he's out of sight before you roll."

Jorge studied the map displayed on his cell phone's screen. Tonight, he and Alonzo were working on a backup plan. They wanted to find places where they could ambush Lucas on a route he often drove. The optimal location would be secluded, where the two hit men could fire their silenced AK-47s without fear of detection.

Jorge felt like he was in command of an important military mission. He glanced at his mobile phone's display. On it, he saw a map and an icon symbolizing Luke's truck. The tracker on the target's vehicle sent location data through the Internet.

Jorge figured alternate plans like this one were important because Mateo often changed his mind.

Lately, Mateo had been as wishy-washy as Jorge's hare-brained girlfriend. First, the drug lord had said, "Kill him and make it look like an accident." Then Mateo had asked them to murder Lucas and hang his body from a bridge. Later, Mateo had ordered them to wait for further instructions.

Alonso put the van in gear after Lucas's truck crested a steep hill and disappeared. "How far back should I be?"

Jorge glanced at his apprentice, Alonso. "Catch up. Keep the pickup in sight. Drive at a steady pace. If you lose him, I'll tell you which way he went. If he turns, pass the place he turned. Stop up the road, turn around, come back to where he turned, and follow his path. I'll track him on my mobile if he changes his route."

While the two men followed Luke's truck, Jorge had an idea for a new way to kill Lucas, should Mateo change his mind again and call for an "accident." He'd seen Lucas's bottle of ginger ale in the fridge in the barn. He could spike the drink with fentanyl. He had gelatin capsules containing super-lethal doses of the tasteless, odorless, and deadly drug.

# SIXTY-FIVE

## LATE SATURDAY, AUGUST 10

THIS EVENING the living room in the Ford farmhouse was lit by dim lamps. A gentle, warm wind wafted in through the screens, carrying the smell of damp vegetation and crops into the house.

A chorus of insects vocalized in the humid night.

Luke felt the comfortable warmness of Layla next to him. Their arms wrapped around each other, they rested on the couch. She buried her face against his chest, holding him close. Little Angela was in bed.

The soothing nearness of Layla made Luke realize he'd missed her a great deal during his Spicer Farm undercover duty.

*I want it to end.*

He took slow, even breaths, and his tension faded.

Layla stirred. "You okay, honey?"

"I'm happy cuz I'm with you." He kissed her neck. "I wish I would'a got out of the Spicer covert thing when I had the chance."

Layla rubbed his chest. "You and me both." She kissed his cheek. "Let's enjoy the moment."

"But I gotta be at the Spicer place tomorrow."

Layla straightened up. "Put your worries aside. Let's get in bed. We need each other."

"I'm thinkin' about the baby. What's he or she gonna be like?"

"I wondered that, too." She kissed him. "Let's talk about girl and boy names and make love." She turned off the lights.

Luke smiled in the darkness. "I like your plan." As he and Layla stood to go to their bedroom, worry invaded his thoughts.

What would Layla do, if a bullet, a bomb, or a knife took his life? He'd committed himself to finding Mark's killer, but was it worth the effort? Mark was dead and gone. In a while, the memory of him would fade away, though he'd been a famous horse trainer. The world would go on whether or not his killer was caught. But at that moment Luke decided he had to catch the murderer to serve justice.

Luke didn't relish the idea of getting out of bed before dawn on a Sunday morning. The forecast called for a gray day with light sprinkles and then a round of heavy rain and thunderstorms to arrive after sunset.

Like artillery during a battle, thunder and lightning would pummel the land. It was as if the Norse god, Thor, was determined to hammer the Kentucky fields and farms. But then again, wasn't Thor supposed to be the protector of humankind, according to lore?

# SIXTY-SIX

WHILE THE THUNDERSTORM RAGED, Luke, still dressed in blue jeans and a work shirt, sat in a chair and peered out the window of his Spicer mansion bedroom. Lightning flashed across the midnight sky, and a bolt struck the woods across the road. The building shook.

Rain pelted his window. All of a sudden the heavy downfall lessened, and the storm lost its intensity. Luke heard the weak wind moan. Then what sounded like a scream of pain echoed through the night. The constant screeches came from the outsized barn. Were the high-pitched shrieks those of an injured person or a horse?

Luke rushed to the back entrance of the mansion, pulled the door ajar, and listened. Mixed with the sound of the smattering of fat raindrops, he now heard distant humanlike groans coming from the horse barn. He stepped into the drizzle of the misty night. He ran, splashing through puddles toward the barn entrance near David's office.

As Luke yanked the door open, a deep, guttural roar came from halfway down the barn's central passageway. He moved at a fast pace past stalls. Horses were vocalizing, responding to his presence.

A sudden crack of thunder sounded near the barn. At least three thoroughbreds kicked at their stall walls and roared.

The odor of ozone drifted into the barn while another wave of heavy rain pounded the roof.

A thoroughbred screamed in pain and kicked the stable wall. The sign above the animal's stall read, "Fast Guy." He was the horse Ali was going to buy for two million dollars. Luke thought the stallion would destroy its stall when the animal kept kicking the wooden walls, bucked, and screamed in pain.

Luke saw a lengthy gash on Fast Guy's side where a saddle would rub. Blood streamed from the cut. "I gotta get a vet to treat it," he said to himself. He raised his voice. "It's okay, boy. I'm gonna help you."

Luke grabbed his phone and tapped David's name on the device's contact list.

"Luke, why the hell are you calling this late?" David's voice sounded like he'd been asleep.

"Fast Guy spooked and cut himself on the stable wall. He's bleedin' like crazy. You gotta call a vet."

"I'll be in the barn soon. The vet's contract says he won't come after five p.m. on weekends."

Luke figured the injured horse was too upset to approach. Instead, he talked to it with a soft voice. The storm weakened, and a gentle rain began to patter on the barn's roof.

Fast Guy was calmer by the time David arrived. He studied the horse before unlocking the stall. Both Luke and David neared the injured animal.

David blinked. "This gash is the longest I've seen on a horse. I hope I have enough iodine and bandages in my office to patch it." He hurried away.

Speaking in low tones, Luke took two steps toward the tall stallion. "Easy. You'll be okay." He stroked the horse's mane.

*Seems to like me.*

The horse peered at him with curious eyes. But the

animal's wound still bled. "Ali will be as mad as a hornet sprayed by bug killer when he hears about you."

David came back with a bottle of iodine and a roll of gauze. "This isn't enough to do half the job." He paused. "Can you hold this?" He handed the medical supplies to Luke.

David withdrew his cell phone from his hip pocket. "I'm going to call Steve, the owner of Kobold Farm down the road. He'll have bandages."

Luke figured David wasn't all bad. At least the Mexican cared for animals.

David had his phone against his ear.

* * *

## 12:15 A.M., MONDAY, AUGUST 12—KOBOLD FARM

Steve, the owner of Kobold Farm, heard his cell phone ring. After a quick sip of bourbon, he set his shot glass on the coffee table. The call was coming from David, the Spicer Farm's barn manager.

Over the previous three years, David had helped him when he needed it. He was more apt to assist him than Mark had been, even though Steve and Mark had been buddies years ago, from boyhood until early adulthood. Steve was glad David was calling. He'd been trying to invent an excuse to contact him.

"Hi, David. I'm awake, having a nightcap. What's up?"

David was breathing fast like he was short of breath. "The storm scared Fast Guy. He spooked and started to buck and bounce against the stable wall. He has a severe cut. We're short of bandages and iodine."

Steve recalled Fast Guy was a superb thoroughbred. "Come over. By the time you are out front, I'll have a box of medical supplies ready."

"I can't go. The horse is bleeding. Our man, Lucas, can pick it up."

"Have him knock on the main house front door." Steve

paused for two beats. "After you get this under control, give me a call. I have to ask you something."

"Will do. Speak to you later this morning. Gotta go."

Steve figured he'd convince David to have a one-on-one private meeting with him. It was of the utmost importance to move fast to make a deal.

# SIXTY-SEVEN

## 12:30 A.M., MONDAY, AUGUST 12—KOBOLD FARM

A LIGHT DRIZZLE was falling when Luke pulled into the Kobold Farm driveway. He guessed his Dodge Ram pickup had been coughing because it wasn't warmed up. He was impressed by the white Kobold mansion, lit by floodlights. It appeared to be twice the size of the Spicer Farm's stately residence.

As his truck rolled to a stop, it coughed and backfired with a noise as loud as a pistol shot. The large house's front door opened. Luke saw a man's backlit shape in the doorway. The man was of average build and five foot ten, Luke estimated. The man waved. "Come in. I heard you arrive." He laughed.

When Luke pushed on the pickup's driver's side door, its hinges squealed. He exited his truck and eased its door shut. "Are you Steve?"

"Yes, sir. I take it you're Lucas." Steve held out his hand.

Luke shook Steve's hand. The man had a weak grip. Luke felt dead tired. "I better git them medical supplies back to David quick. Fast Guy is bleedin' like a stuck hog."

"Step inside out of the rain while I get the box of supplies."

Luke entered the foyer. Its floor was marble, and the walls inside the entrance were paneled in a dark wood. Within seconds Luke sized up Steve, who had brown hair and eyes and a thin face. He wore tan slacks and a short-sleeved sports shirt. He didn't act rich, but he must've been worth tens of millions of dollars.

Steve went from the foyer into the front room and bent down to pick up a medium-sized cardboard box. As he stood, his nose began to bleed. Blood dripped on one of the box flaps. He snatched a handkerchief from his rear trousers pocket and poked the monogrammed cloth into his nose. "Damn. I have an appointment to get my nose cauterized next week."

"I had the same problem. My doc used a chemical swab to treat it, and I never had the problem again."

Steve handed Luke the box. "Thanks for the encouragement."

Luke nodded and left.

Steve waved, still pressing his handkerchief over his nose with his other hand.

After getting into his truck, Luke ripped part of the flap from the box where Steve's blood had dripped. He pulled an evidence envelope from under the driver's seat and put the cardboard into the packet.

# SIXTY-EIGHT

## 9:15 A.M., MONDAY, AUGUST 12—SPICER FARM

SUNLIGHT STREAMED into the windows of the dining room in the Spicer mansion. The severe thunderstorm the previous night had cleaned the air. But high winds and lightning strikes had splintered ancient trees in the woods across from the Spicer Farm's main gate.

Luke sat in the sunshine sipping coffee at a walnut table.

*I'm as sleepy as a bear about to hibernate.*

Finding Fast Guy injured, picking up bandages and iodine at the Kobold Farm, and helping David patch up the horse's severe wound had kept him up until three in the morning. And on Saturday, he'd stayed up late with Layla and left for the Spicer place before dawn.

He glanced out the window and saw the vet's truck leave. Carmen and David stood on the gravel driveway watching the horse doctor depart.

Carmen turned. Luke could tell she'd seen him staring out the window. She waved, and Luke did, too. She appeared fresh, dressed in a short calico dress.

The heavy oak dining room door swung ajar. Carmen entered, smiling. "I heard you were a hero taking care of Fast Guy."

Luke thought the hardest thing he'd done was to splash through puddles. Talking to the horse was easy. "I didn't do much. David did the bandaging while I kept Fast Guy calm."

Seeing no china cups, Carmen picked up a paper cup, filled it with hot water, and dangled a tea bag in it. She sat in the chair next to Luke, and he could smell her perfume. "David said you went next door to get bandages and iodine from Steve."

Luke shrugged. "I'm surprised Steve was still up. He got the medical supplies himself."

Carmen set her paper cup down. "Steve's a hands-on guy. He and Mark had known each other since they were kids."

Luke wondered if the two men had socialized, gone to a bar to drink, or played cards. Would encouraging Carmen to talk about Steve lead to her divulging clues about Mark's murder? "Did the two guys get together much?"

Carmen bit her lip. "Not since I've known them."

"Did they grow apart and go their separate ways?"

Carmen toyed with her cup of tea. "Mark said they were once buddies. When they were kids, they used to hang around at both of their farms. Later, they did a lot together in high school and during their early twenties." She peered at the ceiling as if she were trying to remember details of what Mark had told her. "Then Mark and Zoe started going out. She was Steve's girlfriend throughout high school and after graduation."

"Did they become enemies?"

"No. But they were professional competitors. Mark was a great thoroughbred trainer, and Steve is, too." Carmen paused. "When Mark married Zoe, Steve was broken-hearted, so he broke off his friendship with Mark. But they often talked during their annual farm parties."

"Did Mark divorce Zoe?"

"No, she died of ovarian cancer." Carmen peered at her feet. "Mark met me after her funeral, and we married soon afterward."

Luke rubbed his chin whiskers.

Carmen leaned forward. "Because the two of them didn't forgive each other after Zoe died, it changed their lives."

Carmen stood and added hot water to her cup. "They were rich kids who never learned how to deal with people in the real world."

"How do you know Steve didn't wise up after he and Mark went separate ways?"

Carmen sipped her tea, and then let a breath out. "I've talked with Steve lots of times. Steve's never going to grow up, and he's too effeminate for my tastes."

Luke's curiosity was piqued. Had Carmen bedded Steve? If she had, did he still desire her? It didn't sound like she cared for him. Luke figured he'd keep asking questions. He still hadn't learned enough about Mark, except the man had stolen his friend's girlfriend and married her. Luke took a sip of coffee and gathered his thoughts. "Did Steve ever marry?"

"No. Like I implied, he's not the type many women would prefer." Carmen frowned. "He also holds grudges. When he stopped socializing with me, he'd say brief hellos and goodbyes, but nothing else."

"How'd you meet Mark?"

She swallowed a sip of tea. "I was waiting tables in Lexington at the Palmer Restaurant. It's a high-class place. He asked me out. I loved his personality. We had a whirl-wind courtship and married. In retrospect, even though he was handsome, he *was* eighteen years my senior. He was like an older brother...I shouldn't have said that. Forget it."

"Duly noted." Luke stood and filled his coffee cup. "You're the owner of a famous horse-training farm."

"I didn't want it. I'm not a country girl." She picked up her teacup and trained her eyes on Luke. "This place would've gone out of business if Mark hadn't started to launder drug money."

Luke sat again. "I heard a few horse farms are losing money."

Carmen shrugged. "Steve's Kobold Farm is in trouble."

"You think it's gonna go bankrupt?"

"Who knows?" She tossed her empty paper cup into the trashcan. "I have to finish some work in my office. See you later." She smiled and left.

Luke got up, peered in the wastebasket, and used a pencil to pick up Carmen's paper teacup. Then he put it in an evidence bag.

# SIXTY-NINE

**11:15 A.M., MONDAY, AUGUST 12**

DAVID PULLED his tall pickup truck into the Minnow Creek Recreational Center's parking lot and waited for Steve to arrive in his expensive red sports car.

Why did Steve want to meet in a parking lot away from prying eyes? In case Steve said something Mateo would want to hear, David had put his encrypted satellite phone in his glove compartment. Steve's request to meet had been unexpected and strange.

Steve was cordial and helpful when David needed to borrow a tool, or even bandages for a horse, but something was off about him. Though rich, he acted like a country bumpkin.

When David rolled down his driver's side window, he heard a car rolling over gravel. Steve's sports car stopped next to David's truck.

Steve swung his legs out of his shiny vehicle and stood. He wore a baseball cap, sunglasses, slacks, and a sports shirt. He neared David's open window. "Let's sit in the shade." He pointed to a bench.

"Okay." David wiped sweat from his forehead, reached in his glove compartment, and grasped his satellite phone.

It was quiet and cooler where the two men sat on a bench under a massive tree. Steve leaned forward. "Sorry for all the cloak and dagger stuff, David." He eased back on the bench. "To come to the point in an abrupt way, you guys at Spicer Farm launder drug money."

David's eyes flickered. "What?"

Steve leaned forward. "Years ago Mark and I were buddies. Of late, less so. But I still talked with him once in a while. I heard three years ago he had severe money problems. Then you and the Mexican sugarcane farmer, Mateo, started buying expensive horses from Mark for cash, horses he had trained. Then Mateo resold them."

David shrugged.

"To be specific, Mateo sold them to a Saudi prince who paid by wiring money to Mateo's bank." Steve first frowned at David and then smiled. "Come on, David. Let's stop playing games. I'm not the police. I want to make a deal."

"What are you suggesting?"

"I'll sell my top horses to Mateo for cash. Small denomination bills would be okay. He can board his thoroughbreds on my farm until he sells them." Steve took a moment, seeming to think about what to say next. "To be honest, I have money problems like Mark had."

David rubbed his chin and studied Steve. Steve was no idiot. At least he had accurate information. Mark's thoroughbreds had attracted the attention of the Saudi prince, Ali ibn Saad Ahmad al-Awazim. Two or three years ago Ali had bought two of Mark's horses in a package deal from Mateo for three million dollars. The skinny, insanely rich prince had wired the funds into Mateo's bank account. Ali was awash in oil money.

Mateo had visited Mark's horse farm once after buying the first two horses from him. He'd told Mark he owned a sugarcane farm. Mark must've told Steve.

David put on a smile. "Mateo is rich. He indulges in expensive hobbies."

Steve nodded. "Yep, but one hobby isn't expensive, racing pigeons."

David laughed. "True. I remember Mateo saying it's a lot cheaper to race pigeons than horses."

Steve removed his cell phone from his pocket. He selected the photos icon on the device's display. In three seconds he found a picture of a dead pigeon. It had a mini sack attached to its back. "This is one of Mateo's carrier pigeons. I think you know what's in its backpack."

"It's not one of ours." David felt jumpy.

Steve zoomed in on the dead bird's photo. "It flew with a group of a dozen birds over my farm heading your way. This pigeon must've been sick because it plummeted to the ground. I had my birding binoculars with me. The rest of the birds flew into your horse barn."

David had come to love homing pigeon competitions after Mateo had started his pigeon racing club, *Club de Las Aves*. As part of his deal with Mateo, Mark had agreed to hire David to be his barn manager. Mateo also had asked Mark to allow his pigeons to be housed in the Spicer horse barn loft. Because of the many pigeons roosting in the barn, David had hired two Mexican friends to take care of them. David's wandering mind returned to the present. He fixed his gaze on Steve. "At times new birds will join a flight of pigeons."

"No need to make excuses." Steve smiled. "I won't contact the cops. I want to make a deal." Steve shrugged. "The picture is in a safe place with my affidavit should I die."

David took a deep breath. "I still believe the bird belonged to someone else. But Mateo is always on the lookout for fine horses. I'll give him a call." David pulled his satellite phone from his pocket. "Please wait."

"Here's a fact to mull over before you call. Mark taught you how to train thoroughbreds for three years. But it'll take more experience than that to become a well-known trainer. I'm the top trainer in Kentucky ever since Mark passed away."

"I'll mention it to Mateo."

Steve nodded and leaned back with both his hands behind his head.

David got into his truck and touched Mateo's name on the satellite phone's contact list.

\* \* \*

DAVID GATHERED HIS THOUGHTS. Mateo would be irate when he learned Steve was blackmailing the *Nuestro Club* cartel. Mateo would order his two hitmen to execute Steve.

*I must convince him not to take brash action.* He tapped Mateo's name on the encrypted satellite phone.

The phone rang six times. The cartel leader's distinctive voice boomed through the speaker. "What's happening, David?"

"We have a problem, but also a great opportunity."

"What?"

"A famous thoroughbred trainer who owns the Kobold Farm, which neighbors the Spicer place, Steve, has a picture of one of our pigeons with a backpack of pills. I assume he has the packet of pills, too."

"What's he want?" Mateo's voice sounded as irked as a bully who'd been poked in the ass by a pin.

David had to take a quick breath before continuing. "He wishes to join *Nuestro Club* as a partner and sell us horses for cash. He says small denomination bills would be fine."

"I should have him shot." Mateo sounded like an angry bull.

"Boss, before ordering a hit, please understand Steve has written an affidavit and stored it in a secret place with the pills and pictures. These items would be given to the *policia* should he die."

"You mentioned an opportunity. What is it?"

"Steve is the leading racehorse trainer in Kentucky. Mark had been the best. We've bought the majority of the thoroughbreds with the best bloodlines that Mark trained for the last three years. But now Spicer Farm doesn't have any more well-trained, elite horses ready for sale."

"Wasn't Mark teaching you how to develop winning thoroughbreds?"

"Yes, but I admit I haven't fully mastered the art of horse training."

Mateo was silent for an extended time. "David, you have a cooler head than mine. You are honest with me and give me excellent advice. Let's work with Steve on a trial basis."

"*Si*, Boss."

"I want you to tell him we are members of the Colombian cartel, *Los Hermanos*."

"But he already knows we are Mexican."

"Tell him we started a rumor to confuse the authorities." Mateo laughed. "If he squeals to the cops, they'll go after the Colombians. Lucas is working for them. If Lucas happens to die, the police will focus on *Los Hermanos*, and we'll move our operation elsewhere. I'm considering California."

David had to concede Mateo was shrewd. He was like a master chess player, thinking of possible moves and what the result of each would be. "A fine idea, Boss. I'll convince him we're Colombians."

Mateo was silent again. David imagined him deep in thought. Mateo's voice broke the silence. "If Steve works out, we'll move our operations to the Kobold Farm."

"What about Carmen and Spicer Farm?"

"All Carmen knows how to do is drink, take drugs, and screw. But keep the whore, if you want." Mateo disconnected.

# SEVENTY

CARMEN STRODE out the back door of her mansion into the clean air and sunshine to take a walk. It was a relief to leave her stuffy office.

*Where is Lucas?*

Once in a while, he'd disappear, as would his antique pickup truck. Antique was a generous description. She laughed. It was a mobile hunk of junk. As she thought about Lucas, she sighed.

Even when she'd made blatant passes, she had struck out with him. She had noticed he didn't display his emotions, but held them in check. Yet he *did* like her. She knew it.

*He's an interesting guy for a cartel member. But at breakfast why had he asked numerous questions about Mark?*

Her cell phone rang from inside the pocket of her calico dress, breaking her train of thought. "Hello, David."

"Carmen, I have a surprise for you. Come to my office, if you can."

"I'm on a walk."

"There's a man I'd like you to meet. But he has to go soon."

Carmen wondered why David was insistent and secretive. "Who is he?"

"A member of *Nuestro Club*."

"Be in your office soon. I'm close to the barn." She ended the call. In recent days David had been acting like her boss instead of her employee.

*Nuestro Club* was keeping the farm afloat, she figured. If she agreed to their "business" offer to keep the farm solvent, she'd never get out of it. She'd be trapped in a web of criminality, illegal drugs, and money laundering. She furrowed her brow.

Carmen entered the barn's rear entrance. David's office door was open a crack. Leaning close to the entrance, she heard quiet voices speaking Spanish. She straightened up and rapped on the door.

"Come in." David's voice was half an octave higher than normal, which told Carmen he was nervous. She sensed he was as jumpy as she was. Why was a Mexican member of the *Nuestro Club* cartel visiting?

The office door was ajar. Carmen pushed it. A tanned Latino man dressed in an expensive tropical-style suit sat next to David's desk. A bulky suitcase rested on the floor by him. David straightened in his comfortable desk chair and then pasted what seemed to be a nervous smile on his lips. "Carmen, thanks for coming on short notice." He gestured toward the man. "This is Rafael, our courier."

Rafael smiled, stood, and extended his hand. "Carmen, it's a pleasure to meet such a stunning lady." He grasped her hand. His grip was gentle, yet she felt an urge to take a half step backward. He'd spoken with a slight Spanish accent.

"Nice to meet you, too." Carmen found it hard to smile. She took her hand away from his.

David gestured at two chairs near his desk. "Please have a seat."

Carmen selected the wooden chair nearest the desk. As she settled into her seat, she noticed a brand-new, five-foot-tall safe near the far wall of the office. She pointed. "Where'd that safe come from?"

David sighed. "Mateo thought he'd invest in one." He paused. "Rafael, go ahead and show her."

Rafael hefted his big suitcase and placed it on David's desk. After unlocking it, he clicked the luggage snaps and opened the case.

Carmen's eyes gaped open. Benjamin Franklin's face stared at her from bundles of cash. The suitcase held stacks of hundred-dollar bills. "What's going on?"

"This is our payment for your horse, Fast Guy," David smiled. "Impressive, isn't it? Two million dollars for one thoroughbred."

David tilted his head. "And we'll board it at Spicer Farm until Ali takes the animal off our hands."

Carmen felt blood rush to her face. She hadn't been pleased when David had announced earlier that Mateo had bought Fast Guy, without consulting her first. Her anger grew, but she bit her lip. She blinked. "It's too much money for an injured horse."

"You heard the vet. The cut's not severe." David patted one of the bundles of bills. "This isn't the only cash coming your way. You're now one of our valued partners."

Carmen was silent.

David's smile was ultra-wide, and his teeth gleamed in the beam of sunlight coming through the window. "Mateo and I have come up with a scheme to make life easier for you. I'll keep your cash in the safe, do all the paperwork, and hire tax lawyers and consultants. When you need money, ask, and I'll write a check for whatever you require using a Spicer Farm checking account. For tax purposes, it will appear your draws come from the overall profits of the farm."

Shock hit Carmen's stomach. She felt defeated. Nauseous, she swallowed and tried to smile. *Nuestro Club* already had her in its grasp and under its control. She was snared in a net from which she saw no means of escape. "Are you going to put the money in the safe?"

"Later. Yours is old and not as secure."

She had excellent eyesight.

*I could remember the combination if I see him unlock it.*

David glanced at Rafael. "Can you tell Carmen the curious facts you related to me about the money?"

Rafael grinned. "Ten thousand hundred-dollar bills add up to a million dollars. Each million weighs twenty-two pounds. The suitcase is heavy—in excess of forty pounds."

Carmen glanced at David and tried to remain calm. "When will Ali come to get Fast Guy?"

"This afternoon." David paused. "He wants his trainer to work with the horse on the Diablo Farm. Later, he'll bring him back and board him here."

"What about the gash?"

"The vet said it would heal soon."

Carmen felt an urge to drink. She noticed a fifth of bourbon on David's shelf. "Let's all have a drink."

David stood and grabbed the bottle. He set three shot glasses on his desktop, poured the drinks, and handed one to Carmen.

The bourbon felt warm as it flowed down her throat. Alcohol was her true and loyal friend.

*I'm going to get drunk today. It'll do wonders, at least for the present.*

# SEVENTY-ONE

WHILE DAVID PACKED Carmen's two million dollars in cash into his late-model safe, he decided he'd call Mateo.

*Even if it's stretching the truth, I'll tell him she accepted the cash. At least she didn't object.*

The safe door clicked shut with the sound and feel of a precision machine. David twirled the lock's dial and let out a sigh of relief. Carmen was now a member of *Nuestro Club*. A fine piece of ass, she shouldn't be discarded like a pet her owner no longer desired. Yes, Mateo was now her master, just as Mateo had been David's master for years.

David clenched his fists.

*Mateo's a fickle man. There has to be a way to ensure he doesn't change his mind again about Carmen.*

After unlocking his desk drawer, David grasped his satellite phone, took three deep breaths, and called Mateo's number.

"*Hola*, David. You get the money yet?"

"*Si*, Rafael arrived sooner than expected. Carmen seemed pleased. I believe in reality she's now a member of *Nuestro Club*."

"Excellent." Like he often did, Mateo became silent, as if thinking. Then he spoke. "I don't trust Lucas, as he calls himself. My Bogota contacts have checked into Joseph Murphy, a.k.a. Lucas Blanco. They've learned nothing."

David wondered if he should speak or not, but his urge to do so was strong. "Should I fire him?"

"No. Don't be surprised if he is killed in a mishap. The Colombians won't be upset with us if their spy dies in an accident."

All of a sudden David's throat felt dry. "Carmen will be sad."

Mateo laughed. "She'll find a new lover."

"I suppose she'll continue to cooperate."

"She's one of us, and everybody knows once a member, nobody quits *Nuestro Club*." Mateo paused for two seconds. "Besides, if it works out with Steve and his Kobold Farm, we won't need Carmen and Spicer Farm unless we decide to combine them."

"Boss, I like your idea of combining the two farms."

"Let's see how the situation evolves, and then I'll decide if we'll keep both of them." Mateo hung up.

# SEVENTY-TWO

## 3:00 P.M., MONDAY, AUGUST 12

SAUDI PRINCE ALI rested on the leather seat in the back of his chauffeured black limousine. The air conditioning was nice in this humid Kentucky climate.

Though hotter, the desert air of Saudi Arabia was dry and often pleasant, superior to the sticky air of the Bluegrass State. Even the climate in London, England, where he owned a modest mansion, was better than Kentucky's. True it rained in the UK, but its atmosphere wasn't unbearable.

Ali turned to peer from the rear window of his limo. The truck pulling his empty horse trailer was a hundred meters behind him.

*It's a disaster Mark's dead. If he'd lived, I wouldn't have needed to find a new trainer and take Fast Guy to the Diablo Farm.*

Stroking the mane of his newly purchased animal would calm him. He loved horses. Earlier that day, he'd wired the payment for the thoroughbred to Mateo's bank.

His driver turned Ali's limousine onto Hardwood Lane. In three minutes Ali spotted the entrance to the Spicer Farm and its hundreds of feet of driveway. As his two vehicles followed the gravel driveway, they kicked up a modest cloud of dust. The limo as well as the truck that pulled the horse trailer halted by the front entrance of the Spicer mansion.

Ali saw Carmen sitting in the shade on a fancy lawn chair. She held an iced drink in one hand. She set her beverage on an oval table and got up.

Ali figured he'd never get accustomed to the way Western women dressed. In his country, women wouldn't dare to wear risqué garments such as the one Carmen wore today. A mid-thigh, low-cut dress exposed an ample area of her chest and much of her shapely legs. She wore no head covering, which was considered scandalous in parts of the Middle East. Yet Ali felt pleased, titillated by the woman.

Carmen walked toward Ali's limo in an unsteady gait. The driver opened Ali's door, and he emerged. The humid, hot air enveloped his face and body.

Carmen extended her hand toward him. "Welcome. I heard you'd be picking up Fast Guy." She had slurred her words.

Ali felt her gentle hand as she shook his. He smelled alcohol on her breath. "It is a pleasure to see you again, Carmen. I convey to you my sympathy for the death of Mark. He was the best trainer in Kentucky, one of the finest in the world."

"Thank you. I heard you're taking Fast Guy to the Diablo Farm for training."

Ali nodded. "Herman DeLong is a superb trainer at Diablo. I think I can convince him to work for you." Ali had decided to convey his reservations about David with subtlety. "Mark said he was teaching David to be his backup trainer, but alas, David still has much to learn. But I heard he's a great manager of your farm's affairs."

Carmen was quiet for two beats and then asked, "Are you going to bring Fast Guy back to my farm to board him?"

"Yes, in two or three weeks."

Carmen studied the grass at her feet and then peered into Ali's eyes. "I'm sorry about what happened to Fast Guy last night."

Ali frowned. "What?"

"Late last night, thunderstorms upset Fast Guy. He bucked, and cut his side on the stable wall. Didn't David tell you?"

"No." Ali recalled David had called yesterday afternoon to say Fast Guy was for sale. Ali wondered why the man had neglected to text him or email him about Fast Guy after the horse had been injured. But, of course, the animal had been hurt late in the evening. "How serious is the wound?"

"It's eight inches long, but it's shallow. The second layer of skin was cut for a half-inch." Carmen's words were less slurred. "The vet stitched it and said Fast Guy would heal in two to three weeks."

"Excellent."

*Should I continue to board horses at Spicer Farm? David is a fine clerk, but he needs to improve his communications with his customers. On the other hand, Carmen is a nice lady, though a loose woman. If I can convince Herman to hire on with Spicer Farm, I won't have to change farms. Money greases wheels.*

Carmen smiled in a delightful way.

Ali's loins tingled. "I must meet David to get my horse. It's always a pleasure to see you, Carmen." He patted her hand and left for the horse barn.

# SEVENTY-THREE

**3:58 P.M., MONDAY, AUGUST 12—SPICER HORSE BARN**

TWO MEXICAN ASSASSINS—JORGE, and his young partner, Alonzo—were mucking stalls. Jorge leaned on his shovel. He didn't like the smell of horse shit and piss, but monitoring the communal refrigerator near David's office was crucial. He recollected David's words. "Lucas takes a break in the late afternoon to drink ginger ale."

A half hour earlier, Jorge had reached in the fridge and taken out a sandwich. He had also dropped a gelatin-coated pill of pure fentanyl into a half full plastic jug of ginger ale labeled "Lucas." The opened bottle of soda was Jorge's one option because Lucas's second ginger ale container was sealed shut.

Jorge believed the gelatin capsule would dissolve fast in the acidic soft drink. *Nuestro Club* chemists had chosen a type of capsule made to melt in water in a short time.

Alonzo tapped Jorge on his shoulder. "Why don't you work harder? If Lucas ODs, we need to seem like we're real stable hands."

Jorge's eyes flashed. "You're the trainee. Until you learn the trade, you must do the dirty work when required."

Alonzo kept quiet, scraped the flat shovel across the stable floor and pushed dirty straw into a pile.

Jorge whispered, "He's near the fridge."

Alonzo gazed past the row of stalls and saw Lucas staring into the refrigerator.

\* \* \*

## 4:02 P.M., MONDAY, AUGUST 12

Luke was hot and sweaty. Today's late afternoon was sizzling and steamy humid. He noticed someone had moved his ginger ale bottle aside in the industrial-sized refrigerator.

He snatched his plastic jug and unscrewed its cap.

*This is gonna hit the spot.*

He lifted the container to his lips. Then he noticed what appeared to be a plastic residue near the bottom of the bottle.

*Could be ground up plastic in the ginger ale.*

The ginger ale didn't fizz. He turned to the sink, emptied the bottle, and tossed it into the recycle barrel.

*Lucky I didn't drink plastic crumbs.*

After unscrewing the lid of his second bottle, he swigged ginger ale and felt refreshed. He took the cold bottle with him. He reckoned he could drink it when he visited Carmen. If she was still drunk, he'd try to get her to drink ginger ale like he did.

\* \* \*

## 4:07 P.M., MONDAY, AUGUST 12

Jorge had excellent eyesight. It helped when he was observing, tracking, and aiming at people on his hit list. He noticed Lucas had stopped an instant before taking a drink of the ginger ale and fentanyl mix.

Alonzo stepped close to his older partner. "What happened?"

"He tossed the ginger ale bottle into the barrel without drinking. Then he unsealed a full bottle."

"Why?"

Jorge had the same question. Chances are the capsule had not disintegrated. He'd hoped the cold, acidic soda would've dissolved the gelatin ampoule in minutes. The ginger ale container had felt frigid, though. The icier the liquid, the more time the capsule would take to break down. "I think the kill pill didn't melt fast enough, and he saw it."

"What's Mateo going to say?"

Jorge rubbed his arms. "I dread calling him. But he asked me to report." Jorge paused to reflect. "Next time, I'll wear gloves, stick a pin in the pill, and squeeze the drug into his drink."

# SEVENTY-FOUR

CARMEN LEANED TOWARD A LIQUOR CABINET. Loud knocks sounded on her locked office door. Unsteady, she straightened. Wobbling, she felt as if she were in a carnival funhouse. Her office walls seemed wavy.

*I'm wasted.*

"Wait a second," she slurred. Taking her time, she made her way to the door and peered through its peephole. Luke stood outside and held a green bottle of ginger ale.

After struggling with the deadbolt knob, she unlocked the door. "Lucas, how come you're here?" Her words were unclear.

"I brought you ginger ale." Luke held up a bottle.

*I gotta brush my hair.* She blushed when she realized how disheveled she was. With shaking fingers, she combed her hair, but it didn't improve her appearance.

"Come in." Carmen locked the door behind Luke. She began to think faster.

*Why has Lucas been asking questions about Mark? Does he still work for the Colombian cartel? Is he planning how to take over the Mexican drug business on her farm? Can I trust him?* He'd lied about being Lucas, a simple farm worker.

She collapsed on her couch as Luke stepped to the shelves behind her desk and grabbed two glasses. "I heard you bin imbibing." He filled a glass with ginger ale. "Ginger settles the stomach."

Her nausea made her feel rotten. "I'll try it."

*He's getting me ready for a sales pitch from the Colombians,* she thought.

Luke handed her the carbonated drink. "One of these days, you wanna go with me to a LifeRing session?"

Carmen felt the cold glass in her hand and watched the beverage bubbling. "I think you made up the AA story like you made up a girlfriend."

"No, I go to LifeRing or AA sessions no matter what city I'm in." He paused. "I bin in your shoes. Take a sip of ginger ale. You'll feel better."

Carmen drank half of her soft drink. "Feels nice and cool." She touched her hair. It was mussed. "I'm going to freshen up. Be out in a minute." She pointed at the bathroom door in her office.

Luke nodded, sipped his soda, and leaned back on the sofa as she approached the restroom.

Carmen brushed her hair. Feeling flushed and hot, she removed her calico dress, as well as her sandals.

*I don't give a damn what he thinks.* She pulled on the door-knob, stared at Luke, and smiled.

# SEVENTY-FIVE

VV, Mateo's private investigator, sat in the crummy desk chair in his motel room, tired of being alone. "I gotta get out of this place," he said out loud as he stared blankly at a PGA golf tournament replay on his TV.

He lit another cigarette, blew smoke into the hazy air, and grabbed the local restaurant guide from the desktop. His beer belly rumbled, and he coughed as he lifted the cover of a loose-leaf binder.

Under the headline "Top Quality Eateries" he read, "The Last Furlong Restaurant is rated by customers as four-star-plus for excellent food, drink, and decor."

He scratched his black hair and then tapped in the restaurant's phone number on his cell phone.

"Last Furlong Restaurant," a woman answered.

VV exhaled, and smoke drifted from his mouth. "I want to make a reservation."

"How many and what time?"

"One. How about five tonight?" He sucked on his cigarette. Its tip glowed.

"We're booked until seven."

"Seven's fine." Smoke poured out of his mouth as he spoke. He coughed.

"How shall I list your reservation?"

"Mark it as VV."

"VV?"

"Yeah, those are my initials."

"Thank you. We'll see you then."

# SEVENTY-SIX

AS CARMEN EMERGED from her office restroom, she felt Lucas's eyes on her. It made her feel sexy. "I'm too hot," she heard herself say as she neared him. He was sitting on her sofa. She thought he'd gulped. "I hope you don't mind."

Luke stood. "I'll set the AC to sixty-five." He turned and walked to the thermostat.

He was attractive. Out of Luke's sight, Carmen took off her bra. When he turned toward her, she saw him blush through his tan. She didn't remember him having blushed before. "Sit by me. We've got to talk."

Luke's eyes showed a fire she hadn't seen before. "I can't do this. My girlfriend's pregnant."

Carmen felt her chin quiver. A wave of strong sadness hit her like a tsunami. Her body shaking, she moaned as she wept. She wiped tears from her face and forearm. "I don't want to live anymore." She felt herself panting, and then uncontrollable sobbing began.

*I need a tissue. I can't stop.*

Luke was next to her. He reached into his rear pocket and handed his handkerchief to her. "I'll pour another glass of ginger ale for you."

"Thanks." She felt grateful, but ashamed.

Luke refilled her glass. She drank. The soda's coolness flowed down her throat, and then she set the tumbler down. Without warning, a second spell of weeping struck her.

Luke sat next to her and patted her back. She buried her face in his shirt. It felt soothing.

*Is this the final time he'll be near me?*

"Don't leave me." Her words streamed out without consulting the logical side of her brain. She didn't regret them.

*I'm in love. But it's hopeless.* Her tears flowed again. She understood her emotions controlled her.

Luke studied her. "I wouldn't have said anything if I'd known it would'a hit you so hard."

She peered into his eyes. "It's not your fault. It's me. I fell for a great guy, but you're taken."

"I'll still be your friend and bodyguard." He paused. "You should get dressed and relax. Then we can drive someplace and get a takeout hamburger. I have an idea how to make you feel better, too."

Carmen sniffled and swallowed. "Okay, but give me a few minutes to wash my face and dress."

# SEVENTY-SEVEN

## 5:45 P.M., MONDAY, AUGUST 12—LUKE'S OLD TRUCK

LUKE PULLED on the passenger door of his timeworn pickup truck. The ancient, rusty door hinge squealed in protest. He turned to Carmen. Her face had been blotchy after her crying spell. But now he couldn't tell she'd been weeping.

*She's an expert puttin' on makeup, 'cept her eyes are red.* He realized he was staring at her a second too long. "Sorry about the noise. The hinge needs oil."

"It doesn't bother me." She began to move to the truck's door.

"Hold on. I gotta move my shoppin' bag." Luke could smell the rotten garbage covering the steel box that held his Smith & Wesson pistol. The metal container sat at the bottom of the bag. He grabbed a dried banana peel and a hamburger bun and put them into a white plastic litter bag. Then he rolled up the shopping bag with the box and the weapon still in it. He shoved the paper bag behind the passenger seat. "Wait a sec, and I'll let you in. I'm gonna dump this." He tossed the litter bag into a trash barrel.

After he rolled down the passenger-side window, he helped Carmen get into her seat.

*The smell should go away when I start drivin'.*

Carmen smiled. "I'm hungry. Thanks for taking me out." She seemed happy, even though a half hour ago she'd been depressed and unable to stop crying.

The pickup started with a cough of noxious fumes, like it often did. "We could've taken yur vehicle, but I've got something in the truck you can try after we eat."

From the corner of his eye, Luke could see Carmen was examining his profile. "What do you have in mind?"

"Ever shot a crossbow?"

"No."

"One's hanging above the back window." In the rearview mirror Luke could see she'd craned her neck to view the bow. He'd put it there earlier, so she'd see it.

"Is it brand-new?"

"Yep. It's more accurate than older ones and easy to use. You wanna try it after we eat our fast food?" Luke figured if she shot the crossbow, it would make her feel powerful.

*She's feelin' helpless.*

"I'll try it." She reached behind her and up to touch the crossbow. When she turned back to focus on Luke, she grinned, and her eyes had a sparkle in them.

"You wanna try it before we eat, or are you hungry?"

She shrugged. "I'm not famished yet. Let's shoot."

"Down the road, I have a spot where I set up my target." Luke visualized Granger Park, where they could walk into the woods. He'd lead Carmen to the hill where he often did target practice.

The hillside stopped the arrow-like bolts that flew behind his target. His bow was an advanced design. It propelled bolts at five hundred feet per second and could kill a deer a hundred yards away. Luke figured he'd arrive at the park in fifteen or twenty minutes.

# SEVENTY-EIGHT

LUKE STOPPED his battered pickup truck in the far corner of the Granger Park visitor lot under a massive oak tree. The vehicle's engine dieseled and halted.

Carmen caught his attention. "Where do you practice?" A broad smile adorned her face.

"It's a hill I shoot into. It's a five-minute walk away." *She's either flying in the stratosphere or down in the dumps.*

Carmen unlatched the passenger-side door and slipped out. "It's nice to get away from the farm and all the commotion." She glanced at Luke. "Want me to carry something?"

Luke reached into the truck bed for a surplus Army duffel bag. "You can take the crossbow and quiver. I'll git them out of the truck after I get a hold of this."

"What's in the bag?"

"The target." Luke slipped it from the bag. He'd bought his crossbow target online and was pleased with it. A lightweight cube sixteen inches square, it had handles on the top to make it easy to carry.

Carmen moved a step closer to the target. "Nice design." Easy-to-see bullseyes were printed on four of the cube's sides.

After they arrived at the hill, Carmen watched as Luke stepped off twenty-five yards. He placed the cloth-covered, soft target on the grass against the base of the hill.

When he returned to her, Carmen was examining his crossbow. "Is it hard to load?"

"I'll show you." Luke pulled an arrow-like bolt from his quiver and powered on the green LED light in the nock, the notched tailpiece on the projectile's end.

"What did you do to the tail of the bolt?"

"I powered up an LED light. It'll turn on when the bow string shoots the bolt. Then we can see its flight path better."

Luke balanced the bow on the packed dirt at his feet. Then he put his foot in a stirrup at the front of the crossbow to hold it against the ground. With the weapon's safety on, he used a cocking rope to pull the bowstring up and back, locking it in place. Then he placed an arrow-like bolt on the bow's shooting rail and slid it backward. Finally, he slipped the bowstring into the notch on the nock near the rear tail feathers.

Carmen frowned. "I don't think I can do it. Seems dangerous."

"I'll load it for you." He paused. "Ever fire a rifle?"

"Yes. My dad taught me with a twenty-two. It had a scope."

Luke pointed to the scope on the crossbow. "You shoot a crossbow about the same way." He pointed at a lever on the weapon. "Here's the safety." He handed her the bow. "You go first. Okay?"

"Yes."

"Point toward the target, turn the safety off, aim, and squeeze the trigger." Luke hoped she wouldn't shoot the bolt wide of the target. He didn't relish searching for his bolts on the hillside.

Carmen lifted the weapon, disengaged the safety, and sighted. Luke noticed she didn't shake. After two seconds, she shot the bolt. Its flight path was a green streak, created by the tiny LED light in the nock. The shaft hit the target on the second ring from the bullseye. She laughed. "That shot was better than I thought I'd do."

"You did great." Luke pulled a second bolt from his quiver. "Let's shoot a half-dozen, and then we can find a fast-food joint."

"This is fun." She paused. "Do you hunt with this?"

"Yep. I plan to go deer huntin' this fall." He took the bow from her hands to reload it. "This bow's the latest model. The older ones can kill a deer at fifty yards. This one is effective up to a hundred yards."

Carmen nodded. "Wow. But is it as accurate as a rifle?"

"No, but if it's not too windy, I can shoot a pattern an inch across at a hundred yards."

"So, the new bows are much better than the old ones."

He began to reload his bow. "Yep. Let's see if I can hit the bullseye."

# SEVENTY-NINE

## 6:58 P.M., MONDAY, AUGUST 12—LEXINGTON

VV, the PI, pulled into the Last Furlong Restaurant's parking lot and stopped near a picture window. He saw four Lexington Police squad cars parked nearby.

*Cops must be having a party. Or they're on a call?*

Pushing his heavy body up and out of his car, he felt winded.

*I gotta eat less. Yeah, right. I've tried that. I'll never lose my extra thirty pounds.*

VV had arrived at the restaurant at his reservation time. While his table was being prepared, he told the greeter he'd wait at the bar.

The pert blond hostess smiled. "I'll come get you when your table's ready."

VV spotted one of two unoccupied barstools. Easing up onto one of them, he glanced to his right. Six police officers stood and others sat in a glassed-in private room. He recalled having attended similar gatherings when he'd been a Louisville policeman. Two more officers entered the separate dining area as he watched.

*One man in the crowd must've retired.*

The bartender caught VV's attention. "What'll you have?"

"Scotch on the rocks."

As the bartender turned away, a lanky Lexington policeman in uniform sat next to VV and nodded.

VV smiled. "Crowded for a Monday."

The young cop shrugged. "This place is always filled whenever I come in. It's the food and the atmosphere."

VV surveyed the barroom. Photographs of racehorses covered its walls. Glass displays encased colorful jockey silks. "I see what you mean." He paused. "What's going on in the private room?"

"Sergeant John Reilly's retiring. It's gonna be fun."

"I've been to similar parties when I was with Louisville PD." VV's mind flashed back five years ago to his own retirement party. He sighed.

The thin policeman grinned. "Brother, wanna join us? I bet you miss the camaraderie of being with fellow cops."

VV felt uplifted, less melancholy. "You sure it'll be okay?"

"No problem. I'll ask the lieutenant. He'll say it's fine."

"Thanks. You going to join them soon?"

"After the bartender brings my usual."

Within fifteen seconds the bartender set VV's scotch on the rocks on the bar and placed a pitcher of draft beer and a mug near the rail-thin cop. The two men left greenbacks for the barkeeper.

VV got off his barstool and grabbed his drink. "I'll catch up. I gotta cancel my reservation."

The policeman hefted his beer pitcher. "No need to do it. I'll tell the little blond doll up front you're with us."

"Thanks." VV shook the cop's hand. "I'm Victor, but everybody calls me VV."

"They call me Parker."

# EIGHTY

**8:30 P.M., MONDAY, AUGUST 12—LAST FURLONG RESTAURANT**

VV SURVEYED the noisy dining room filled with cops. He took his time to turn his head because the room seemed to sway.

*Being buzzed feels good.*

He was confident he was still in control of his wits. True, normal voices sounded distorted, but he could listen and remember. Officer Parker had said the words "task force" loud enough that VV zeroed in on the man. But as Parker continued to talk with retired Sergeant John Reilly, Parker lowered his voice. VV no longer could understand what the man was saying.

*I gotta hear more.*

VV's inner voice sounded as clear as an operatic aria, even though his thick tongue made it hard for him to pronounce words. "Excuse me," he slurred as he slipped past two conversing policemen. They sipped drinks and ate delicious-smelling meatballs from paper plates.

VV strained to listen. Parker was speaking. "…it's a long name," Parker said indistinctly in a quiet voice. "Ah lemme see. It's the…Task Force…Anyway LPD's in it with the FBI,

DEA, ATF, IRS, and a bunch of other…Something's going on with drugs and horses…"

"Holy Christ," VV whispered below the noise of the loud talk in the room. He couldn't hear what else Parker said. *I gotta call Mateo.* VV waved at Parker. "Thanks for the invite, Parker. Gotta go."

Parker smiled and waved back.

As VV headed for the men's room, he muttered in a low voice, "Loose lips save ships, too." He'd call Mateo from the inside of his rental car. His encrypted satellite phone was in the vehicle's glove compartment.

# EIGHTY-ONE

AFTER HE'D STAYED awake for almost two days, Luke lay on top of his bedspread, still dressed. His heavy eyelids closed, and he saw soothing darkness. It was as if he were viewing a black screen in a movie theater.

All of a sudden, a colorful panorama popped into his vision, and he was aware he was dreaming. He saw green, rolling hills. Beautiful horses grazed behind hundreds of yards of wooden, chocolate-brown fences on both sides of a blacktop country road. He stood on the highway, peering up at where it crested a steep hill. Should he get off the roadway before a speeding pickup truck barreled down onto him?

He tried to move his legs. They wouldn't budge. It was as if he were bonded to the blacktop. While he struggled to get his body to work, he heard the distant, echoing gallop of a horse on the pavement. Luke's eyes searched ahead to the top of the hill. A horse with a man atop it crested the hilltop, traveling at breakneck speed. Then the swarthy Latino came racing down the hill, his Mexican sombrero flapping in the wind. The sound of the pounding hooves of the tall, jet-black animal hammering on the asphalt increased. The rider raised a rapier above him like a cavalryman. He whipped the weapon's blade back and forth.

The sharp cutting edge whistled as it sliced through the air. Still stuck to the pavement, Luke struggled and felt his eyes open wide. His heart galloped like the steed, faster and faster. He tried his hardest to move. Fear hit him like a sudden storm. He tried to scream, but not even a whisper would come from his mouth. He couldn't breathe. The horse was close. Luke saw the beast's wild eyes.

Grinning, showing his bright teeth, the rider swung his razor-sharp, gleaming sword down at Luke's head. Black shadows invaded Luke's dream.

Luke felt like he was floating. All of a sudden, he saw his decapitated head rolling on the blacktop road. Terror coursed through his body like an electric shock. The dream seemed real. As his heart pounded yet faster, a frigid blackness descended upon him. He closed his eyes, and his fear melted into relief, as if he'd died and rested in peace.

The wind whistled.

He asked the darkness, "Where am I?"

"Open your eyes, and ye shall see." The voice had been deep and sinister.

Luke struggled to lift his eyelids. A full moon shone above him in the night sky, visible through a misty fog and the bare, dead branches of a tree. He cast his eyes downward. Lit in the pale light of the moon, Layla held a baby and grasped little Angela's hand.

Three tears ran down Layla's face. The drops sparkled in the moonlight. Layla stood near a tombstone in the blowing mist. Luke felt icy. He squinted. The headstone read, "Under this soil lies Deputy Sheriff Luke Ryder, who died in the line of duty."

On the verge of hyperventilating, Luke awoke all of a sudden and sat up straight. He got out of bed and washed his face.

# EIGHTY-TWO

## 8:51 P.M., MONDAY, AUGUST 12—THE LAST FURLONG RESTAURANT PARKING LOT

VV HELD a bottle of ice-cold water. He sat in his rental car in the restaurant parking lot, nauseous. He swallowed a sip of the water. He wished the frigid liquid would dilute the bile in his stomach. He'd vomited three times into a toilet pot in the men's room until he had dry heaved.

"I'm gonna have a hell of a headache tomorrow." He'd spoken to the emptiness in his vehicle. "But getting plastered was worth it."

He hoped he wouldn't puke again. He'd left the driver's side door ajar just in case. "Gotta call Mateo ASAP." His words were distorted.

After filling his lungs with air, he exhaled and gulped water. Then he reached into the glove box to remove his satellite phone. Resting against the back of the car seat, he forced himself to relax. He touched Mateo's name on the device's display.

"VV, why the fuck are you calling after business hours?" Mateo's ferocious voice battered VV's brain. In the background, VV heard a woman's voice and the squeak of a mattress spring.

"We got trouble, Boss." VV spoke in a drunken voice. "A federal task force is investigating drugs, horses, and money laundering in the Lexington area." He'd spoken indistinctly, and he wasn't positive Mateo understood him.

"How do you know, you drunken sonofabitch?"

"Cuz I had dinner with a bunch of plastered Lexington cops." Though his words were clear in VV's mind, they sounded drawn out like an audiotape playing back at slow speed. "One talked about what he should've kept secret."

Mateo was quiet for at least three seconds. "Victor, sorry I jumped on you. You did a terrific job, even if you had to get hammered to get it done." He laughed and then paused for at least five seconds. "We need to take action." His voice sounded serious.

"What do you want me to do, Boss?"

"Confirm your finding." Mateo again was silent as if he were planning a chess move. "I'm going to pull the plug on the Spicer Farm operation. If you hear from people in our gang, tell them to follow Plan A."

"Plan A?"

"Yeah, they'll know what to do. By tomorrow night at this time, they will have left the farm, after destroying all the evidence they can. They'll leave one by one to arouse less suspicion." He paused. "I'm sending the jet to Knoxville to pick up our men."

"Anything else?"

"I'll let you know." VV could hear Mateo breathing in and out. "I'll wire a healthy bonus to your account. When we regroup, I'll let you know our substitute location should you decide to rejoin us."

VV felt his stomach was ready to erupt. "Thanks, Mateo."

"I must wake up David and two others. Gotta go."

VV hung up and puked on the parking lot surface.

# EIGHTY-THREE

HIS ENCRYPTED SATELLITE phone rested on the sheets next to David, whose snore was as disturbing as the growl of a Rottweiler.

The phone rang. David coughed, sputtered, awoke, and snapped on the bedside lamp. The brightness of it blinded and roused him. After he snatched his satellite phone, he saw Mateo was calling. "Shit." David's voice echoed in his single room.

On the seventh ring, David smiled, trying to lessen his displeasure. He answered in an easy-going voice. "*Hola*, Mateo. What's up?"

"We have severe trouble. VV learned a federal task force is investigating horses, drugs, and money laundering in the Lexington area."

"Shit."

"I've set Plan A in motion. Our jet will pick up you and the guys in Knoxville. I'll let you know when later."

"*Si, Senor*." David rubbed his eyes. This was a turning point in his life. What would the coming days bring? A rush of adrenaline streamed through his body.

"The final flight of pigeons should arrive by four tomorrow afternoon your time. Unload all product and dispose of it. You'll be the last to leave except for the two *sicarios*. Evacuate the rest of the men at intervals."

"Yes, Boss." David felt his mouth dry up. "Will the *sicarios* take care of Lucas?"

"Yes. Lucas is still a member of *Los Hermanos*. There's no doubt he's spying for them. The *sicarios* will make his death appear to be the work of the Colombians. This will help us make the authorities believe you and the men are from Bogota."

"But everybody knows we're Mexicans."

"To the task force, it will seem like we lied about being Mexicans to deceive law enforcement. The feds will go after the Colombians. In a year or two, when everything's forgotten, we can come back to Kentucky."

"You mean at Kobold Farm?"

"It's a possibility, but not with Steve as a partner. We'll see." Mateo paused. "Get going. I've got to roust the *sicarios*." He disconnected.

David perched on the edge of his bed and tossed his phone aside. It bounced on the mattress.

*I'm not going to sleep for a day or two. I'll get a cup of coffee and wake the guys.* A rush of regret hit him. Watching over the farm and the horses had been a joy. Now it was over.

\* \* \*

## 1:30 A.M., TUESDAY, AUGUST 13—SPICER BUNKHOUSE

Jorge had expected Mateo's call ever since David had awakened him to say Plan A was in effect. Jorge was not pleased he and Alonzo were to stay behind and take out Lucas.

Jorge and his trainee, Alonzo, sat in the dim interior of their mid-sized, run-of-the-mill sedan. The vehicle was in the far corner of the Spicer Farm's parking lot.

Jorge wondered, *What's Mateo going to require this time for the Lucas hit?*

Tapping his foot on the car's floor, Alonzo coughed. "How are we gonna get away, if everybody else is taking the jet?"

"We'll be on a long road trip in this car, *amigo*. Don't fret."

Alonzo blinked, obscured in the low light inside the sedan.

Jorge's satellite phone rang. "Hello, Boss."

"You know about Plan A."

"*Si*."

"Are you ready to act?"

"*Si*, Boss."

"Do you still have the items to make it seem like the Colombians killed Lucas?"

"*Si*. I wrote on a white blanket with a black marker, 'Death to those who cross *Los Hermanos*.'"

"Perfect, but add, 'This is what happens to snitches.'"

"Consider it done, Boss." Jorge took a quick breath. "Should we hang the body from a bridge?"

"No. I prefer you get away as fast as possible."

"Anything else, Boss?"

"I also want you to deal with Steve Kobold, who owns the farm abutting the Spicer place. He tried to blackmail me. This is how I want you to handle it…"

# EIGHTY-FOUR

## 10:30 A.M., TUESDAY, AUGUST 13—INSIDE LUKE'S TRUCK PARKED ON HARDWOOD LANE, OUT OF SIGHT

HIS PHONE AGAINST HIS EAR, Luke waited while Jim's cell phone rang.

"Hi, Luke. Anything happening?" Jim's voice was upbeat.

A fluttering sensation in Luke's stomach felt strange. "Nothing. That's why I'm callin'." All of a sudden Luke recalled the end of his vivid dream. In his mind's eye, Layla held their newborn baby. His tombstone with its epitaph appeared. In rapid succession he asked himself, *Am I losing my nerve? What'll Jim think?*

"Still on the line, Luke?"

"Yep." He paused. "We're not gettin' anywhere." Luke's lips seemed to be working without his control as if they had a mind of their own. "I should leave the farm, and the task force can raid it. They'll find plenty of evidence, including drugs and money. Carmen will talk, and she'll be a lot safer after y'all raid the place."

Luke heard Jim begin to breathe faster. "Let me take it up with Rita and the rest of the task force." He paused. "I'm glad you came to your senses. You'll soon be a new father."

Luke felt a wave of shame combined with guilt rush through his body for having asked to end his undercover role.

*Am I a coward?*

He decided to change the subject. "Do you have results from the DNA I bagged at the farm?"

"Nothing yet. I asked the lab to put a rush on it. We should have answers in a day or two."

"Thanks, Jim."

# EIGHTY-FIVE

ON THE OUTSKIRTS OF LEXINGTON, sunlight beamed into Rita's motel room. It served as her temporary office while on deployment from the Louisville FBI Field Office.

She sat at a desk. Her nimble fingers tapped on a laptop computer's keys. In her role as a member of the Spicer Farm Task Force, she was updating a plan for a joint FBI/DEA raid of the farm. As she thought of how to word her next sentence, she paused and gazed through her window at the green grass and trees.

*We have probable cause. We shouldn't delay.*

Her cell phone sounded, cutting short her train of thought. "Hello, Jim."

"Luke called minutes ago. He believes he's hit a dead end. Said he doesn't think he'll dig up anything new."

"I thought the same thing." She sighed. Luke's judgment and his intuition were excellent. Of course, nobody was a hundred percent perfect. But he was often three steps ahead of everyone else.

Jim's strong voice grabbed her attention. "Luke thinks he

should leave the scene, and the task force should raid it soon."

"Guess what? I'm updating the plan to raid the farm."

"When do you suggest we act?" Jim's words came quicker than normal.

"ASAP. We should coordinate with the team leaders this afternoon in the motel's meeting room, let's say at two?" She paused. "We could hit the farm tomorrow."

"I'll pull Luke out later tonight."

Rita smiled. "See you at two." She hung up.

*Dick the DA may not approve of the raid, but politics shouldn't get in our way.* Rita figured Dick would be happy after the raid was done. *He'd get plenty of credit for the arrest of the cartel members.*

Rita began to call the task force members, starting with the DEA agent in charge.

\* \* \*

## 10:40 A.M., TUESDAY, AUGUST 13

Jorge and Alonzo rested in their black sedan parked on a turnout on a country road. The little-used gravel lane led to Granger Park's rear entrance. The vehicle's air conditioning blew a cool breeze on Jorge's face. After Mateo had given them the order to kill Lucas, Jorge had devised a new plan.

Glancing out the car window, Jorge caught sight of the dark green sedan he'd leased first thing that morning to drive to the airport, where he'd leave it. If he couldn't hire a helicopter, he and Alonzo would take out Lucas in the park instead of from the air.

Jorge tapped Kentucky Helicopter's phone number on the keypad of his mobile phone. The company operated from Lexington Bluegrass Airport.

"Kentucky Helicopter. This is Felix."

"I'd like to hire a helicopter able to seat at least three passengers for a flight late this afternoon until after dusk." Jorge spoke with a Spanish accent.

Jorge heard Felix flipping through papers. "We have a chopper available."

"What's the cost?"

"Five hundred dollars an hour per person, payable in advance." He paused. "We'd use one of our larger military surplus birds."

Jorge wouldn't use a credit card. He preferred to pay cash. Mateo had agreed to wire money from an untraceable account in the Bahamas to the charter flight company if cash was not acceptable for some odd reason. "How can I pay?"

"By credit card."

"Do you take cash?"

Felix yelled something Jorge couldn't understand. He figured the man had put his hand over the phone's mouthpiece. Then Felix came back on the line. "We'll take cash. How many hours do you think your flight will be?"

Jorge shrugged. "Two hours. I'd like to take off at seven." Sunset would be around eight-forty p.m. He'd board the helicopter by himself, unarmed. He was staring at the field near the turnout. "I have a special request."

Felix sounded like he'd sipped coffee or water. "What?"

"This flight is a surprise birthday present for my brother, Alonzo. I'd like you to fly me to a field by Granger Park and land. My friend is taking Alonzo to the park. He knows nothing about this. When the chopper lands, he'll be astonished."

"Since you'll be by yourself for the first leg of the flight, I'll reduce the bill by five hundred bucks."

"Thanks. It's generous of you." Jorge paused. "I'll pay you twenty-five hundred, okay?"

"Yes. Try to arrive by six-thirty."

"Okay." Jorge hung up.

Alonzo took a quick breath. "What should I do if Steve gets wary?"

"Pull your gun, handcuff him, and shove him in the trunk." Jorge smiled. "Don't worry. Mateo said Steve wanted to make a deal with us. He'll be cooperative. But remember, tell him we're with the Colombian cartel."

Alonzo seemed less nervous. "Mateo was smart when he told Steve he would meet him in person."

Jorge smiled. "Yeah, Mateo's shrewd. And he's trying to make it seem like the Colombians have been running Spicer Farm, not we Mexicans. It'll give us a better chance to get away."

Jorge exited their black car and headed for the green sedan he'd leased.

# EIGHTY-SIX

3:45 P.M., TUESDAY, AUGUST 13—SPICER FARM HORSE BARN

LUKE KNEELED behind a stack of bales in the horse barn's loft. The bales of hay had a fresh, sweet smell. He'd rearranged them so he could peer through a crack and see the pigeon coops and roosts. *Might as well do somethin' useful on my final day.*

Pigeons often arrived in the late afternoon, and then one of the Mexicans would climb the wooden stairs to the loft.

*They could be takin' drugs off the pigeons and hiding them in the loft.*

The noise of someone's shoes coming up the rough pine steps caught his attention. He'd felt a microsecond of surprise and then prepared to act. Taking his cell phone from his hip pocket, he was ready to shoot a video. He was surprised when David stopped at the top of the stairs.

*First time I seen him near the pigeon coops.*

David held a shopping bag. After surveying the area, he walked to the pigeon coops, unfolded a lawn chair, and sat.

*He's waitin' for the pigeons.*

Two minutes later the first of the birds fluttered through the loft window.

One by one, David removed the diminutive packs from

the backs of the pigeons. He tossed their undersized parcels into his shopping bag.

Luke counted the pigeons as they arrived. David continued to gather their packets. After a dozen birds had come through the window and he'd snagged their cargo, David left.

Luke wished he could've taken one of the pigeon's bundles and put it in an evidence bag, but it was not to be.

*At least I got a video of it.* He shared the link to the video on the cloud with Jim and Rita.

After he'd checked that no one was around, Luke descended the wooden steps and headed for his bedroom in the mansion.

"It's a relief to be leaving," he whispered. He felt happy as a dog with a ham bone.

He figured he'd pack his personal belongings and toss his suitcase in his truck. At dusk, he'd stop at Granger Park on the way back to his rented farm to practice with his crossbow.

Jim had said he'd let Luke know if he was supposed to take part in tomorrow's raid. Jim and Rita were scrambling to organize the team. He reckoned they'd be awake most of the night.

# EIGHTY-SEVEN

THE HELICOPTER VIBRATED like a massage chair as it flew over the rural gravel road leading to Granger Park. Jorge spoke into his headset microphone. "I'll blow your brains out if you don't do what I say." He held a big blue pistol against the back of Felix's head. The helicopter's left side door had been slid back. Air was whipping at Jorge's face as he peered down at the winding country lane. Both he and Alonzo occupied the rear, left-hand side seats of the chopper. From them, the two *sicarios* could fire their silenced AK-47s.

Felix was breathing hard. Jorge realized the guy wasn't in a panic. He was mad as hell. Felix turned his head toward Jorge. "If you shoot me, we all die."

Jorge was beginning to like Felix. He had balls, but Jorge figured he'd have to set the man straight. "If you don't follow directions and land this thing before I say, you'll die." He paused. "If you'd like to make better money, cooperate and come down to Bogota, and we'll increase your pay four times." Jorge was glad he didn't have to kill Felix. Mateo had ordered Jorge to convince the pilot that he and Alonzo were Colombian.

Alonzo inspected his cell phone's screen. "He's up the road about a mile."

Jorge scanned the road ahead. He spotted Luke's time-worn truck driving at a snail's pace. "When I tell you, swoop down and dive toward the old truck ahead." Jorge glanced backward at Steve Kobold, who was handcuffed to a pole in the back of the military surplus whirlybird. He appeared to be scared shitless. *He should be,* Jorge thought. *He doesn't have much time to live.*

The helicopter began to descend. Jorge and Mateo grabbed their AKs.

* * *

## 8:40 P.M., TUESDAY, AUGUST 13

The sun had set minutes ago. Luke had just turned onto the gravel back road leading to Granger Park. The night began to darken in this secluded place, and his dingy clothes blended with the dim light of dusk. The ancient pickup's headlights cast flickering yellowish beams ahead.

His muscles relaxed, and Luke sighed.

*It's a relief to leave Spicer Farm.*

He anticipated stopping at Granger Park on his way home so he could target practice in semidarkness with his state-of-the-art crossbow. He touched it and the quiver on the passenger seat. Like his Smith & Wesson, the crossbow was a friend.

He planned to use his side vision to sight his portable target when it would be lit by moonlight and the stars. Hunting a deer in twilight would be easier, but if he could make out and hit a target later in the evening, he'd be ready for hunting season.

After he'd gone a half mile on the gravel track, he saw the dim outline of a black car parked on a turnout. Then the whop-whop-whop vibrating sounds of helicopter props assaulted him from behind. A loud bang sounded at his right ear. It rang. The truck's back window and windshield shattered. Bits of glass showered him and the pickup's front seat.

He saw shiny bullet holes in the pickup's hood and dashboard.

*Bastards are shootin' at me.*

He slammed on the brakes. The truck slid on the gravel like a sled on snow.

The chopper hovered over the field to Luke's right. Two men sat on the whirlybird's left side facing out. They lifted their rifles. The weapons flashed and spit sparks. Luke heard bullets impact the right side of the truck as he dove down to his left. He twisted his back and hit his right shoulder on the steering wheel. It felt like he'd been punched. *Am I hit?*

In an instant, he snatched his crossbow and quiver. He kicked the driver's side door open.

*Lucky the dome light ain't been workin'.*

He rolled onto the road. Gravel bit into his side. The pickup's engine burst into flames. The explosion warmed his body. He rolled into a six-foot-deep ditch. The odor of singed hair made him realize how close he'd come to being incinerated.

Water in the bottom of the trench soaked his boots. He stepped forward. His feet felt like muddy suction cups had grabbed them. He peered over the top edge of the deep ditch. His truck was burning like a giant bonfire. It lit the surroundings in an eerie orange light.

Bam, bam, bam. Sharp reports of exploding ammunition came from inside the thirty-year-old truck.

*The SOBs burned up my Smith & Wesson.*

It was still jammed behind the passenger seat. Luke grabbed for his phone in his hip pocket. The device was gone.

*Must of fell in the water.*

The chopper's rotor noise changed pitch. Luke watched the whirlybird land in the field.

*I should load the crossbow.*

He put the bow's stirrup on a flat rock and grabbed the cocking rope from his quiver.

* * *

AFTER THE DEAD LEAVES, weeds, and dried grass kicked up by the helicopter's wake had settled, Jorge stepped onto the ground. He watched the flaming pickup. It lit the lonely gravel roadway in a fierce, ruddy-orange glow. When the chopper had landed, he thought he'd seen motion behind the truck in the dancing shadows beyond the fire.

*My eyes could be playing tricks on me.*

Jorge peered past the flames into the weeds on the far edge of the road. But the brilliant fire made seeing into the blackness futile. "Damn," he mumbled. He caught Alonzo's attention. "Cuff Felix to the landing struts." He turned on his flashlight. "I'll confirm the kill. Follow me when you're done."

Alonzo trained his AK-47 at Felix. "Get out."

A flashlight in one hand and his rifle in the other, Jorge started walking toward the burning truck.

* * *

LUKE SCRUTINIZED THE HELICOPTER. The silhouette of a man appeared near the mechanical bird. This man held a flashlight. Its beam moved back and forth across Luke's position.

Luke felt a short shiver of fear. He touched his side and felt his little SCCY pistol. It made him feel confident, though it was a weapon of last resort. The SCCY was a deterrent under fifty yards—better at twenty-five paces. But his new bow was accurate up to a hundred yards. Little wind was blowing. It wouldn't have much effect on the flight of his arrow-like bolts.

As the two assassins neared the burning truck with their AKs at the ready, Luke low crawled left on the bottom of the ditch. His stomach was burning like he'd swallowed battery acid.

*Damn, what a time to get heartburn.*

His temples pounded and sweat rolled down his brow

into his eyes. They stung. With his sleeve, he wiped perspiration from his forehead and eyelids.

The assassins were a hundred and ten yards away on opposite sides of the burning truck, approaching the effective range of Luke's crossbow.

*I'll shoot one. The second one won't know where the bolt came from.*

Luke leaned forward on the edge of the ditch between dense weeds and aimed at the man on the left. When his enemy was eighty yards away, Luke squeezed the bow's trigger.

The bolt zipped ahead, a trail of green light streaking behind it. With a thud, the projectile hit the assassin's chest. The *sicario* fell backward, the arrow-like bolt pointing upward from his chest at the night sky. The man made no movements.

Luke gulped. *Shit. I forgot to turn off the LED light in the nock.* The second gunman had to know Luke's position.

Luke dove down into the ditch. Within two seconds the second assassin fired a burst of three rounds from across the road—a hundred yards away. The slugs clipped the top edge of the ditch where Luke had been a microsecond before.

Luke's heart pounded. He kept low and crept to his right. His foe would assume Luke would flee left, away from where the shots had come.

After smearing mud on his face, Luke kept still in murky shadows under the lip of the ditch.

*I can't reload the bow.* He'd need at least fifteen seconds to do that. There was no way he'd stand up to do it and create a tempting target.

The second killer moved closer. He was sixty yards distant. Luke pulled his SCCY 9mm pistol from his holster. He cocked the weapon under his flannel shirt, trying not to make a noise.

*Come closer.*

If he fired his short-barreled weapon from fifty yards, Luke reckoned he'd have a fifty-fifty chance of hitting his enemy. But from twenty-five yards or less, he'd be certain to hit the assassin.

As the aggressor moved nearer, Luke picked up a stone with his left hand. He tossed it into the ditch water to his right. The rock splashed. Luke's enemy fired two bursts of three rounds. The bullets whizzed through the overgrown weeds, severing their woody stems.

Luke leveled his petite pistol. He aimed at the middle of the assailant's chest. Luke squeezed the trigger. The loud crack of the shot echoed along the ditch. He fired again. And again. He had eight rounds left. The bullets thudded as they hit home. The offender grabbed his shoulder. He dropped his AK. A fourth round smacked his knee. He fell like a bag of concrete.

Luke pushed himself over the lip of the ditch. He rushed forward. He kicked the AK aside and picked it up. He slid his SCCY back into his holster.

"Yur under arrest for attempted murder." Luke felt relief. "Make the wrong move, and yur dead meat. Lay flat on yur belly."

The man obeyed.

Luke felt pain in his lower left leg where his shinbone had been screwed back together. He ripped one of the man's sneakers off his feet and tied the offender's hands behind his back with shoelaces.

*He ain't goin' anywhere with those wounds.*

The ringer on Luke's cell phone disturbed the silent roadway. He glanced toward the edge of the ditch. The phone's display was lit. As he moved toward the device, his left shin throbbed. Grabbing his phone, he saw Jim was calling. "I need backup."

"What happened?"

"Two men tried to kill me, but I'm okay. I'm on a gravel road a mile from Route 42 near Granger Park. One perp's likely dead and the other's wounded. They flew in on a chopper. It's still runnin' in a field 150 yards north of me. My truck's on fire."

"I'll send in the troops. Maybe the highway patrol can send their chopper. Hold for a sec."

Luke thought Jim was taking too much time to get back to him. But the man was calm under pressure and had to be working as fast as he could. Luke heard him pick up his phone. "Cruisers and a chopper are on the way." He paused. "How are you dressed, and how are you armed?"

"I'm wearin' black jeans and a blue flannel shirt. I smeared mud on my face. I got my crossbow, my 9mm SCCY, and one of the perp's AKs."

"Hold again. I'm gonna radio out the info."

After three minutes, Luke heard Jim grab his phone. "Hey, Jim. A pilot must be with the perps' chopper. Chances are they don't know how to fly."

"Noted. Sounds like you've taken out the bad guys, though."

Luke heard helicopter noise. A spotlight beamed down and scanned the area near him. "The highway patrol chopper's above me." Luke, lit by the burning truck, waved at the pilot. The helicopter began to descend. "He's gonna land on the road."

"I'll hang up." Jim sounded relieved.

Distant sirens wailed, and their noise increased. An ambulance skidded to a stop.

* * *

KENTUCKY HIGHWAY PATROL SERGEANT BROCK MCCOY surveyed the scene below from the hovering police chopper. The remnants of a pickup truck smoldered in the roadway below. Occasional flames came to life from the burned wreck and then went out. The whirly-bird kicked up dust from the gravel road as the craft landed. Brock glanced at his pilot. "Must be the deputy in the dark pants and shirt."

The pilot nodded. "Fits his description."

Brock scanned the scene as he jumped from the chopper. The destroyed truck reeked of smoke.

The man in the dark clothes held an AK-47 while he spoke to an emergency medical technician and pointed to a man flat on his back in the field. The EMT and his partner ran to the person in the field. Beyond the EMTs a civilian helicopter stood in the meadow. Brock squinted. He saw a man sitting on the ground near the front of the distant chopper's landing skid.

Brock turned his attention to the man in dark clothes. As Brock approached the supposed deputy, he kept his hand on the butt of his Glock. A person lay flat on his stomach with his hands tied behind him.

*He must be one of the perps. I need to confirm the man in black is law enforcement.* "Sir, give me your name, please."

"Deputy Sheriff Luke Ryder. I don't have ID. I was undercover."

Luke appeared to be calm despite his brush with death. Brock gestured at the man lying prone on his stomach. "Who's he?"

"One of the two men who shot up my truck."

Brock nodded and then saw the EMTs running back toward him. As they came closer, Brock recognized one of them. "Jack, how's the guy out in the field?"

"Dead with an arrow sticking in his chest."

Luke pointed at the tied man at his feet. "This guy's wounded. I shot him in the shoulder and knee."

Jack glanced back and forth at Luke and Brock. "A man's sitting by the helicopter in the field and another guy's in the back seat."

Brock nodded. "I'll check it." As he turned to face the civilian whirlybird, he heard sirens and saw emergency lights in the distance. Within fifteen seconds, three squad cars arrived.

* * *

A HALF HOUR LATER, Luke's mobile phone showed Jim was calling. "Jim, the scene's secured."

"I'm on the way, Luke." Jim paused. "But I want to pass

on good news. The lab did a DNA test on Steve's blood from the chunk of cardboard you turned in. We also tested a drop of blood Alice found on the dead leaves near Ethan's body. It was Steve's blood. Odds are he killed both Ethan and Mark. Nice work bagging the bloody cardboard."

"Seems like I didn't waste my time grabbin' DNA after all. See you soon."

"Hang in there, brother." Jim disconnected.

# EIGHTY-EIGHT

## 3:30 A.M., WEDNESDAY, AUGUST 14—LUKE'S RENTED FARM

TIRED BUT ALERT, Layla sat at the wooden table in her farmhouse kitchen. She hadn't slept since Jim had called to say Luke had been in a shootout, but he wasn't hurt. She'd been worried because Luke had been due home at least an hour before Jim's call.

She recalled Jim's words. "I'll drive him home, but it won't be for hours. We have a lot to do tonight, but his undercover assignment is done. I wouldn't stay up waiting."

She'd felt relief and joy. "Y'all caught Mark's killer?"

"Keep it quiet. Yes. It's because Luke found key, incriminating evidence."

Layla's mind was busy. Even though Jim had advised her to go to bed, she knew she couldn't sleep.

A key turning in the back door lock and clicking it alerted her. She stood. A surge of delight traveled through her body.

Luke stepped inside. His clothes were filthy, encrusted in dried mud. "Layla, I didn't expect you'd be up."

She ran to him and hugged his chest, feeling his strong body next to hers. Her warm tears began to flow. "I'm glad it's over." She tilted her head backward and used her soft tongue to French kiss him. After what seemed forever, she pulled her lips from his.

He let her go, kneeled, and reached up to hold her hand. "I bin thinkin' of doing this for weeks." She could hear him choke up. "Will you..." He sucked in a lungful of air. "Will you, Layla, marry me?"

Layla found herself speechless, and tears streamed down her face. Luke was crying like a baby, too. "Yes, yes, and yes again. I love you, Luke." She fell to her knees. They caressed and kissed. Layla couldn't remember a time when she had been happier. She felt warm and content, yet excited for the future.

# EIGHTY-NINE

## 10:00 A.M., WEDNESDAY, AUGUST 14—DA'S LEXINGTON OFFICE

DICK, the DA, sat in his office at the head of his shiny walnut conference table.

*This prosecution is going to be easy*, he mused. *Steve Kobold is going to be locked up for life*.

Luke and Jim sat by one edge of the table, and Dick's assistant was on the opposite side near a conference phone. It was connected to a digital audio recorder.

Brilliant daylight streamed from the window behind Dick and lit the well-shaped face of the public defender, Jennifer Castro. She occupied a chair at the foot of the table. A Spanish speaker, she represented Alonzo, the teenaged Mexican hitman who'd survived the shootout with Luke.

Young and petite, Jennifer had bleached blond hair. An up-and-coming defense lawyer, she was as perceptive as a young female bald eagle. Dick had no doubt she'd soon establish a private practice.

Dick recalled the first phone call he'd had with Jennifer about Alonzo's case. She'd convinced her client he would be better off if he trusted her to represent him. She'd mentioned Alonzo's alternative counsel was a high-priced lawyer. He often represented drug cartel members, but he prioritized the cartel's interests over those of individual defendants.

Alonzo was willing to sing for the right deal, according to Jennifer. Alonzo remained in the hospital under guard.

Dick focused on Jennifer's brown eyes. "What do you propose?"

"My client is willing to plead guilty if the terms are agreeable."

Dick leaned forward in his swivel chair. He recalled Jennifer had said the *Nuestro Club* cartel had forced Alonzo to train as an assassin. The teenager also claimed he hadn't killed anyone. "We can reduce the charge to assault third, a class D felony, for his attack on a police officer. Alonzo would serve five years." Dick paused. "Because of his age, I'd argue to enroll him in our rehabilitation program, if he agrees to enter it."

Jennifer grinned. "We agree to the terms."

Dick smiled. "Excellent." He loved the benefits of Mark's murder having been solved. Convicting Steve Kobold for first-degree murder would assure Dick's re-election. Reducing Alonzo's charge was a worthwhile trade. Dick caught the attention of his assistant. "Chester, call the number."

Chester tapped a phone number into the disk-shaped conference telephone. A deep male voice answered, "Officer Conroy."

Chester leaned closer to the conferencing telephone. "This is the office of District Attorney Dick Troft. Could you please put Alonzo on the line?"

A bumping sound came from the speakerphone as the officer handed a handset to Alonzo. "Hello. I am Alonzo."

Jennifer leaned forward, her blond tresses dangling onto the tabletop. "Alonzo, this is Jennifer. We have a deal. Tell the DA what you know."

"Mateo, the boss of *Nuestro Club*, tell Jorge and me kill Lucas cuz Mateo say he spy for *los Colombianos*. Jorge ordered me drive Steve from Kobold Farm to turnout on gravel road close Granger Park."

Dick squinted. "Why did Jorge ask you to do that?"

"Cuz he say Steve ask Mateo for deal to launder drug cash. Mateo say he would fly in on chopper and meet Steve in field by park. But it a lie. Mateo want Steve dead. We was to kill Steve—dump body next to Lucas body and put white blanket with fake message from *los Colombianos* near them."

Dick felt a tingle of excitement. *This kid's testimony is great.* "Why did Mateo want Steve killed?"

"Cuz Steve have one of David's pigeon—it die and fall on his farm. It have pill packet on back. Steve blackmail Mateo. Steve said he would give a picture of the dead bird and drugs to police 'less Mateo start cleaning cash at Kobold Farm."

"Anything else?"

"Mateo say he know Steve kill Mark with drug powder. Mark partner with Mateo. Mateo say he mad after Tau Lang sell fentanyl powder to Steve."

"Who is Tau?"

"Top *Nuestro Club* dealer in Louisville. He say ain't no reason for user buy powder. Too strong. He think Steve do Mark."

"Anything else you want to say, Alonzo?"

"I scared *Nuestro Club* kill me in jail. Need protect me."

Dick sighed. "We'll figure out something if you continue to cooperate." He caught Jennifer's attention. "Anything else we should cover, counselor?"

"We're up-to-date for now."

Dick focused on the conferencing telephone. "Alonzo, thank you for your cooperation. Jennifer and I will be back in touch with you from time to time."

"*Gracias, Senor.*"

Dick nodded, and Chester disconnected the phone. Dick stood and shook hands with Jennifer. He felt her feminine touch, and then let go of her hand. "Thank you, Jennifer. I'll be in contact soon."

She smiled and left, closing the door after her.

Jim stroked his chin. "Alonzo will be an excellent witness."

Luke shifted in his chair and caught Dick's attention. "What are you thinkin' of doing about Carmen?"

Dick glanced down at his folded hands. Then he eyed Luke and Jim. "Unless I get solid evidence she did something illegal, I'm inclined to leave her alone. Her husband was murdered, and based on Luke's observations, she had no idea Mark was laundering money until after he died. David's been handling all the farm's financial transactions since Mark hired him. Luke said she was surprised when David sold an expensive thoroughbred to Mateo without her permission. We found no money in David's safe, and no drugs anywhere on the farm. Mark's safe had been cut open, and it was empty. I assume the Mexicans took the cash and drugs with them when they fled." He paused. "Jim, do you have any late word if the task force has a bead on the Mexicans?"

Jim rubbed his forehead. "We have no new developments." He furrowed his brow. "We figure somebody in the task force tipped off the Mexicans. I've been in touch with the Mexican *Agencia de Investigacion Criminal*. They have no record of a Mateo Guerra or a David Braga. The names are aliases."

Dick slumped. "Since they escaped in their vehicles, I'd think we'd get them soon."

Jim leaned forward. "What about the Saudi Arabian, Ali?"

Dick bit his lip. "We have no evidence he was aware he played a role in money laundering."

Jim's eyes flashed. "Have you ever met an Arab who doesn't know what's going on?"

Dick shrugged. "The feds will follow the money. They may charge Ali with something. Who knows?"

Jim sat up straight. "You gotta admit Ali's got balls to stay in the country."

Dick shifted his gaze to Luke. "To change the subject, congratulations on your upcoming marriage. I also want to commend you on getting the key blood evidence Steve dripped on the cardboard box. His DNA connected Steve to Ethan's murder."

Luke shrugged. "The credit should go to the crime tech, Alice Strom. She decided to check a drop of blood with a darker color than the rest of the blood on the leaves near Ethan's body. If she hadn't noticed the blood color difference, we wouldn't have nailed Steve for Ethan's murder."

Dick nodded. "Duly noted." He turned to Jim. "Could we give both Alice and Luke bonuses—and an extra week of leave? Luke and Layla should have a decent honeymoon."

Jim grinned. "I'm working on it."

# NINETY

## NOON, PDT, SATURDAY, AUGUST 17—MATEO'S COMPOUND NEAR TIJUANA

A YOUNG, tanned woman wearing a bikini carried a tray of lunch to Mateo's shaded table next to his Olympic-sized swimming pool. Mateo could smell the ribeye filet steak. He felt his mouth water.

"*Gracias, Angelita.*" Mateo admired her figure.

Angelita smiled like a Hollywood actress as she returned to the kitchen.

Mateo stood by the pool's edge, drying off from his swim in the cool water. *I better call David to see if he's settled in.*

Before he sat at his table, he grabbed his bottle of Tennessee whiskey and poured a shot. He sipped it and set the shot glass on his tray next to his plate.

*Whiskey goes well with steak.*

He sat and slid the metal chair closer to his table, causing a metallic screech.

He touched David's name on his secure satellite phone and heard a ringing tone.

*I hope nobody's figured out how to break into these phones. Messenger pigeons are fun, but they're slow.*

He heard David's voice. "*Hola,* Boss."

"Hi, David." Mateo smiled. He felt relaxed, and the smell of the humid swimming pool water combined with the taste of whiskey made him feel drunk and lazy. "I am calling to find out if you and the men arrived at the new location."

"California's like home. We made it with no trouble, thanks to the IDs you put on the plane."

"You're welcome." Mateo paused. "I have learned Lucas is a policeman, and he's Murphy's double. VV learned the real Murphy died in a car accident in Houston before Mark died."

"We all must have a twin someplace on Earth."

"Lucas killed Jorge and wounded Alonzo." Mateo sipped his whiskey. "I'm considering whether or not to put out a contract on Lucas—or Luke Ryder." Mateo was quiet for a while. "But Luke found DNA proof sufficient to put Steve away for life."

"Steve must've been nuts to kill Mark because of an old dispute."

"I liked Mark—a lot." Mateo exhaled noisily. "Steve tried to blackmail us. He's a snake. I should have him killed in prison."

David sighed. "But Mark was a loyal friend."

"Yes. I'll call you in a week so you can report your progress in restarting operations. Gotta go." Mateo hung up.

# NINETY-ONE

DRESSED in a short-sleeved shirt and jeans, Luke carried a stack of dinner plates to an extra-long picnic table. It sat on his farm's wooden porch, shaded by its roof. Luke could hear cicadas buzzing in the distance, and the air felt less humid than it had during the last three days.

Luke began to set plates on the tablecloth. His mind began to wander.

*I gotta let the guys know what to do for the hemp harvest.*

Jim had volunteered to supervise the farm hands Luke had hired to harvest his hemp crop while he and Layla were on their honeymoon in London, England. Luke's sister, Rene, would watch little Angela.

Luke heard crunching gravel in the driveway behind the house. In less than a minute, Jim climbed the porch steps with Carol Cuddy, the psychologist, on his arm. Jim grinned. "Luke, I see you're already domesticated."

"Layla has me wrapped around her little finger." Luke all of a sudden felt proud he was remarried, and his bride was pregnant. For years he had been unsure a second marriage would work for him. But when he'd proposed, he was positive he was right to remarry. He felt hopeful, happier, and ready to face whatever the future held with confidence.

Carol held an apple pie. "I'm going to go in and help Layla and Angela so you guys can talk." She made a beeline for the screen door and went into the kitchen.

Jim took a half step closer to Luke. "There are new developments in the Spicer Farm investigation."

Luke sat at the picnic table. "Have a seat and give me the lowdown."

Jim settled on a bench. "The Colombian cartel guy—Murphy, your double—died in an auto accident in Houston in April."

"Lucky the Mexicans didn't find out when I was undercover."

Jim nodded. "I gave our little crime scene specialist, Alice, the bonus you lobbied for."

"She deserves it."

Jim blinked. "Alice also tested gelatin capsules we found in the hitman Jorge's luggage. They each contained enough fentanyl to kill a man—sufficient to make death appear to be caused by an ordinary OD. Could be they planned to use them on you."

Luke rubbed his chin. "Being poisoned by fentanyl would've been hard to stop." He paused. "How's it going with Carol?"

"I like her. I know why you two were a couple. She's sweet and intelligent."

"I'm glad it's workin' out. Carol needs a man in her life." Luke paused. "Okay if I borrow her for a quick powwow? I wanna ask her about Carmen before she arrives."

"Carol will be happy to talk with you, I'm sure. By the way, the feds are still investigating Ali." Jim turned toward the screen door at the same time Carol pushed it ajar. "Carol, Luke wants to talk with you. I'm going in to help Layla."

Carol set a jug of lemonade and silverware on the table. She sat next to Luke. "What's up?"

"I gotta ask about Carmen."

"Ask away."

"Based on what I told you before, do you think she needs therapy?"

Carol sat up straight. "Yes. To be blunt, she's a classic nymphomaniac if all the rumors about her are true."

"Is it curable?"

"Therapy would help." Carol took a breath. "Two main aspects of nymphomania are loads of sexual drive, and many partners. Women with the problem often aren't satisfied by sex. They feel guilty and ashamed and could have problems with alcohol and drugs."

Luke bit his lip. "You described Carmen." He watched Carol's eyes. "Could you convince her to go into therapy?"

"If I get a chance to chat with her today, I'll try. I'd take her as a patient if she asks." Carol leaned on her chin.

"Thanks." Luke turned his head. "I think I hear a car comin' down the driveway."

"Anything else?"

"Ali has taken a likin' to her. He started to board two of his six horses at the Spicer Farm. And he helped her hire a barn manager and a master horse trainer. Plus Ali gave her an interest-free loan so she could keep operating the farm."

Carol glanced toward the sounds of footsteps around the corner. "I could help Carmen learn strategies to make her relationship with Ali last."

"The feds are investigating his money dealings." Luke paused a moment. "Keep it on the QT."

"No problem."

Carmen strolled around the corner.

Luke stood. "Welcome."

Carmen gave Luke a platonic hug. "Thanks for inviting me." She held a two-liter bottle of ginger ale in one hand. "I know you don't drink alcohol, so I brought this."

"Thanks." Luke nodded toward Carol. "I'd like to introduce Carol, who's a good friend. She opened a psychology practice a month ago."

Layla stepped out onto the porch. "I see another guest has arrived."

Luke reached for Layla's hand. "Layla, this is Carmen."

Luke sensed Layla was leery of Carmen, but neverthe-less, Layla grinned. "I'm pleased to meet you. Why don't you come in and let's chat while I check the chicken in the oven."

Carmen followed Layla.

Luke sat down again next to Carol. "I want to ask you about Steve, too. You remember I told you Mark's first wife, Zoe, died of cancer, and she'd been Steve's high school sweetheart?"

Carol nodded. "And from what Carmen said, Steve and Mark ended their friendship after Mark convinced Zoe to marry him."

"Based on those facts, what do you think of Steve?"

Carol leaned on her elbow and took a breath. "He's the sort of person who holds grudges for years and feels he must get even with all of those he thinks wronged him."

Luke folded his hands and peered at the sky. "He also killed Ethan, the drug pusher."

Carol sighed. "Steve has the personality type of a serial killer." She peered at Luke's farmland as if she was recalling something. "I've met Steve at least four or five times. He's charming in a fake way and manipulative. People say he's a habitual liar, and he thinks he's superior to everyone else. From what I heard from Jim, Steve showed no remorse for the two killings we know he committed. Losing his high school soulmate was traumatic for him. He may also have suffered abuse and neglect during childhood."

Luke leaned back. "If we wouldn't have caught him, yur saying he could'a killed a lot more people?"

"Yes." Carol turned her gaze to the screen door. "They're carrying out the food. We better help."

They stood.

Soon the group was eating and talking. Luke felt relaxed. *Can't wait to be on the plane to England.*

# NINETY-TWO

**7:30 A.M., FRIDAY, SEPTEMBER 6**

TERMINAL 8 AT New York's JFK airport was crowded, but Luke had a song in his heart. He held Layla's hand as they peered out the immense window at the British Airways jet. It would fly them to London's Heathrow Airport. Beyond the plane, the upper atmosphere was blue, and the warm sun was shining through the clear, cloudless sky.

Luke guided Layla closer to him and peered deep into her eyes. "I'm feelin' like it's Christmas in September."

"Me, too. Feels like butterflies are bumping around inside me."

Luke sucked cool air into his lungs and felt a smile form on his lips. He cast a glance at the crowd rushing by. "Let's not worry what people think." He pulled her against his chest. Her lips felt warm and tender as they kissed. They paused.

People stopped and smiled. Layla concentrated on Luke's eyes. "Kiss me again. I don't care if they see us, cuz I'm in love."

"Me, too." Luke kissed her with passion, and a dozen people clapped. Others cheered. He felt carefree, like he was soaring across the sky though he was still on the ground.

# IF YOU LIKE THIS, YOU MAY ALSO ENJOY: THE FINGER TRAP

## A TONY FLANER MYSTERY BOOK ONE
## BY JOHNNY WORTHEN

*When half measures don't get you the whole truth...*

Tony Flaner is a part-time comedian and full-time commitment-phobe who has never been able to stick with anything in his life. After his fourteen-year marriage ends in divorce, Tony's life takes a dramatic turn when a drunken party ends in murder.

With his life on the line, he must uncover the identity of the mysterious girl who was murdered and how they ended up together in the first place. This undertaking is not just about clearing his name—Tony needs to prove to himself and everyone else that he can finish something for *once in his life*.

But when Tony discovers that his fate is intertwined with that of the mysterious girl he hardly knew—and that their lives are connected like a Chinese finger trap—he unknowingly embarks on a journey full of twists and turns around every corner.

*Can Tony Flaner finish this one task and clear his name before he gets sent to prison for a murder he didn't commit?*

*AVAILABLE NOW*

# ABOUT THE AUTHOR

John G. Bluck was an Army journalist at Ft. Lewis, Washington, during the Vietnam War. Following his military service, he worked as a cameraman covering crime, sports, and politics—including Watergate for WMAL-TV (now WJLA-TV) in Washington, D.C. Later, he was a radio broadcast engineer at WMAL-AM/FM.

After that, John worked at NASA Lewis (now Glenn) Research Center in Cleveland, Ohio, where he produced numerous television documentaries. He transferred to NASA Ames Research Center at Moffett Field, California, where he became the Chief of Imaging Technology. He then became a NASA Ames public affairs officer.

John retired from NASA in 2008. Now residing in Livermore, California, he is a novelist and short story author.

www.ingramcontent.com/pod-product-compliance
Lightning Source LLC
Chambersburg PA
CBHW010817250626
47156CB00011B/3101